RACE

THE RED

HORIZON

- THE FLIGHT OF THE PTERONAUT -

M. JONATHAN JONES

RACE

THE RED

HORIZON

- THE FLIGHT OF THE PTERONAUT -

M. JONATHAN JONES

Brandyke Books
www.brandykebooks.com

First published in 2016 by Brandyke Books
www.brandykebooks.com

Copyright © M. Jonathan Jones 2016
Cover illustration © M. Jonathan Jones 2016

ISBN 978-0-9935200-1-3

The right of M. Jonathan Jones to be identified as the author of this
work has been asserted by him in accordance with the Copyright,
Designs and Patents Act, 1988.

This is a work of fiction. Names, characters, places, incidents and
dialogues are products of the author's imagination or used fictitiously.
Any resemblance to actual people, living or dead, events or locales is
entirely coincidental.

Author's note

Pteronaut. From Greek *ptero-* 'wing' (cf. *pterodactyl, archaeopteryx, helicopter*) and *-naut* 'traveller', (cf. *astronaut, cosmonaut, aquanaut*).

01

Daylight comes creeping across the cold dead deserts, chasing away the darkness of night. Another day dawning in the long tale of days. Where the shapeless dark has been before, a new terrain comes into being, of rust-red plains and a brilliant blue sky above them. Sand and sky, red and blue, each is a mirror of the other, reflecting its pristine perfection: always faultless, forever empty.

Trapped between earth and sky is the restless wind, the master of all movement on the plains. It is the wind that sings the dust-devils into being and laments their passing, smothering the tracks that they make. It is the wind that hisses across the dunes, building their slithering slopes and driving them on their march towards the eternal horizon. It is the wind that whistles around the rocks and the cliffs and the outcrops, taking the dust that was once part of them and turning it against them, grinding them down, leaving only endless emptiness in their place.

Day after day, this is the way that things are and the way that things have been for untold ages past: blue sky, red rock, and the wind's many voices.

But not today. Today is different. Today, there is another note that rises and falls across the sands.

A ragged red plume flares up into the sky, a rising smoke-streak that scatters the whirling winds before it. The track it leaves is straight, an unerring line that cuts across the dust-devils' countless criss-cross trails. It does not deviate; no graceful curves or dizzying loops are left in its wake. It brings an unnatural order to the ageless dunes, a new geometry that scars the landscape.

At the head of the dust-plume is a splinter of metal and glass that glints in the daylight, moving faster and more purposefully than any dust-devil. The velocycle's massive wheels churn up the sand, one fore and one aft. The coming day strikes sparks from the supple arch of metal that connects them, and beneath the arch, the barrel of the engine drums away, drowning out the wind. Held out ahead, as if it is trying to outrun its own wheels, is the jutting dart-shape of the cockpit.

The velocycle thief lies face-forwards beneath the glass of the canopy, watching through the goggles of his facemask as the horizon streams towards him. Noise fills the cockpit. Noise fills everything. The hammering of the engine burrows into the thief's bones, shaking all the way up his spine past his ribs and into his skull until his teeth rattle. Still he does not relent. For mile after racing mile, he keeps the accelerator-stalk pressed as hard as he can, pushing the velocycle to its absolute maximum.

Ahead and to the left, the horizon shifts and grows, buckling into the silhouette of some highlands. The thief glances down at the radar-screen, and smears away a spatter of drying blood-drops with one red-gloved hand. The screen shows nothing. Nothing and not nothing – only the glowing dot of his vehicle at the centre, the outlines of swelling dunes, and the rocky outcrops up ahead; nothing for the thief to worry about. But he knows that the radar-screen will not remain empty for long.

He kicks back into the steering-stirrups to angle the velocycle towards the rising cliffs. High ground is where he needs to go, and he is determined to get there by the quickest and most direct path.

It is an uncomfortable ride. The thief is still learning to read the shades and textures of the ground-radar, but even when he can, it makes no difference. Boulders or sand, hollows or ridges, he does not care what lies between him and his goal. The speedometer peaks when he cuts across a stretch of hard-baked rock pavement or on the empty flats, and drops away when the wheels plough into deep-piled dunes. The studded tyres spin and skid, but still the thief presses onwards. No matter what the obstacles, he carries on carving out his route towards the highlands, knife-edge straight.

Another number on the instrument-display catches his eye, and he glances quickly at it. The thief guesses it shows how much fuel is left in the tanks, and it is falling steadily towards zero: his reckless dash across the plains is drawing to a close.

The silhouette on the horizon hardens into the dark stripe of a plateau. The thief cannot tell how far away it is, not from the radar – he is used to judging distances by eye. Those eyes peer out through the goggles of his facemask and study the way that the outline of the plateau shifts with each passing mile. He gauges the distance to it by the angle it cuts across the sky and how the perspective changes the shape of its slopes. All those signs tell him that he might have twenty-five or thirty miles to go – a few minutes at the speed he is travelling. Just a few minutes. Maximum speed, no detours or delays. That is all the thief needs if he is going to survive.

When he looks down at the radar-screen again, it is there: another vehicle. The glowing dot flashes strong and steady behind the smudged back-scatter of the velocycle's dust-wake. They have found him; just as he had expected they would, but far sooner than he had hoped. The miles and miles of empty desert between them will not matter now. Even as he watches the radar, the distance between his velocycle and the other vehicle shrinks, eaten up by the speed of pursuit.

The thief checks and re-checks, looking from the rushing view of the deserts outside to the instrument-display, to the radar, to the instrument-display, and back to the deserts again.

Highlands, speed, radar, fuel.

Highlands, speed, radar, fuel.

It becomes a ritual, and every time he looks at the radar, the glowing dot that follows him is closer. Unmistakably closer. There is no doubt: his pursuers are approaching him faster than he is approaching the high ground.

9

The thief glances up from the blood-spattered radar-screen towards the plateau, willing away the distance. Another jolt. Another drift. Another stretch of bare bedrock where the wheels roar with sudden freedom.

Out there, in the cold dead deserts, the margins of survival are always so small. A finger's width. The blink of an eye. One wrong step. Margins too small to be sure of their impact. Still the thief tries to measure them, to count the costs and to even the odds. His pursuers might not reach him in time. He still has a chance. But if they do catch him, he will not give up without a fight – they know that now.

Another few minutes, another few miles, and the dot has crept right up until it is almost directly behind him. The thief glances over his shoulder through the rear section of the canopy, but the view is obscured by the trailing dust-clouds thrown up from the wheels of his velocycle. Then for a moment the clouds clear and he sees the metal and glass teardrop of the other velocycle, a mile or so behind him. Its steering-fins twitch eagerly, waving and gesturing from their recesses in its streamlined outer skin, urging it into a subtle new angle of pursuit.

Unlike the thief, the pilot of the hunter-velocycle reads the grey-green shadows of the ground-radar like an expert. Every hollow, every drift, every obstacle that slows the thief down, the hunter-pilot avoids. Where the stolen velocycle lurches forwards from one jarring impact to another, crunching over half-buried edges or jolting across the choked-up scar left by some long-dead river, its pursuer takes a weaving detour. Despite its meandering route, the hunter-velocycle is closing the distance. Soon, the two vehicles will be head-to-tail, and the shadows that reach out from the highlands are still miles away: those fine margins of survival are becoming finer by the second.

The dot comes closer. Closer. Closer. Closer. Then the next time that the thief checks, the two dots in his radar-screen have become one, and the hunter-velocycle is behind him. It darts in and out of the billowing wake thrown up by

10

his wheels, looking for a way to draw level. Its pilot is too close now to care about the obstacles that the thief blunders through. There is no way to bring the pursuit to an end trapped in the plume of dust thrown up behind his quarry, and the hunter-pilot knows it – he has to come alongside.

The thief knows it too. Every time the hunter-velocycle veers out to one side or the other, he matches it with a blocking move of his own, keeping his wide rear wheel directly in front of his pursuers. His steering is clumsy, but it has the desired effect. Again and again, he counters. Again and again, he keeps his lead.

But it is a game that the thief cannot win. The attempts to draw level have ceased to be random; the pilot of the hunter-velocycle only ever tries to overtake on the right-hand side. Every time, the thief is forced to steer slightly right-wards to block the move, and gradually, the hunter is pushing him away from the highlands and away from safety. With the cliffs now running almost alongside instead of ahead, the thief has a decision to make: keep his lead, or keep his course.

He kicks back hard into the left-hand steering-stirrup. Fins and vanes flare out down one side of his velocycle, catching the wind and pulling the vehicle back in the direction of the cliffs. In an instant, the pilot of the hunter-velocycle does the same. The thief is back on course, but he has lost his lead; the hunter-velocycle has come alongside, throwing up a parallel dusty streak.

The two vehicles dance a duet, their tracks snaking alongside each other across the flats. The thief glances over at the pilot of the hunter-velocycle, huddled forwards like him in the same prone pose beneath the canopy. He cannot see the pilot's face through the transparent visor of the helmet, but he does not need to – they all look the same, each and every one of them.

Abruptly, the thief turns away and glances forwards, first at the rising cliffs, and then down at the radar-screen. Only a few miles left. Five minutes, no more. In the supply-pouch in

11

the small of his back, he can feel the weight of the pistol he took. He only has four shots remaining. Not enough, perhaps, when the fuel runs out and it comes to a stand-off, but four shots will have to do.

Except the hunter-pilot will not let it come to a stand-off. The hunter-velocycle bucks slightly as the rear section of the canopy lifts and slides backwards. A passenger sits upright out of the cockpit and into the full force of the wind. The currents catch hold of the hunter-velocycle, slowing it, buffeting it, rocking it on its axis, and the pilot struggles with the steering as the streamlining vanishes.

The movement catches the thief's eye. He glances over at the hunter-velocycle and he sees a new threat: the cold hard glint of daylight running down the barrel of a rifle.

The gunman turns sideways on to the wind and pulls the rifle back into his shoulder, setting the telescopic sight as close as he can to the visor of his helmet. He struggles to stay upright, aiming slightly to the rear of the canopy of the stolen velocycle where the thief's legs are stretched out behind him. Even now, after all that has happened, they will not kill him. Not outright, anyway.

The gunman holds his aim, holds his breath, and squeezes the trigger. The sharp crack of the shot is torn away by the wind.

At the very last instant, the thief veers away. Drowned by the noise of the engines, he does not hear the shot itself. He feels its impact somewhere aft, a dull thud against the rhythm of the engine. No warning-lights flash. No alarms sound. The shot has failed to end the chase.

The gunman steadies himself for another attempt, unbuckling the safety-harness that restricts his movement. He finds a different angle this time, so that the shot will count wherever the bullet strikes.

Lying face-forwards in the cockpit, the thief can do nothing but watch. There is nowhere to go, nowhere to hide – he will never reach the safety of the plateau.

A warning buzz jolts him back into the moment: the fuel is almost gone. For a heartbeat and no more, the thief eases his grip on the accelerator-stalk and hits the brakes. The gunshot comes as the hunter-velocycle flashes on past him at full speed. It misses his legs, misses all of him, and punches through one of the windows in the cockpit-canopy.

The decompression-alarm howls, its keening audible even above the engine-noise and the low-fuel warning. Breathable air vents out and the choking atmosphere of the desert floods in. An emergency oxygen-mask pops out from one of the solid sections in the canopy-roof, swinging from a twisted stalk of plastic tubing. The thief bats the mask away and scrapes and paws at the kaleidoscope of canopy-glass that now lies scattered across the radar-screen. He has seen something there that even his unaccustomed eyes have learnt to recognise: loose stones.

With a yank back on the accelerator-stalk and a kick of his right foot, the thief veers away from the highlands and towards the pebble-field. A blinding cloud of dust and grit sprays up from the wheels of his vehicle, and he feels his stomach slip backwards.

Behind and to the left of him, the hunter-velocycle barely slows, slews around, and accelerates in pursuit, but the hunters have lost their advantage. The gunman holds the rim of the open canopy with one hand, his rifle useless for the moment as the hunters come up quickly behind the stolen velocycle's solid rear wheel.

Inside the cockpit, the thief glances down at the radar-screen. He watches the dot of the hunter-velocycle creep up behind him again, cutting away his lead. The thief has no chances remaining; his timing will have to be perfect.

The pebble-field appears ahead, strewn across a wide landscape that might once have been a river, losing its power as it spread out towards a long-dead ocean. The noise from the racing wheels changes to a rumble. Together, nose to tail, the velocycles jolt and judder across the sweep of stones.

13

The thief keeps his eyes on the radar-screen. The dot of the hunter-velocycle creeps closer. And closer. And closer. The fuel warning-light seems to blink in time with the rise and fall of the decompression-alarm, becoming a metronome, ticking away, marking out the time to act.

One; two; three...

Without warning, the thief pulls the stolen velocycle around into a sudden switchback turn, aiming at the cliffs and cutting across the path taken by his pursuers.

It is a move that an expert pilot might manage to make one time in ten, and the thief is no expert. The angle of the turn is too sharp to be made at one hundred and thirty miles an hour – too sharp even to be made at sixty.

The back wheel skids out from under him, carving across the sands and sending a scudding fan of crimson dust into the air. The thief fights to maintain control, steering one way and then the other, but it is no use. His velocycle slides over onto its side, spinning wildly. Stones scatter in all directions. Out of control, the velocycle tears a gouge into the ground, shearing off all the steering-fins on one side. Shreds of metal and plastic fly into the air, joining the hail of gravel from the wheels.

Too late to steer a safe course, the pilot of the hunter-velocycle brakes. All the steering-fins punch out at once, but the hunter-velocycle is too close to stop. The studded front wheel rams into the underside of the stolen velocycle, slowing both vehicles almost instantly to a walking pace. The impact sends the gunman flying out of the open canopy, and the hunter-velocycle flips end-over-end over its prey.

Almost weightless, it seems, the hunter-velocycle spirals gracefully into the air, looping slowly high and far. And then, gathering speed, it comes back down to a splintering crash on its back among the boulders. Fuel from its shattered tanks ignites, fed by a stream of leaking oxygen from the cockpit. Fire races across the wreck, quick and hungry flames that leap high with a whoofing roar. They flare, breathing the last of the air in the cockpit. Then almost as

14

quickly the flames become a whispering flicker, fanned only by the thin ration of oxygen in the poisonous atmosphere.

A smear of smoke mixes with dust, red and black, and lifts across the shining blue of the sky. It flutters there proudly, and as the flames die back to almost nothing, the plains fall silent once again.

02

The smoke from the crash does not fly unchallenged for very long. Soon the wind comes and takes hold of it, pushing it, twisting it, folding it inwards and then turning it outwards until it vanishes. The dust-cloud that the crash kicked up into the sky is also hastened on its way, and then the wind is once again master of all movement on the plains.

In just a few days, the aberration will be gone. The wind will cover the wrecked velocycles, burying them beneath a new dune and hiding them from the sky, making the desert clean and smooth again – as things should be. It has already started to soften the edges of the tracks that the velocycles left behind them, and a sprinkling of rusty sand has been heaped around the broken bodies of both vehicles. It will take time for it to put things right, but time is all it has.

Gently, the wind reaches into the interior of the stolen velocycle where the glass of the canopy has been smashed. It piles fine dust-grains around the red-suited figure that lies inside, making a tomb for him.

But the thief is not dead.

He twitches a hand and lies still. His hand twitches again, and then he moves one of his legs, kicking away the smothering dust. Consciousness returns to him slowly. From somewhere close by, he can hear the whistle of the wind as it explores the canopy, and for a moment he thinks he is somewhere else, somewhere high and far and safe, looking down at the desert plains from a distance. Then the note of the wind falls, and he hears the rattle and hiss of the sand-grains as they creep around him.

Behind the round goggle-lenses of his facemask, the thief opens his eyes, but he is confused by the fragments of canopy-glass that he is lying on. They swirl around and around, and he cannot tell which way is up and which way is down. Beyond the glass, he tries to focus on the first fingers of the dunes that the wind has brought in with it. Their shallow swells confuse him still more. Are they near or are they far away? The thief cannot be certain, so he closes his eyes again. In the dark, near or far does not matter. In the dark, he can rest. Sleep is so close; he just has to let go.

How long since he has slept? Days? Hours? He cannot be sure anymore. Not since the sandstorm. Not since the noise of thunder in the night. Not since they found him and took him.

Slowly, the velocycle thief remembers where he is, and how he comes to be there. And with the memory comes a sense of urgency. If he sleeps, they will come and find him, just as they did before. He must get up, and he must get up now.

With his eyes still closed against the confusion of his surroundings, the thief concentrates through the shifting dark, trying to recall how to get up, which muscles to move, and which direction to move them in. His gloves slide and scrape on his bed of glass, and finally he collects his limbs beneath himself and pushes himself upright.

The movement brings the blood pounding to his head and rushing to his ears, and he realises that he can taste blood too. Its iron tang on his tongue mixes with the acrid smell of burning plastic and rubber from outside, and of dead flesh roasting. He swallows, and then coughs warily, but there is no sharp pain deep down, no rush into his mouth from some internal injury. Just a cut in the lip or the cheek where he has bitten himself beneath his facemask. He can move his arms and legs with no discomfort. Everything feels just as it should, only distant, still numbed by the fog of unconsciousness.

The velocycle thief possesses an uncanny sense of balance and orientation, and without it, he might have lain there many minutes more. But even so, it is a moment or two before he can open his eyes fully.

He ignores the surroundings that refuse to remain still and focuses instead on the figures that are projected onto the inside of his goggles. At first, he struggles to make sense of them, too dazed to read their meaning, but there is no alarm sounding in his ears, so he knows that the skin-suit is intact. As they swim out of the haze, the internal pressure-readings seem to be fine. Internal and external temperature-readings also look normal. Only his water and air-supplies are low, desperately low, but they have been low for days. There is nothing new for the thief to worry about. Just the old familiar worries.

With his wits returning, he crawls around inside the cramped wreck. The cockpit of the velocycle still defies his first attempts to make sense of it, lying over at an angle. Then he finds the handle to open the canopy and tries to slide it back, but he cannot move it. On its side, all the velocycle's weight is pressing down onto the frame, wedging it into the sand; the thief is caged inside.

Hidden behind a glass panel, he finds the emergency escape lever. He punches through the glass and takes hold of it. Using all the strength he can, he leans back until he feels the lever click. Release-bolts fire above his head with a loud *crack-pop* and a section of the canopy soars a dozen feet into the air. It flaps against the sky and crashes to the ground a few yards away. The thief pushes an arm up through the rectangular opening that is left gaping in the canopy and catches hold of the fuselage.

Slowly, he wriggles out into the daylight. First his head, then his other arm. He heaves his body free of the cocoon of the stolen velocycle, slithers across the wreck, and drops down onto the sand. All across the scales of his skin-suit, red and black patterns of camouflage shift and change, like the shadows of unseen clouds, regulating his body-temperature now that he is out in the open.

The thief lies in the sand for a few more moments, breathing the filtered desert air with his eyes closed.

Outside in the daylight the smell of burning flesh and leaking fuel is stronger, and it makes him feel sick.

His eyes flick open again; he must not stay in the dark. The goggle-display tells him that the external temperature is nudging five degrees below zero already and it is still early. The day is going to be hot – it might even reach one or two degrees above freezing – and that will play in his favour if he can make it to the cliffs.

Using the wreck of the velocycle for support, the thief stands upright and checks himself over. The scaly exterior of the skin-suit shows a few minor cuts and grazes, but they will heal. Already, the wounds have scabbed over with dark resinous sealant. Searching with his fingers, he reaches around behind his back, checking the shield-shaped carapace that he wears there. That too seems to be intact and undamaged. The thief has been lucky. But luck must be paid for, and he sees the price of it attached to his right ankle. The sturdy silvery loop of metal that fixes the tracker-tag to his leg is also unscathed; it is too much to hope that the crash might have rid him of that.

One single sip of water through the drip-tube inside his facemask sets a warning blinking on the edge of his vision. The thief swats it away with a quick gesture to his temple. Water will have to wait. He looks back in the direction he has come from. Above the rippling haze of the horizon he can see nothing. The wide desert plains look as empty as ever beneath the blue sky. Deceptively empty.

With a growing sense of urgency, the thief leans back inside the wreck of the velocycle. The emergency water-flask is gone – he has seen that already – and wrenches the supply-kit from its fixtures. It is half-empty, its vital contents plundered in piecemeal fashion over the years. Any ration-bars it once contained are now no more than crumpled wrappers thrown back into the case. He will have to make do with the food that he carries in the supply-pouch in the small of his back.

19

Next he checks the toolbox. It rattles unpromisingly as he prises it free from its mounting. Mixed in among the detritus of broken springs, lengths of half-stripped wire, and oily valves is nothing of any use. Nothing that might cut through the metal loop of the tracker-tag around his ankle. He has not been able to prise it off with his knife, and he cannot shoot it off. For now, he is stuck with it.

The thief pulls the pistol from his supply-pouch and paces towards the heat of the flames that have taken hold of the other velocycle. He shields his goggle-eyes and the skin-suit turns a pale red to reflect the heat. Twisting coils of black smoke trickle out of the cockpit, and any canopy-glass that remains unbroken is smudged and inky on the inside. Anything not destroyed in the crash has been fuel for the fire. What is left of the hunter-velocycle offers nothing for him to salvage.

Next he searches for the gunman. Caution is unnecessary. Thrown from the open cockpit at full speed, the gunman's body is a hundred paces from the wreckage, lying among some boulders and bent back on itself at an impossible angle. A wide tear flutters along one side of the gunman's suit, exposing a bloody gash and a thrust of broken ribs, still steaming in the cold air. The thief slips the pistol away and turns the gunman's body over.

A scarlet slick has congealed across the visor of the helmet, hiding the face that he knows is inside, the face they all have. Only what the gunman wears – the symbols that have been daubed across the exterior of the suit and the jangle of drift-metal charms hanging around his neck – make him any different from any of the others. One of the charms sticks upright from his chest where the impact of the crash has embedded it – so much for the protection of the gods.

Quickly, the thief examines the gunman's body. The suit is inflexible and rigid, all metal and plastic. Inert. As dead as its wearer. The only similarity with his own skin-suit are the rows of gill-cells that run from spine to breastbone around the gunman's ribcage. On one side, above the ragged wound in the chest, the mesh protectors of the gill-cells have been torn open. The filters inside are almost black from exposure to the air, and red dust already peppers them, clogging the pores. They are useless.

On the other side of the gunman's body, three of the cells are intact, and the thief pops open the mesh protectors one by one and slides out the filters. The tapering lozenges he finds inside are not quite the same shape and size as the filters of his skin-suit, so they will not function with maximum efficiency, but judging by the grey-blue colour and spongy texture they have been replaced recently.

Careful to shield himself from the dust-laden wind, the thief seals off the respiratory-capillaries to his internal air-supply and exchanges the grey and crumbling filters he carries for the ones he has scavenged. He takes a few deep breaths, and watches the air-supply readings in his goggle-display blossom with a healthy green glow. Enough air for about a week or so. Not long, but longer than his supply of water will last.

Once more he glances over at the horizon. The straight red line still looks empty beneath the sky, but he knows that if he does not move soon, none of his calculations and rationing of supplies will make any difference. Beyond the wreck of his velocycle, a mile or so distant in the opposite direction, the cliffs rear up into the heights he needs. It is time to go.

He hoists the body of the gunman over his shoulder, walks back to the stolen velocycle, and dumps the body inside through the open escape hatch. A sticky mass of congealed fuel is smeared across the bodywork of the velocycle from a gash in the fuel-tanks, half-frozen now that its liquefying additives have boiled off. The thief picks up a section of broken steering-fin and uses it to scoop up a good amount of the freezing fuel. Once it is pasted inside the cockpit, he takes hold of the emergency oxygen-mask which still dangles there, and slits through the tangled coil of its supply-line with the knife from his belt. With a hiss, what is left of the emergency oxygen-supply seeps out.

A glowing piece of rubber tubing from the other wreck is all it takes to start the fire. The thief steps back as the fuel catches. Rippling waves of blue and yellow flame wash across the interior of the velocycle, lapping tongues that take hold of anything flammable. Plastic whines and pops as the flames gut the cockpit, and a thick black cloud of smoke drifts upwards. It can be seen for miles, a sure marker of the thief's location. But with the tracker-tag still attached to his ankle, that does not matter, and he will leave nothing behind that can be used against him.

03

The high wall of the cliffs casts a long shadow out across the dunes. Ages before, the plateau might have been an island in a shallow sea, and the cliffs the ramparts of its coastline, or the edge of the continental shelf. Now, the seas have dried to nothing, and the rivers that once cut valleys through that high wall have trickled away to unknown ends in the choking sand.

The thief crosses into the shadow, and the temperature-readings in his goggle-display plummet to twenty degrees below freezing. Despite the super-insulated layers of the skin-suit he feels the chill deepen, and the suit responds by burning some of its store of sugars to keep him warm. Even so, he quickens his pace to stave off a shiver.

Less easy to deal with than the cold is his hunger. His stomach growls. He has bled the pigment from two transparent sections of the skin-suit, exposing the blue-purple swirls of the photosynthesising tattoos across his chest and shoulders, but in the shadow of the cliffs the output of the tattoos is minimal. The sugars they provide will just about keep him going – he feels them trickling into his bloodstream already – but they are no cure for the gnawing hunger of an empty stomach.

With one hand, he shuts off the capillary-tubes that feed oxygen into his facemask. With the other, he reaches into the supply-pouch that nestles beneath the shield-shaped carapace on his back and fumbles around until he finds a ration-bar. In one swift practised movement, the thief unclips a section of his facemask, hinging it down, and squeezes half the contents of the foil wrapper into his mouth, saving the rest for later. The desert air bites at his lips, cold and dry, and he quickly repositions the facemask and turns the air-supply back on. It is not much of a meal, but it will expand in his stomach and keep him going.

Worse even than the lack of food is the lack of water. He follows the mouthful of the ration-bar with another careful sip at the drip-tube. The few drops of water he swirls around his sandpapery tongue only intensify the burning thirst, and the low-water warning blinks back into the goggle-display. He swipes it away once again, but it will not be long before it remains on the edge of his vision. Down in the constant cold beneath the cliffs, the dead rivers are places to dig down to the permafrost in the hope of finding water-ice to melt, but the thief has no time to replenish his supplies.

As he gets closer to the plateau, the reason for his haste becomes louder. Something echoes back at him from the walls of rock, something that might be the ghosts of sounds he has never heard, of rolling waves and crashing breakers. But the thief knows those sounds for what they really are: the rise and fall of engine-noise, carried on the wind.

Behind him, the plains look more and more empty by the minute. Already the outlines of the wrecked velocycles and the tracks they cut across the dunes have become blurred and indistinct – even the trail of his bootprints is hard to see. The thief is not fooled. The emptiness of the desert is an illusion, no more real than the shimmering islands of a *fata morgana* that float above the sands.

Beyond the mirage, a new plume of dust rises up into the sky, a swirling red cloud, bigger and more threatening than that made by any velocycle. By now the wrecks of the velocycles have finished burning and only a faint inky smudge hangs in the air to show where they are. But whatever drives the dust-cloud onwards, it needs no signposts; there is no doubting the menacing intent that steers it straight towards the cliffs. It moves more slowly than the velocycles, making barely half their speed, but that is still many times faster than the thief can run. Even so, there is nothing else he can do – at the sight of the swirling red cloud, the thief runs.

24

The land starts to rise towards the plateau. At first the incline is gentle, but then it steepens, and the thief is forced to slow his pace, bent almost double by the angle of the ascent. At their base, the cliffs are littered with fragments that frost-heave and wind-erosion have brought crashing down. Boulders lie in heaps where they have fallen, like irregular eggs on nests of smashed stone.

The thief looks up at the cliffs, and then back at the growing dust-plume. If he can find an easy way up, he might climb high enough above the plains before the cloud reaches the wrecks, but it will be close – the chase and the crash have eaten away at his headstart more than he had realised. He needs a quick and easy way up.

Quick and easy are rare qualities in the desert. As he gets nearer to the cliffs, the thief can see the curves that the wind has carved across them. Extending to a height of twelve or fifteen feet above the ground, their vertical faces are almost perfectly smooth and utterly unclimbable, undulating in silken waves that offer no purchase; he will need to find a recent rockfall to make a start.

He turns aside, running parallel to the cliffs. Up ahead, part of the cliff wall seems weaker than the rest. Perhaps it is a flaw in the million year-old rocks that have been laid down layer by layer, or just the way that the formation is standing half in the full glare of daylight, half in shadow, so that the freeze-thaw actions of day and night are particularly aggressive. Either way, it is a place of crevices and terraces that the thief can use to gain height above the plains.

Staring up at the rockface, glancing across the fissures he can see, he clambers over the rubble at their base. As he goes, his eyes follow near-invisible networks so far, reading them like a map. Time and again his gaze turns aside as he sees how each possibility becomes an impossibility, trailing away into smooth stretches of nothing, or ending at an impassable obstacle. None of the routes he can see leads high enough.

25

Then the thief finds a path, a crooked crumbling path, a difficult and dangerous climb, but not quite impossible. It is a route he has to take. Over his shoulder, the dull rumble grows on the edge of his hearing, and he can almost feel the ground trembling as the dust-cloud approaches. The thief restores the camouflaged sections to his skin-suit to cover his tattoos and starts to climb.

His first step is not really a step at all. The lower sections of the cliff are still polished smooth, so he takes a running jump, up an untidy ramp of boulders, and then leaps as high as he can. Arms and legs outstretched, the thief slams against the cliff-face and somehow he hangs there, finding the merest faults to cling to.

He has started his ascent, and right from the very beginning, it takes its toll on his strength and skill. In his goggle-display, the graphic that shows his air-supply pulses with the rise and fall of his chest; every in-breath turns it green, drawing the toxic desert air through the filters of the gill-cells, blooming red again as he breathes out. The skin-suit breathes with him, adding a little of the oxygen it exhales to the supply from the gill-cells, keeping him going, making every breath count for two. And beneath its red and black scales, the skin-suit's muscles work in concert with his own. They knot and flex, sensing the movements of his body as he stretches and strains, helping him to climb.

Tacking backwards and forwards across the cliff-face, working always at the maximum extent of his reach, the thief goes as quickly as he dares. As he climbs higher, away from the scouring action of the sand, handholds are easier to find, but the walls get steeper.

There are places where fragile sections of rock give way under his hands and leave him scrabbling for purchase. What seem like stable ledges tumble away beneath his boots, clattering down among the boulders at the base, so that he has to jump to the next foothold and trust to luck that it will take his weight. Sometimes it does. Sometimes it is only another fragile leaping-off point from which to make one more desperate lunge.

Even with the assistance of his symbiotic second skin, the thief's arms and legs burn from the effort. But despite all the difficulties and the dangers, again and again, from one handhold to the next, foot by foot, he heaves himself upwards.

At two hundred feet, a great vertical sheet of the cliff-face has fallen away, leaving a stepped ledge. The fall must have been recent, because the handholds and footholds are sharp-edged and unweathered. For a few minutes, the thief makes good progress, and then he allows himself a quick glance back across the desert plains.

The billowing column of dust has almost reached the remains of the velocycles. Waves of sand and gravel foam up all around the thing that makes it, obscuring its vastness, and the snakeskin pattern of its tracks is strung out behind. For a moment, the blood-red clouds drift away, and the thing at the centre of the dust-storm reveals itself.

Daylight slants across the storm-shields on its flanks, glittering where they have been polished to burning silver by century after century of wind-blown dust. The rays break into dazzling streams across a riddle of girders and pipework, splintering from the cranes and drill-masts that rear up above the armoured upper-deck. Streamers of smoke and steam snag around revetments and battlements, torn into tatters as the metal monster thunders along. Beneath the vast shadow that it casts, parallel rows of tracks churn, a clanking army of toothed metal plates that leave their marks on the shifting sand.

It is the Crawler. Undaunted. Untiring. Unstoppable.

Almost half as high as the plateau itself, the Crawler does not look like it should even stand upright, let alone move at such speed. But it is moving, and the noise of it shakes the cliffs, sending powdery streams of dust and showers of rock-fragments cascading down.

The Crawler did not slow as it neared the charred remains of the velocycles. They were rare treasures, lost in the age-old wastes, dug out from some dune and made whole again with half-forgotten skill and ingenuity. Now their blackened bones offered nothing to salvage, and the Crawler had a greater prize to play for. It did not stop and it did not swerve aside. It ploughed on over the wrecks, grinding them and shredding them and flattening whatever was left, burying them back beneath the sands. The hunt was on, and it would not be distracted.

In just a minute more, the Crawler had reached the steep incline at the base of the plateau, defying the shadows that gathered there with its silvered sides. It knew that its prey was there among the rocks somewhere; the tracker-tag told it that. But the accuracy of the signal was limited and it was no use any more – the last strike had to be made face-to-face.

The thunder of its engines faded away and the Crawler rocked to a halt. At some secret signal, hatches opened all along its steel flanks. Figures emerged from inside, a suited swarm of them, daubed with symbols to bring luck in the hunt. Like a flood they came pouring out, running along the external walkways, seeking out the best vantage-points. War-masks of metal and plastic covered the transparent visors of their helmets, shielding from view the one face that they all shared.

The Crawler's drones turned towards the cliffs, an unmoving army, intensely quiet. Only the bone ornaments that were tied along the balustrades made any sound as they swayed and jingled against each other. Hidden behind the dark slits in the masks, unseen eyes searched for the thief.

Wedged between two boulders, the thief has stopped dead. The mottled scales of his skin-suit hide his outline perfectly, red and black against the rockface and fissures at his back. He stares at the Crawler, now just a few hundred feet away, an iron and steel counterpart to the cliffs he has just climbed. Metal and rock, the two heights make a dark and narrow valley with a thin strip of sky at the top, and he is trapped between them.

Standing as still as the stones around him, the thief's arms and legs start to shake from the effort. He relaxes the muscles and then tenses them again by turns, shifting the burden of his bodyweight slightly each time. Even with the strength of the skin-suit to help him, it is little relief. The tendons running beneath the sole of his foot feel like they will snap any second. Willing his aching muscles to respond, the thief presses his foot harder against the cliff-face, grinding away the flaking surface to make the slightest of indentations. But the change in the direction of pressure only makes things worse. His foot starts to cramp. He has to move. Striking out suddenly, the thief leaps from cover, lunging for the next handhold.

As one, the Crawler's drones turned in his direction. They had seen him. A tremor ran through their ranks. Some rushed forwards wielding long-barrelled harpoon launchers, firing them into the face of the cliff. Pitons drove deep and cams expanded to grip the rock. Each harpoon trailed a line behind it, and each line bristled with swarming figures that crossed the gap.

Using the lines to aid them, a handful of drones reached the top of the plateau. They stared down at the thief, ready with long poles that were fitted with hooks or the loop of a noose, seeing which way he would go next. Others tried to follow him, or to second-guess where he would turn aside. A cautious shot rang out, a failed attempt to herd the thief into the path of one group of net-wielders – shooting out his legs would do no good now – and the bullet struck splinters from the rock barely two feet from him.

More and more lines hiss into the cliff-face and the thief climbs as quickly as he can. But no matter where he goes, the web is closing in. He twists and turns, trying to keep to his route as the rockface seethes around him.

The thief changes direction suddenly, pushing off from one ledge and catching hold of another. The nets are closing in. He turns again, and again, leaping for handholds that seem like sheer rock, finding purchase on the merest faultline.

The hunt is almost over.

Almost surrounded, the thief reaches a spur of the cliff that juts out into space. There he stops – his ascent can go no further. An overhanging lip of rock projects above him like a shelf, barring the route to the top of the plateau. He can overcome it, but it will be slow and careful work, and the Crawler's drones will be waiting for him at the summit.

The thief is trapped.

But it is not the summit of the plateau that the thief was ever aiming for. Standing on the spur of rock, he does not look up; instead, he stares across and down, gauging his height and the distance to the armour of the Crawler's upper-deck. Only for a second he stands there, his eyes taking it all in. And then he moves.

Mute and motionless, the Crawler's drones can only watch as the thief takes two rapid steps towards the end of the spur and kicks off into the empty air.

As he leaps out above the drop, the thief finds the handles that are hidden away at his shoulders. Grasping them tightly, he depresses the thumb-locks, and in one swift movement, he extends his arms upwards and forwards in a sweeping arc.

From within the protective housing on his back, a framework of struts and spars explodes outwards. Overlapping leaves of tissue spread and stretch, section by section. Folds fan out and flatten themselves. Wires go taut, pulling, tightening, locking everything into place. In the next instant, chaos becomes order, and two broad wings catch the currents.

With a crack and a snap, the thief beats the wings once, and then once more. He has left the ground behind and taken to the air – he is a Pteronaut again!

04

The Pteronaut is in the air, but he is falling, not flying. His launching leap can still end in death among the boulders at the foot of the cliffs. For now, the Crawler and its drones are forgotten; gravity is the enemy that he must battle.

He pushes his feet into the tail-spine that extends from the wing-case, bracing himself against it, and beats the wings harder and harder. The sliding spiderweb of struts and hinges on his back translates the frantic movements of his arms into curving cyclical motions of the wings. Efficient soaring upstrokes follow graceful sweeping downstrokes, stitched seamlessly together with a sinuous *sneek-sneek* of the mechanism.

Efficient and graceful it might be, but it is not working. Beat after beat fails to halt his fall. Gravity is too strong. Even without the readings for altitude, airspeed, and climb-rate that have appeared in his goggle-display, the Pteronaut can see that. Beyond the translucent constellation that the readings form, the red rocks rush towards him. He has not climbed high enough, and the Crawler is too close – there is nowhere to go but straight down.

The Pteronaut beats the wings faster, desperate to carve an upwards path. Struts creak. Wing-tissue strains. He angles his wings against the flow of air and tries to defy the unforgiving vertical grain of his fall. His chest heaves. Pure oxygen seeps into the facemask; the skin-suit has sensed the urgency in his rapid breaths and is fighting gravity with him.

Another fifty feet go by.

More oxygen.

More beats of the wings.

A hundred feet.

He cannot counter the downward force. The cliffs flash past, a blood-red smear. The silver slopes of the Crawler

32

sparkle as they mirror his doom. The Pteronaut stares into the bone-splintering smile of the boulders below.

Suddenly he has it. From one instant to the next, the fall becomes a dive, and then the dive becomes a swooping glide. The currents that were hurtling him to his death now respond to the beats of his wings and keep him aloft. The pull of gravity is held at arm's length.

The Pteronaut is flying, but he cannot fly far. He is trapped within a narrow chasm. The cliffs he took such risks to climb are behind him, the Crawler ahead, and the freedom of the blue sky shines bright above him, criss-crossed by the taut tangle of the harpoonists' lines. He angles the wings and arches his back, flexing his spine like a bent bow as he tries to turn. There are inches to spare. His wing-tip strokes the Crawler's sides, and as his back straightens, he finally faces along the length of the chasm.

For two or three seconds, he keeps the wings utterly still, his arms tense and unbending, and holds the line of the glide as the spars creak and the wing-tissue flutters. Then he hears the noise of descent change to ascent, and he starts to beat the wings again, mastering his course through the air. Two flicking beats lift him higher, carrying him on through the narrow chasm towards freedom. The Pteronaut is flying, really flying, and despite his gasping breaths, it feels good.

In another second, the metal wall of the Crawler's flanks comes to an abrupt end. The Pteronaut flies beyond the Crawler's bulk and out from shelter, emerging into the full force of the winds that sweep off the plains.

Air-currents break into jagged eddies across the boulders at the base of the cliffs. Gust after gust threatens to flip him over. The Pteronaut grips the wings tightly, fighting the invisible turmoil. He is too close to the plateau and the ramparts it throws up in the way of the wind. See-sawing from side to side in the turbulence, he adjusts his flight. He must get higher and into smoother air. There the currents will help him instead of hindering him, lifting him above the unassailable obstacle of the plateau. Escape is fifty feet away. Forty feet. Thirty feet...

But the Crawler did not stand idly by and watch its prey escape. Its engines roared with fury and its smoke-stacks spouted black streamers high into the sky. The drones hurried away from the cliffs, racing back across the lines that they had fired. They knew that the Crawler would not wait; any who were too slow would be left behind.

The roar of the Crawler's engines became a rumble, and the rattling mountain of metal heaved itself into motion. The toothed track-plates span beneath its bulk and the rows of separate drive-units swivelled in their sockets, slithering across the sand as they changed direction. Trailing the last broken lines from the harpoons behind it, the Crawler churned up the dust and ground the boulders into gravel. The hunt was on again.

Two hundred yards ahead of the Crawler, the Pteronaut fights his way above the turbulence and finds some lift. He soars up against the cliffs with the wind under his wings. But it is too little, too late: the Crawler is moving and he feels it close behind him, closer and closer by the second. The Pteronaut does not have the strength to outrun it, and the updraughts cannot carry him high enough fast enough. He feels the bow-wave building as the Crawler shoulders the air out of its way. Anywhere else, that wave would have aided him, lifting him as it approached, but so close to the cliffs it is a hurricane that jostles him with one sideways gust after another.

Failed by the currents, trapped against the cliffs, the Pteronaut has one chance remaining: the desert. It stretches out to the horizon on his left. He flicks the wings into a new shape, banking sharply across the buffeting bow-wave of the Crawler, and veers sideways across its snout. For one deadly second, the roar of the Crawler is louder than ever in his ears, the dust from the tracks robs him of his sight, and their churning cuts the air-currents into shreds. Then the terror and the turmoil is behind him, and he is out of the dust-cloud and soaring across the sand.

The Pteronaut's escape is still not certain. His speed falls to almost nothing as he heads straight into the wind coming off the plains. If he cannot go forwards, he must go upwards. Angling the wings in their sockets, the Pteronaut tries to get as much lift as he can. He climbs, carving a steep and rapid ascent out of the air. Then he swoops towards the sand again, trading height for speed. At the end of every racing dip, he must climb again. And again. And again.

It is exhausting. There is no way that the Pteronaut can outrun the Crawler on the plains, not even with the muscles of his skin-suit and the extra oxygen it supplies. Fatigue means nothing to the turbines and drive-shafts of the Crawler, and he is already tiring. Every wing-beat is an illusion of freedom, a desperate attempt to hold off the inevitable fall to the ground. And it is an illusion that is coming to an end.

The Crawler was far less manoeuvrable than its prey. Its tracks skidded and slewed as it tried to change direction. Gears crashed and pistons hammered in protest. Just as the birdman fought gravity in his fall, so the Crawler railed against its own inertia, spinning up the dust as it struggled for control. Unable to stop and turn quickly like its prey, it thundered along in the shadow of the cliffs.

Then at last the Crawler mastered its momentum. The chaotic clanking of its tracks faltered, becoming ordered as it slowed enough to align its drive-units and forge a new path across the plains. With the noise of an iron avalanche, it turned away from the plateau. Engines drumming, its tracks a billowing blur, it came tearing after its prey at full speed.

Running ahead of the Crawler, a few desperate yards and no more, the Pteronaut feels the force of its bow-wave like a blow from an invisible fist; he can even see its effects, lifting the top-most layer of sand from the ridges of the dunes. He has to keep ahead of it. Behind the crest of the bow-wave, the onrushing currents will suck him in and flip him around. Then the Crawler will have him.

Seconds before the full force of the blow falls, the Pteronaut's wings fill with the sudden rise in pressure. That is what he has been waiting for. He bends the wings to catch it and soars ahead of the lift-zone it forms, stealing as much height as he can. It is a knife-edge of air and no more, and if he stays too long within it, it will bat him out of the sky.

The knife-edge passes him by. The currents start to break up. That is the moment when he must act. The Pteronaut banks sharply. Almost stalling, skirting the unseen edges of the bow-wave, he twists back on his own flightpath and converts all his height for speed. A hand's width from his wing-tips, the silver scales of the Crawler sweep past. Then, dipping and accelerating once more, he is heading back towards the cliffs, leaving the Crawler to chase his fading slipstream.

For a few seconds, the Pteronaut holds his arms out straight on either side, gasping for breath. He swoops towards the plateau in a gliding dive, faster than before. The rushing wind sings between spars and struts. The taut tissue of his wings beats like a drum, then goes silent. Beneath him, the desert blurs, and the Pteronaut flies low enough to hear the hiss of the sand-grains running before his shadow.

Just when it seems that he must crash headlong into the dunes, the air-currents start to rise. For countless miles, they have hurried above the desert, meeting no barrier other than the impermanent slopes of wind-driven sand. Now the angular solidity of the plateau thrusts up above the plains, and the air-currents quicken as they reach it.

Like he is riding on a wave towards the ancient shoreline, the rising air carries the Pteronaut upwards. He turns aside just before the wave splinters against the cliffs, staying out of the ragged eddies that batter the rocks. Parallel to the summit, at right-angles to the wind, he keeps within the lift-zone. All the long and difficult climb up the precipice rushes past in a flicker, the rapid descent of his launch in reverse. Twitching the wings to stay stable, he soars higher and higher with every breath.

Then the Pteronaut is suddenly above the plateau, with the freedom of the blue sky all around him. He has done it; he is back in the sky, high and safe and out of reach. He has escaped from the Crawler.

05

Back down on the plains, the Crawler had made its turn. It roared towards the plateau as fast as its tracks could carry it, but the birdman had already made his lead count. Stranded beneath the high walls of the cliffs, the Crawler watched the birdman follow the edge of the plateau, becoming a distant speck as he soared with the currents of air until they lost their upward power. Then the speck turned away over the plateau and vanished from sight.

The Crawler slowed as it approached the towering cliffs, a glittering thunderstorm trapped down on the plains. Its turbines rumbled and its deck-plates juddered. The echoes of its engine-noise battered the rocks that blocked its path, but the rocks stood unmoved. The Crawler could not follow the birdman up onto the plateau. Even with all its immense power, it would take a hundred years for it to smash a route that it could climb. It had to search for another way.

Slowly, the Crawler's tracks started to roll again, carrying it along. The birdman was lost behind the barrier of the old coastline, and minute by minute he was getting further away. But although the Crawler had lost sight of its prey, it had not lost hope. Not yet.

Even if it could no longer track the birdman in the visible spectrum, the ringing call of the tracker-tag he carried on his ankle was still clear enough. He would have to travel far across the plateau to outrun the range of the tag, and the Crawler was tireless. It would skirt the high walls of rock, and sooner or later, it would find a way to climb them. Somewhere there would be a ravine that was wide enough to admit its bulk or a canyon that opened low enough for it to reach. It just had to find it.

The Crawler would not give up. If it had to search for a thousand miles, it would find the path it sought. And the birdman could not fly during the freezing hours of the night. When the deadly cold of darkness came, he would have to roost somewhere, and then the Crawler would catch up with him.

06

The Pteronaut needs a thermal. The wind against the cliffs has carried him several hundred feet above the plateau, but it is still not enough. Every few seconds, he has to beat his wings to claw back the altitude that he loses steadily from his gliding flight. His shoulders and trunk ache from the effort, and his arms feel almost too heavy to stretch out. Maintaining a constant height above the ridges is more than he can manage. He lets the skin-suit take the strain, but its power needs direction, and he cannot keep control for much longer; not for the hours of flight that he needs to outrun the range of the tracker-tag. First the climb, then the fall, then the battle of his escape – the Pteronaut is exhausted.

The barrier of the plateau will keep the Crawler at bay, but the Pteronaut can see the dust-cloud that its tracks send churning into the air. He knows that the Crawler will not rest. It will find a way to follow him and hunt him into the night. Landing on the plateau and running is no escape. The Pteronaut is a creature of the air, and only in the air is he free. Anywhere on the ground, he is trapped. His one hope of survival is to gain as much altitude as possible and then to glide on for what is left of the day, hanging beneath the wings, regaining his strength. When night comes, he will need to have put many miles of desert between himself and the Crawler.

And to do that, he needs a thermal.

Behind the goggle-lenses, the Pteronaut's eyes go searching for darker rocks that heat faster than their surroundings. Even just a few degrees' difference will set the air in motion, causing it to spiral upwards. The day is warming – the temperature-readings have risen steadily – but telling cold dark shadow apart from warm dark rock is no easy task, even for his well-practised eye.

If there were any moisture in the desert, the Pteronaut could look for clouds forming as warm damp air rose and then cooled. There is no chance of that: the wastes beneath him are as dry as his own water-stores, and the sky is as empty as ever; he has not seen any clouds for months.

But the Pteronaut is a creature of the air, and he does not need to see thermals to find them. Blue thermals are what he seeks, invisible columns of rising air. He must use the touch of the currents themselves as a guide. Reading the airflow around him is as easy – or as difficult – as reading the cliff-face for a path to climb. Down so close to the rocks, his sense of the contours within the air is blinded by the unseen turmoil as it rushes over the peaks below. The currents are a maze of pathways going this way and that, changing constantly.

He banks further away from the cliff-edge, beating the wings slowly and steadily, climbing up to where the air is smoother. Between wing-beats he pauses to feel the currents settling around him, and with every foot he climbs, the patterns in the trackless sky become clearer.

On such a warm day, with the temperature touching freezing, it takes no more than five minutes before he feels it. There is something over to his right, the merest breath of an updraught. It is the beginning of an invisible upwards slope into the sky, as impermanent as the desert dunes below, but to the Pteronaut, just as real. He has found his blue thermal.

Angling the wings in their sockets, he cuts across the wind towards it, feeling the power of the updraught grow as he approaches. The flow of air quickens. The spars of the wings creak and the tissue that is spanned taut between them crackles and hums. All around him, the currents speed up as the draw of the updraught sucks them in. Buffeting breezes are marshalled together, aligning and ordering themselves as they hurry higher. And the Pteronaut goes with them, rising effortlessly into the sky.

He no longer needs to beat the wings to climb, yet still he cannot rest. Maintaining control is crucial. If rising air gathers too much under one wing, it will flip him over onto his back, or lift him so fast that he stalls and falls feet-first to the desert below. So he is cautious. He holds the hand-grips tightly and spills a little air from one wing or the other if he feels the slightest tremor.

Keeping his flight steady, he takes his time swerving through the weaker updraughts that swirl around the edges of the thermal, fitting in with their corkscrew currents until he reaches the plume of maximum lift at its very centre.

There is a jolt as his wings fill with the warmest air and his stomach flutters at the rapid upwards acceleration. Spiralling up above the highlands at a thousand feet a minute, he watches his shrinking shadow until it vanishes into the jigsaw of the canyons below. His heart soars as the sky broadens out around him on all sides, spreading further and wider, pushing back the rust-red rim of the solid horizontal world. This is where he truly belongs, carried by the wind through three dimensions.

Up and up the Pteronaut goes, rising in the vast tower of air. As the ground recedes, he fixes his gaze on the readings in the goggle-display. Figures for altitude climb while those for temperature and pressure fall. Five thousand feet. Six thousand feet. Seven. Eight. And still he keeps on rising.

For every foot that he climbs within the thermal, he must glide for many more when he leaves it behind. He must take an easy and effortless path above crevasses and ravines and ridges that will delay the Crawler's progress. Hours in exchange for minutes are what he seeks, a chance to spend a restful night in shelter and to fly again tomorrow. The Pteronaut knows that his escape will not be won fully in one day; the deadly cold of a long dark night stands between him and his salvation.

Every foot matters, but he cannot let the towering updraughts carry him to their very top, twelve or fifteen thousand feet above the highlands. The Pteronaut is a creature of the air, and yet he is not the master of it; temperature and pressure conspire to keep him below a certain altitude.

As the pressure falls, so too the lift provided by the wings decreases. More effort will be needed to stay aloft, and already, at close to nine thousand feet, the Pteronaut is pushing the wings and the skin-suit to their absolute limits. If he goes too much higher, the freezing temperature of the air, already searingly cold outside the thermal, will overcome any protection the skin-suit can provide. Hypothermia will set in. His scant supply of water will not freeze, protected deep beneath the scales of the skin-suit, and while the fatty acids and saccharides in the suit's own tissues will keep it supple and moving, the Pteronaut has no such immunity. Frostbite will steal into his fingers and toes, robbing him of the control he needs to land.

Oxygen is another problem. Long before he loses consciousness to hypothermia, he will pass out from loss of breathable air. Above a certain altitude, the gill-cells will cease to function properly. The emergency reservoir of pure oxygen from the skin-suit has already been depleted by the escape from the cliffs, and the small amount his photosynthesising tattoos supply directly to his bloodstream will barely keep him conscious.

So the Pteronaut keeps a close watch on the goggle-display as the readings change, waiting for as long as he dares. It is a deadly game he plays, betting gliding-height against the cold and the thinner air. Minute by minute, those fine margins of his survival become slimmer and slimmer.

At close to eleven thousand feet, the highest he has ever gone, and with the plume of warm air weakening, the Pteronaut knows that he has gone as high as he can. He banks out of the thermal.

From one instant to the next, the upwards pull vanishes and the rippling wing-tissue becomes still and silent. Only his gliding flight will keep him airborne now. In the goggle-display, the temperature-readings retreat in shock away

43

from the levels that they reached within the thermal. Hastily, haphazardly, the red and black camouflage rearranges itself across his body to minimise heat-loss. He feels a tingle of warmth against his skin as the suit burns some more of its store of sugars to counteract the drop in temperature. Even so, a prickle of ice-crystals grows against his cheeks and lips inside the facemask, furring the inner-surface with his first frosty breaths. The crystals freeze and thaw in time with the rise and fall of his lungs, and stop just short of levering the facemask away from its airtight seal. The Pteronaut has almost climbed too far, but now he is gliding down through the sky, dropping gradually back into the warmer layers of air below.

He drinks what he can as the water-vapour in his out-breaths turns to ice in the facemask and then melts again, slurping up the pools it makes against his lips. The skin-suit recycles almost every drop of water that leaves his body, but it will be hours before it has gathered so much as to afford one half-mouthful. The few sips he manages are a debt that the Pteronaut will be forced to pay back later, but temporarily, at least, his thirst is satisfied.

His goggle-eyes sweep across the desert plateau, so far below him. At last, he can rest for a while. He clicks the button on the hand-grips and locks the wings into a new position, one that will carry him on with minimal effort. Hanging at ease, he looks over to the distant curve of the cliffs and finds the searching smoke-trail. The Crawler is still out there, still seeking a way up onto the plateau. He knows it will not rest.

The Pteronaut turns away. Thousands of feet below him, his crucifix shadow skitters across the broken terrain as he picks out the most difficult path for the Crawler to follow, racing the red horizon and the coming of the night.

07

Wreathed in red dust down on the plains, the Crawler rumbled along. The cliffs towered impassive and unassailable on its left, throwing out their shadows further and further as the day wore on. For nearly twenty miles already, it had skirted the plateau, but it had not found what it sought. There was no easy and accessible way up onto the old continent, no wide valley, no gentle slope. The rock walls stood as they had stood for long ages, unbreached and unbreachable.

Tireless in its search, the Crawler was undeterred. It cut a dusty track across the plains, probing every rockslide and every faultline. Laser-light flickered into cracks and crevices as it measured the gradient of the slopes, the angle of the rocks, the stability of the mountainsides. It scanned the numbers that came back to it, seeking a path. None could be found. Too narrow. Too steep. Too unstable. The Crawler's pistons pounded with greater urgency.

Soaring high above the plateau, miles away and getting more distant by the minute, the tracker-tag sent out its silent signal, clasped tight around the birdman's ankle. He had half a day of gliding ahead of him, and if the thermals and the landscape worked in his favour, half a day's gliding could take him beyond the range of the signal from the tag.

The Crawler knew it. It sensed that its prey was getting away. It saw how quickly and how easily the birdman flew, and it guessed that every turn and every change of direction in the signal's progress marked a new obstacle in its path, a new hurdle that it would have to overcome. Ravines. Crevasses. Ridges. Canyons. Steep slopes of scree. Not just the speed and the distance, but the vagaries of the terrain and its geology were being used against it. The Crawler should have been dismayed, but it had remembered something that would tip the odds of success in its favour.

For long ages, the Crawler had travelled the desert wastes. It had criss-crossed the wide red plains a thousand times. They were always the same, and they were always different. Dunes came and went, rewriting the landscape with their own restless wanderings, and sometimes the Crawler found things that the sands had first covered and then uncovered; buried treasures from an age before the deserts ruled.

Some of the things that the Crawler found, it could understand. It saw immediately why they had been built and how it could put them to use, like the velocycles. Other things had uses that were unknown or unclear to it, uses which the Crawler had to reinvent or to rediscover, like the tracker-tag that had been shackled to the birdman's ankle. And in some cases, it found something built for a purpose that it could not even guess at.

The Crawler had something stowed away in the dark depths of its cargo-holds, something that it had once found buried deep in the sands, whole and undamaged. For a long time, that something had been a riddle to it. Then somehow the Crawler had solved the riddle, only to forget the solution again. Now it had remembered once more, and it was searching for this once-useless thing.

A section of its armoured upper-deck slid back along squealing rails, the surface mottled where fleeting streaks of steam from leaks and vents had rusted it. An opening was revealed, deep and full of shadows, and it led down into one of the Crawler's storage-holds.

High above the deck, a crane-arm swung around stiffly and lowered its hook inside, paying out yards and yards of cable as the Crawler groped around among its treasures. The wire stopped, and then the motors started to reverse as it was winched back in; the Crawler had found what it was looking for. Carefully, the hook and its burden were hoisted up from the depths.

A smooth pyramid of folded white metal and plastic came into view. It rocked precariously as the crane-arm swung it away from the opening of the storage-holds and deposited it onto a flat section of the upper-deck. A handful of drones hurried across the Crawler's battle-armour, busying themselves with what had been placed before them. They unclasped the hook from the lifting-girdle and unwrapped the chains that held the pyramid together. Some of them clambered up over the tapering bodywork, folding out the triangles of its wings and locking them in position. Others hinged its tail section into place, and attached the propeller. Somehow, they too had remembered what this once-useless thing was for.

Slowly, the flying-machine took shape, and one of the drones clambered inside the glass bubble of the cockpit, studying the controls, testing the systems, preparing it for launch.

08 The thermal has been left far behind, and high above the plateau, the Pteronaut continues his glide. He is so high that the breaths he draws in from the gill-cells have been warmed only slightly during their passage through the skin-suit's capillaries. Each one is a dagger of ice in his throat and he keeps his breathing shallow.

He does not need much effort to stay airborne as he soars on the wind. Even so, he beats the wings from time to time, just to warm his muscles and to stay alert. If he shivers, his arms will tense and he will lose control. Inactivity is dangerous enough, but the Pteronaut cannot just let the wind take him wherever it will; to have any chance of escape, he must map out the most difficult path for the Crawler to follow.

From so high up, he can see exactly where he needs to go, and he sees that the plateau is not an island, a single free-standing slab of rock – it is just the start of something much bigger. The high cliffs run away on either side to the very edge of his vision. There they meet the blue bowl of the sky, marking out the boundaries of an unknown continent that stands imperiously above the seas of sand, a continent with its very own dunes and ridges and mountains and valleys.

Looking down at the desert from such a height, the landscape appears much more varied than it does closer to the ground. A few thousand feet lower, things seem to merge imperceptibly one into the other, but from where he glides at the limits of the skin-suit's powers to keep him alive, the Pteronaut can see all the variations at once together.

Colours shift starkly. Bright blood-red becomes rust, rust becomes crimson, and crimson becomes a red so deep and dark it is almost black. Textures change suddenly too. Silk-smooth ribbons of fine sand, miles and miles long, wind sinuously across hard expanses of wind-scoured rock pavements, trailing out unfinished where the winds die away. Where the winds strengthen, rows of dunes form crescent-shaped armies of light and shadow, rising up into marching ranks of seifs and great slope-sided barchans. Where the winds clash, the dune-armies break up into squabbling patches, or join together into spirals and stars.

Wherever the Pteronaut looks, the wind is now master, but between the sand-strewn plains, the scars of an older terrain occasionally show through, a terrain that has been shaped by very different forces. Fingers of choked riverbeds clutch out into the dust, and strand-lines of pebbles curve across stony stretches of bare rock, giving it the texture of honeycombed froth. These are orphan landscapes, uncared for by the wind, isolated and unrepeatable. Their time is gone, and the desert is always waiting to erase them.

Cold, red, and dead, the Pteronaut is blind to the stark and striking beauty of the deserts below. He looks at them and sees only the patterns of the prevailing winds, or where the best places to launch and land might be found. Now, he studies the landscape with other more urgent needs. This is a part of the wastes that he has never visited before, far from his usual flight-paths. As he flies above it, the Pteronaut turns his head, seeking out the landforms that will give him the best chance of escape. In the blink of an eye, his shadow ripples across deep canyons and tumbledown ridges, sliding effortlessly up and over all the obstacles that nature can build for him.

Out in the free air of the empty sky, hanging at rest with the daylight working on his photosynthesising tattoos, the Pteronaut can regain some of his strength. The ache of his flight-muscles ebbs away. The toll taken on him by his climb up the cliffs is fading, and the skin-suit, too, is restoring itself as it keeps him alive. The noise of the wind soughing through the wing-spars is familiar and comforting, almost a lullaby.

After a little while of listening to the wind's soft song, the Pteronaut becomes aware of something else, a different tone mixed in with the noise of his gradual descent. There is a buzz, almost too distant to hear, but getting louder. He angles his head from side to side, trying to localise the source of this new sound. Whatever it is, it is not the low rumble of the Crawler, and nor does it sound like the racing engine of a distant velocycle.

He scans the broken contours of the mountains below him for any signs. Nothing. There is no dust-plume fluttering up from anything moving on the ground. He reaches up to his temple and touches the goggle-controls beneath the scales of the suit, using the telescopic sight to magnify the ravines and crevasses. Again he sees nothing. And yet there is something out there.

With a quick decisive movement, the Pteronaut unlocks the wings and cuts an s-shape through the air. It is a costly manoeuvre in terms of gliding height, and he listens carefully through the shifting currents for the location of the buzzing. It grows louder and more insistent. He looks across the red earth for what is making it, scowling and squinting behind his goggles. Yet still he can see nothing moving there except for the slow shift of the shadows marking time.

But then he spots the source of the noise, and it is not below him at all – something else is in the sky.

The flyder is white, as white as a bleached bone against the crimson desert, an angular unwieldy shape that hangs awkwardly in the air. Immovable wings jut out on either side of a stubby body, with a bulbous glass canopy bulging between them, and the landing gear fixed beneath. Mounted at the front is the spinning blur of a propeller.

The Pteronaut stares at this newcomer to his sky, almost disbelieving. Many times he has seen the wreckage of similar vehicles scattered through the dunes, half-buried carcasses, shattered and broken. It never occurred to him that they might have flown through the air as he does, with their brittle skins and their heavy metal skeletons. But this one flies, ploughing laboriously through the sky, and it is heading straight for him.

With little more than a shrug of his shoulders, a lazy liquid movement, the Pteronaut shifts into a new course. Another costly move: he loses some more of the height from his glide. But he can keep the thing in view from a safe distance as it changes course to track him.

He watches intently. The flyder does not soar as he does; its movements are slow and clumsy, and it rocks and teeters, as if it were balancing on an unseen wire strung through the air. Behind the cockpit, the rudder jostles and twitches in the jutting fin of the tailplane, and the flaps in the wings flutter uncertainly. Cramped up inside the glass dome of the cockpit, the Crawler's drone is busy making constant adjustments.

For a few minutes, the Pteronaut is absorbed in his observations. Then, the shining white vehicle seems to overbalance completely; it pitches over sharply to one side and comes diving down fast and true, straight at the birdman.

The swiftness of the movement takes the Pteronaut by surprise. With no time for anything else, he spills the air out from under his wings and loops off to one side in a half-spiral. The flyder flashes past him, the eddies and vortices of its wake dragging him off balance. End-over-end he falls, tumbling through the air for another hundred feet or more before he regains control and levels off. When he looks down, his shadow is noticeably larger against the landscape below. The altitude-reading in his goggle-display tells him exactly how much precious height the manoeuvre has cost him.

The sense of balance and orientation that helped the Pteronaut to recover so quickly from the velocycle crash enables him to locate the flyder again almost instantly. It has levelled off a hundred feet below him, but inside the cockpit, the pilot is already looking around again for the birdman, ready to start climbing for another diving assault. Their eyes meet and the chase is on again. The engine of the flyder pants as it struggles to regain altitude.

The Pteronaut keeps the flyder in view, undeceived now by its stuttering ascent. He changes course, zig-zagging above the steep valleys, but he can do nothing to stop the next attack. Within a few minutes, the flyder is high enough to make another dive, and once again it rolls over and plunges towards him. Once again, he slips sideways and downwards out of its path, falling haphazardly and ending up another three hundred feet closer to the desert below.

They are not dangerous in themselves, the dives. The flyder is a clumsy hunter. Any movements are preceded by tell-tale jerks of the ailerons and the rudder-flap, and the Pteronaut is learning to read its slow-witted semaphore. Gradually, he comes to understand how the thing changes its position in the air, and that gives him an extra second in the turn. With his flexible wings and his feel for the currents around him, there is never any danger of a collision. But the flyder-pilot is not trying to knock the birdman out of the air – this is a game of attrition.

Another heavy-handed fly-past brings the Pteronaut two hundred feet closer to the chasms and knife-edged ridges below. Above him, the sky has lost the brightest blue of noon. The light is failing, imperceptibly but inevitably. Already, the thermals will be starting to lose their strength. Minute by minute, his chances of finding another updraught are slipping away; the Pteronaut needs to take the initiative and finish this duel. That is the only way will he have a chance to reach safety before nightfall.

The flyder climbs laboriously again for another diving attack. The Pteronaut cannot climb above it, and he cannot outrun it. Slow and sluggish as it is, the flyder will not tire as he does. And there are no hiding places in the empty sky. The only hope that the Pteronaut has is to fight back directly – he has four shots left in the pistol in his supply-pouch.

The note of the flyder's engine changes and it lurches forwards and downwards. Once more the Pteronaut spills the lifting air from under his wings and angles them in their joints, falling into an evasive dive. This time, he stays clear of the flyder's wake-turbulence, and he levels off again sharply and cleanly, with the flyder still pulling out of its own dive some distance below him.

That is his chance. He locks the wings in position, reaches inside the supply-pouch where the pistol is stowed away, and draws it out. With the wind humming away at the wing-tissue, he angles his bodyweight against the tail-brace, banking in a slow and steady arc towards his target.

He fires once, and then once again, steadying himself against the recoil. But the shots have been wasted; fighting the currents to stay level in mid-air, the Pteronaut has fired well wide. The flyder flips over and curves away out of his line of sight. Now the Pteronaut only has two shots left, and he needs both hands free to fly. Hastily, he repockets the pistol and unlocks the wings before the flyder can dive at him again.

The birdman's gamble had not paid off, and now the flyder-drone understood the danger that it faced. Looping up above the birdman, it cut a tight circle through the air, watching its prey carefully. It had seen how the birdman turned only slowly with the pistol in his hands: he could not shoot and manoeuvre at the same time. If the flyder-drone kept the birdman on the move, it had nothing to fear.

Once again, the flyder dashes down at the Pteronaut, sending him tumbling through the air. For a moment, despite his excellent sense of balance, the spinning pattern of red earth and blue sky makes him dizzy, flashing past, red and blue, red and blue. But only for a moment, and then the Pteronaut has control again, finding his path through the air towards the bone-white dagger of the flyder below.

This time, the Pteronaut does not level off. He sweeps back his wings and plunges into a dive. Beyond the readings in the goggle-display, his shadow ripples across the hard edges of the canyons. In a matter of seconds he has fallen a hundred feet and he keeps on falling. Two hundred feet, three hundred feet...

There is the flyder hanging in the sky. Its flat white shape seems almost motionless. The wind roars and hisses in the Pteronaut's ears. At the last instant, when he is so close he cannot miss, he lets the wings fold away into the case on his back and braces himself for impact.

With a thud and a judder, he hits the wing.

The Pteronaut often roosts on ledges no bigger than the flyder's wing, good places to get an easy launch the next morning. But he has never landed at such a speed, or on something that moves.

His body bounces against the camber of the wing, and his arms and legs go flailing for the edges, trying to get a hold. Windblast and gravity are formidable opponents taken separately, and now the Pteronaut is wrestling against both of them at the same time. Fingers that have saved his life in many a climb search for something to grip, but the tapering wing is smoother than any cliff-face. He slithers across it, fighting for a hold on the curving leading-edge. The toes of his boots squeak and squeal across the slippery white surface.

Then the Pteronaut's left hand has a hold on the leading edge of the wing, and in the next moment his left foot finds purchase at the wing-tip. A second later, his right boot hooks around the trailing edge. He is almost safe – as safe as he can be, hanging from the wing of a flyder – but his right hand can find nothing to grip.

He is close enough now to see the drone's face through the helmet-visor. That one unchanging face. Moving as carefully as on any cliff-face, the Pteronaut reaches back to the supply-pouch with his free right hand. His fingers slip past the overlapping folds that keep everything safe inside, searching for the hard grip of the pistol. They tighten around it, and he draws it out. Two shots left. Two shots have to be enough; so close to his target, he can hardly miss.

The pilot-drone saw the muzzle of the gun, the danger so close, and it put the flyder into a steep dive. Twisting and turning through the air, it corkscrewed around in a bid to throw the birdman off the wing. The flyder banked and rolled, soaring up and then diving again, trying to pitch its unwanted passenger off into the air. The stakes were life and death, not win or lose, and the pilot no longer cared if the Crawler's prey fell to deadly ruin among the rocks below.

Upwards, downwards, spiralling around, the Pteronaut is still there, clinging on desperately. One moment, his body is thrown clear, his limbs straining to hold on. The next, he slams hard against the wing, bouncing and jolting against it. He needs to grip with both hands, but he cannot bring himself to let go of the pistol. It bangs uselessly against the smooth white surface of the wing. There is no way to take that shot, the only hope he has of breaking the deadlock.

Something of the Pteronaut's desperation slips away from him, and his finger, already tense, squeezes the trigger. The flailing motion of his arm sends the bullet singing into space. Another precious shot wasted, and the move has jeopardised his hold. As taut as wires, the fingers of his left hand threaten to snap.

The pilot puts the flyder into another roll and the Pteronaut sees his chance. The wing-flap lowers fully in front of him and he rams the pistol hard into the open angle that it makes. With the heel of his hand he hammers the pistol tight between flap and wing, twisting the grip around, wedging the flap and locking it open – the flyder is trapped in its spin.

The Pteronaut claws for safety with his empty hand. He finds the edge of the wing and lies at full length across its white width. For an instant, he remains motionless, arms straight, facing headfirst into the dive and the rushing wind.

Then with a last look across at the uncomprehending drone, he releases his hold and goes tumbling away.

The tailfin of the flyder slices past his head, and the Pteronaut flips away from his plunging foe. Falling so fast in that shapeless blue-sky, red-earth whirl of colour, he cannot activate his wings. The currents rip at him, sending his body spinning. Every second that the Pteronaut plummets downwards brings him closer to the point at which turning fall into flight will be impossible. Then he finds an opening in the onslaught of the currents. Arms and legs outstretched, body flattened, his speed slows slightly, spinning less and less. He cannot afford to wait any longer. Still falling too fast, falling too far, he reaches for the wing-grips and presses down on the thumb-locks, tensing his muscles against the shock.

With a whip-crack, the wings flare out and catch the currents. The spars and struts shudder with a neck-breaking jerk. The force of the blow drives all the air from the Pteronaut's lungs, almost wrenching his arms from their sockets. Torn free from his fall, for one tortured in-breath he hangs there, crucified against the sky. And then he moves again. Sideways, the Pteronaut slips into another fall.

But this time, it is a fall with wings.

The Pteronaut jams his feet into the tail-brace, pushing against it to master his path through the rushing currents. He bows the crackling wings in their sockets, straining them into a new shape that will resist the pull of gravity. The ripple of the wind across the wings changes. They fill with air and the Pteronaut is flying once more.

Below the birdman and still falling, the flyder-pilot was also fighting against gravity, but the pistol was wedged tight in the flap and nothing could dislodge it. The drone could not recover from the roll.

The wings of the flyder creaked. The fuselage cracked and popped. The bone-white triangle spiralled towards the rising landscape. Jagged peaks filled the drone's view. No longer a protector, the glass cage of the canopy hemmed it in. None of the charms it wore could save it, the symbols it had painted on its armour were powerless.

One of the landing wheels caught an outcrop of a slant-edged butte, and instinctively, the flyder-pilot raised an arm to ward off the blow. The flyder changed direction abruptly, spinning through the air towards another rocky edge. The tailplane hit an outcrop of the mountain and shattered into splinters. The nose of the flyder crunched against the cliff, and slivers of metal from the propeller went slicing in all directions, cutting the fuselage to ribbons. Fuel enveloped the falling flyder. With a sudden spark, it blossomed into flame, leaving a wreath of smoke behind it as it went bouncing and bumping from rock to rock.

Safe up above, the Pteronaut watches the fireball fall. It seems to slow as it nears the ground, and then it spreads flat in all directions as the red earth takes it. The sky is his again, but struggling out of the dive has taken its toll. He passes above high ridges and lonely ledges, maintaining what altitude he has with slack beats of the wings. Any one of those ledges would make a good roost, a place where he could rest and recover. An hour, that is all he needs.

But the red plume that marks the Crawler's pursuit is out there behind him somewhere, and the power of the daylight is waning. The seductive safety of those ledges is illusory. Rest must wait.

The Pteronaut banks over to where the wreckage of the flyder has come to a halt far below, a scatter of white plastic and metal, strewn like confetti across the rocks. It is still blazing, the flames fed by the last gasps of oxygen and fuel that remain in the tanks. There is nothing to salvage there. Nothing for the Crawler, at least.

The Pteronaut flies closer. He can feel how the heat from the blaze sets the air above it spiralling upwards. Not fast, and not high, but enough for now, until he can find a stronger updraught. He steers into the rising currents of the mini-thermal and soars up with it for another thousand feet, taking whatever advantages he can from his victory.

09

Silence fell. Not quite silence; the terminal hiss of static. The location signal from the flyder had vanished. The Crawler slowed where it travelled the plains beneath the plateau's walls.

For a hundred miles since it had launched the flyder, the Crawler had been skirting the cliffs, bombarding them with sonar, radar, x-rays, infra-red; turning the spectrum inside out in its searching. But the rockfaces had defied every effort to find a way in. Rather, the cliffs seemed to resent the Crawler's intrusion, and reared up higher against it – six, seven, eight hundred feet – getting steeper as they did. They would not relent. The Crawler had searched through the arsenal of weapons that it had dug out of the dust, looking for something that might change its fortunes. Nothing it possessed would be powerful enough. The cliffs were impregnable; there was no point trying to force a way through them.

So it had searched on patiently. For a time, the location signal from the flyder had overlapped with the intermittent chirrup from the tracker-tag as the birdman and the drone had fought their aerial duel. The Crawler had been content to wait, listening to the chirps and cheeps as the two signals dived and swooped above the plateau. Its plan had been working, and while the birdman's glide was interrupted, it had continued its search, patiently and methodically.

And now suddenly this: static, as bleak and as empty as the dunes.

The other signal still called out from the birdman's tracker-tag, but it was changing. For a few moments, the Crawler monitored it intently, sensing nothing else, listening to the small variations as the tones in the signal slid past each other. The tracker-tag was on the move; the birdman was still flying.

The Crawler sped up again. The search for an easy route had failed. If it delayed for even just a few minutes more, the birdman might manage to fly beyond the signal range of the tracker-tag in the hours of daylight that remained. With favourable winds over difficult terrain and strong thermals, he might yet escape. And if the signal vanished off the edge of the Crawler's scopes, it might be hours, days even, before it could be found it again. There was even the chance, the very real possibility, that the Crawler might *never* pick up the signal again, and it was not prepared to let that happen. It could hesitate no longer.

A few miles further on, the Crawler rocked to a halt at the foot of an incline. The incline was steep, but the ascent looked steady. There were no ledges or sheer cliffs barring the route up onto the plateau, just an angled slope, covered thinly with dust and a scatter of loose rock. The Crawler probed the surface with its sensors, scanning its depth and its composition. The slope would slip a little, but it was solid – it would not slide away beneath the tracks.

Even so, the Crawler was not built for such a climb. Right at the summit of the tall drill-derrick that bored down through the permafrost to find liquid water, the Crawler towered almost four hundred and fifty feet above the plain. A hundred feet below the peak of the derrick, the Crawler's armoured upper-deck spread out, and below that, tier after tier of metal, perched and piled up above the tracks that drove it forwards. On a slope as precarious as the one before it, the Crawler could easily become marooned with its drive-units off the ground. Or worse – it could even overbalance and come crashing down. Built as it was, ascent was unthinkable.

But the Crawler did not have to remain built as it was.

Motors clattered and pistons hissed. Halfway up the Crawler's silver sides, metal tracks swung out from where they had lain hidden, retracted and folded away beneath the decks of the middle sections. Like steel spines, they projected out into space. More motors started up. Cogwheels creaked. Elevators whined. Within the chaos of walkways and segments that formed the Crawler's body, a metamorphosis was taking place. The huge irregular bulk was shifting shape. First on one side and then on the other, the middle tiers jostled each other and realigned themselves. Gangways were hinged back. Drawbridges were raised. Pipework was untangled. Slowly, an order emerged, and the Crawler's stacked strata separated themselves from each other, leaving ladders hanging suddenly with nowhere to go. When that was done the Crawler paused, as if it were summoning the strength it needed for the next stage.

With a grunt, hydraulic rams started to move, pushing metal against metal. Sheets of ice-bound dust crumbled and fell from the Crawler, an old skin being shed. Rust formations that had grown long shattered and showered the ground beneath with their fragments. Foot by foot, the middle layers of the Crawler crept along the parallel trackways that thrust out from its sides, gasping and grinding into mid-air until they reached the buffers and shuddered to a halt.

Again the Crawler paused for a moment, sensing the void that had opened up within itself. Then with a squeal of sliding steel, the disembodied upper sections started to move, descending down vertical rails into the space that had been vacated below them. Inch by inch, the Crawler's upper storeys sank down until they too juddered to a standstill, and the armoured upper-deck came level with the projecting middle tiers. Finally, the crane masts and the drill-derrick hinged and folded over onto the patchwork island of the Crawler's wider squatter body, bowing down to touch its broad back.

The Crawler was ready. Its metamorphosis was complete. Below its flattened metal bulk, the rows of tracks rumbled around in their sockets to face the incline, and the Crawler started to climb the slope.

10

Night is falling. For hours after the flyder battle, the Pteronaut has glided from one updraught to the next, hopscotching across the desert. None of the thermals has carried him quite so high as the first, and his glides have become shorter and shorter. Now the light is failing. All around him, the bowl of the sky darkens, its blue shading into purple as the daylight fades. And as the light bleeds away, so too does what little warmth it carries with it. A chill is on the air, as cutting as a knife-blade even as the Pteronaut swoops closer to the ground. He needs to find a roost for the night.

The Pteronaut needs water too. Every sip on the drip-tube brings the low-water warning blinking more urgently on the edge of his goggle-display. Soon it will remain there. He cannot fly for more than a day or two without replenishing his stores, and that will mean digging for water-ice.

Deep beneath the sands, great quantities of water-ice are locked into the permafrost. In some parts of the deserts, massive polygonal mounds of ice-crystals have been thrust upwards by the long and lazy process of freeze-thaw, but the Pteronaut has seen none of those icy upwellings in the new continent. At other places on his usual flight-paths, the deeper rocks are hot enough to keep the water from freezing, and sometimes, the hot regions shift. Some change of an underground faultline will bring a sudden surge of liquid water bubbling up through the sand and gravel. An icy scar will be left for the dust to cover, and the sign of a recent rushing flow down a hillside is a good place to look.

But the Pteronaut cannot spare the time to search for water now. The flyder duel has cost him dearly, and he has no idea how much of his advantage remains. If the Crawler finds him during the night, he is lost. And night has come: it has crept slowly across the sky until only the edges of the horizon still remain light. The Pteronaut has flown as far as he can. If he delays any longer in finding a roost, he will not have enough light to land by.

For another couple of minutes, he holds out against the dark and the cold, passing over another couple of miles of jagged terrain. Then, with the temperature falling fast, he unlocks the wings and shifts out of his glide. Wheeling through the twilight, he scans the landscape in all directions. The Pteronaut loses more height, swooping down as low as he dares, coming in close to the buttes and mesas below.

The air-currents around him fret and become confused as they meet the rising land, and he holds the wing-grips tightly. Looking past the readings in the goggle-display, he searches for somewhere that is easy to land on and good to launch from; never an easy combination. For the landing, flat level ground is the best option; for the launch, a high ridge will be safest and require the least effort. A certain trade-off will be needed.

He spots a mesa with a table-top summit and goes in for a closer look. Every landing is a calculated risk, and something that appears solid might turn out to be too soft and sandy to take the weight of those first thudding footfalls. A blanket of dust spread over fine shifting gravel is the worst; the gravel will swallow a boot and lock around it, bringing the touchdown to an abrupt end. A broken leg or arm would be as good as fatal to the Pteronaut, even without the Crawler on his trail. Broken wings would be even worse.

The summit of the mesa looks solid enough, but on the far side its slopes are too shallow to deter the Crawler. The Pteronaut catches a ridge-current and turns away. Over on the edge of his eyesight, silhouetted against the horizon, he sees three spires towering up between smaller hills. They look promising, and he angles the wings and flies towards them.

Down beneath the spires, the land has already been drowned by shadow. Their summits stand marooned in the last of the light, dusky islands in a dark sea. The Pteronaut flies over the narrow peaks, looping a gentle figure of eight to check them from all directions. The top of each spire is a stack with sheer sides, held high above the valley floor on a crumbling tower that will be impossible for the Crawler's drones to scale. Even for him, the spires are near enough unclimbable. They are just what he needs.

As he comes in closer, the Pteronaut begins his calculations. He feels how the airflow plays across and around each stack, judging how the wind is broken up by the hard edges that it encounters. Reading the invisible patterns of the currents is vital for success, but it is only part of the equation. Angle of approach, airspeed, rate of descent; all of them are critical if the landing is going to succeed.

He swoops lower. The low-light indicator shows in the corner of the goggle-display. Shadow is creeping up the stacks now, slowly swallowing each pinnacle. Definition and depth have all but vanished. Judging distance is going to be difficult, but still the Pteronaut does not switch into the grey-green of his night-vision. Second by second there is less natural light for the landing, but even that gives him more chance of success than the flat and grainy images of the goggles' low-light mode.

The Pteronaut turns away from the pinnacles. He has made his choice of roost. Of the three spires, one has a slightly broader summit, half a dozen paces wide, and with a deep cleft running across it. It is not quite flat, but the angle is not so steep that he cannot stand upon it. That is where he will shelter for the night.

Beating the wings regularly, short shallow flicks, he heads away from the pinnacles, giving himself time and distance for the final approach. When the wind feels right, he doubles back on himself and banks towards the summit. He loses height, turning it into speed. Then he loses speed, holding each beat of the wings a moment too long and too full of air before the next upsweep, braking his descent.

A click of another thumb-button, and the wings change their shape again. Joints flex and struts scissor together. Folds slide past each other. Wires creak, taking the strain as the wings bend from upstroke to downstroke, helping the Pteronaut to eke out every last breeze. He spirals closer and closer to the summit.

Timing is everything now.

The spirals that the Pteronaut makes become tighter and tighter. At their centre the pinnacle grows larger and larger, but still it is no more than a footprint, a tiny patch of solid rock six hundred feet above the desert – a small target that sweeps past in half a wing-beat.

The Pteronaut has to judge the size and the tightness of his spirals to precision. A turn too close and his speed will carry him past the summit; a turn too far and he will lose too much height and strike the side of the stack. With each foot of altitude he loses, the stakes become higher – failure that does not end in instant death will leave him stranded on the plains.

His perception sharpens. Seconds stretch out into minutes in his mind. The rocks come close enough to see the texture of the grains that form them, every fissure and every fault-line is etched in perfect detail, every angle clear. The currents part and the Pteronaut makes the turn. Too close to stop, too near to overshoot, the summit flashes past below him. His arms stiffen, halting the wings between beats. At the very last instant, he seems to hang in mid-air. In a single movement, he unhooks his feet from the tail-spine and releases the wings.

Ten feet straight down, the Pteronaut drops from the sky.

Shhkaaarshhh!

The Pteronaut's boots skid out from under him, scraping sideways across the slope of the summit, and he falls onto his outstretched hands. Face down, he slides towards the drop. His boot-caps score the flaking surface of the pinnacle, trying to dig into it. His fingers clutch at every fissure that the wind has worried into the rock, seeking purchase from the whorls and ridges of his gloves.

He does not stop. Does not even slow. Dislodged fragments of rock go tumbling and spinning over the edge. He pushes harder, fighting against the slope. Every joint locked, he resists the pull that is taking him towards the drop. No more than two feet from the lip of the precipice, friction bites, and the Pteronaut comes to a halt. For a moment he waits, just to be sure. And then he stands up.

The Pteronaut has landed.

Even after just a few hours of flight, the solidity of the rock beneath the Pteronaut's feet feels alien and unreal; the unyielding surface is a barrier, an intrusion into his world of constantly moving currents. He stamps his boots against it a few times, as if to convince his muscles of the reality of it, and then he climbs up the incline towards the cleft in the summit.

The cleft started as a tiny split, a hairline fracture. Flake by flake and chip by chip, ages and ages of night-frosts have widened it and deepened it. Now it is a sheltered V-shaped gully filled to half its depth with gravel; the perfect place for the Pteronaut to spend the night.

The sky above the desert is dark purple, and the horizon is indistinguishable from the distant dunes. The temperature is ticking down in the goggle-display and the rocks crack around him as the frost bites deep. The Pteronaut needs shelter fast.

He reaches into the supply-pouch. Inside, lodged securely in the innermost and safest fold, his fingers find what they seek: a hard cylinder of tough plastic, a little longer than the distance from his wrist to his finger-tips. He draws it out and starts to unscrew one end, working quickly. Already his fingers are tingling from the cold. He stoops and takes a pinch of red dust from among the gravel-grains in the gully – even way up at the summit of the pinnacle, the dunes are trying to take hold. Then he sprinkles the dust inside the cylinder, and presses the open end of it against a nozzle in the exterior of the skin-suit, a teat, hidden in a hollow below the gill-cells. The suit excretes a few drops of acidic liquid, and the dust inside the hard plastic cylinder starts to fizz. The Pteronaut screws the cap back on, lays the cylinder down into the gully, and stands to one side.

Wrapped around the outside of the cylinder is a sheath of red and black plastic, its surface webbed with tiny hexagons. Squeaking and wheezing, the plastic expands as the network of double-walled cells fills with gas. Steadily, the strip stretches and inflates to become a tubular sleeping-chamber, wedging itself tight between the rocks. Within less than a minute, the insulated tube is at full size, its tough plastic skin bloated and distorted to fit securely into the cleft.

The Pteronaut unbuckles his wing-pack from around his shoulders and kneels down at one end of the sleeping-chamber. He finds the taut overlapping screens of the entrance-slit, and with the wing-pack held out in front of him, he creeps inside the tube, out of the reach of the cold and the dark.

The day is done and he has made the most of his chances. All he can do now is lie safe in his roost and sleep, hoping for a bright sky and an empty horizon the next day.

11

The Pteronaut wakes suddenly. He clicks on his low-light vision and peers around. The corrugated inner-surface of the sleeping-chamber shows up starkly, illuminated by a glowing red dot set between the lenses of his goggles. In normal light, the dot is almost too faint to see, but in the darkness inside the tube its reflection skips across the plastic walls and paints a dazzling flare across his vision.

The walls of the sleeping-tube tremble and shake. Outside, the wind plucks away at the Pteronaut's refuge, despite its protected position in the gully.

For a few minutes, the Pteronaut listens hard, out beyond the muffling walls of the tube, out into the howling dark. There is no engine-noise, no clatter of tracks. It is just a night storm, the wind whistling around the rocks. He lies down on his stomach, and is asleep again within minutes.

When the Pteronaut wakes again, the chronometer in the goggle-display tells him it must be almost dawn. He stretches as much as he can in the confines of the tube and tests his flight-muscles after the rigours of the previous day. There are a few aches here and there, but nothing too bad – just the aftermath of the escape at the cliffs and the duel with the flyder. Another day's gliding flight and the aches will be forgotten.

The Pteronaut yawns inside his facemask and takes a small sip of water from the drip-tube, almost daring the low-water indicator to flash its warning at him. Today, if he starts well and flies far and fast, he must land before nightfall and seek water-ice. Tomorrow he will be down to his very last mouthful.

With that thought on his mind, he fumbles around in the corners of the sleeping-chamber. Sometimes ice collects there, freezing in little rivulets as small amounts of water-vapour escape from the suit and condense against the walls. Holding his breath, the Pteronaut slips off the facemask and dabs what he finds onto his tongue. It is meagre harvest, but he is glad for it all the same. Then with the facemask still off, he eats a mouthful of one of his ration-bars.

That is when he hears it.

It starts with no warning – even a landslide begins with a few creaks and cracks – and becomes in an instant a deafening avalanche of engines and steel.

CRASH!

The pinnacle shakes. Inside the sleeping-chamber, the Pteronaut feels the world around him judder and sway. The fury of acceleration and impact dies away as abruptly as it began, replaced by the splintering scatter of stone on metal armour. Outside, beyond the din of destruction, he hears the Crawler reverse back along its own track-marks, ready to ram the rocky pinnacle head-on once more.

In a heartbeat, the Pteronaut has the facemask back on. In another, he is out of the sleeping-chamber. As he stands upright, he drags the wing-pack on around his shoulders and buckles it into position. The summit of the tower is grey in the half-light of dawn. Night has not left the sky completely, and only the horizon glows with the start of another day. Even so, he is in luck – it is cold still, but no longer deadly cold. The Crawler has found him sooner than he hoped it would, but if it had discovered his roost just a single hour earlier, the heat-sapping chill would have trapped him inside the sleeping-chamber. The flight of the previous day has given the Pteronaut a chance.

The Crawler knows it too. Its engines roar with frustration and the pinnacle shakes again with the fury of another impact. The collision sends the birdman stumbling. He reaches inside the sleeping-chamber and activates the slow-release valve on the inflation-cylinder. The sleeping-tube shudders as he withdraws his arm, and starts to shrink gradually back to normal size.

Pressing himself close to the rocks, the Pteronaut creeps to the edge of his roost and looks out.

Two hundred feet below, the Crawler drums into life again. It moves backwards, shaking a jumble of shattered rock from its back. The first rays of daylight touch its masts and cranes, making them sparkle like spears. The Crawler has drawn itself up tall again to navigate a way through the narrow canyons and valleys, but it is still not tall enough to reach the top of the pinnacle.

It stops momentarily, and then the tracks spin in the dirt as it races forwards, smashing its armoured snout against the roots of the pillar for a third time. The pinnacle sways and creaks. Loose rocks cascade down, bouncing off the thick metal scales of the Crawler's upper-deck.

As the Pteronaut waits for the swaying pinnacle to settle, the Crawler retreats again, but not straight backwards as it has done before. This time, it veers to one side as its tracks reverse, lining itself up to ram another of the nearby pinnacles. The birdman watches to be certain. The Crawler pauses, rotates all its drive-units to face in the direction of its new target, and then it powers forwards, crashing into the second pinnacle at speed.

There is no mistake: just as at the cliffs, the tracker-tag has led the Crawler to its prey, but the signal lacks the precision to be certain which pinnacle is his roost. Once again, the final strike must be made face-to-face.

The Pteronaut crawls away from his vantage-point, eager to take his chances while he can. He clutches up the deflated cylinder of his sleeping-chamber, thrusts it into the safety of his supply-pouch, and runs towards the side of the summit that is furthest from the Crawler.

In three quick strides he is there. His boots hit the edge, the last lip of solidity jutting out into the free air, and he leaps out into nothing. Half-way between suicide and salvation, he sees the drop open up beneath him and finds the hand-grips at his shoulders. Slotting and clicking into position, the wings extend, sweeping out to catch the morning breeze.

Almost immediately, the Pteronaut sees his mistake. Startled with the frenzy of the attack and fresh from sleep, he has made his getaway in haste. The Crawler cannot locate the signal from the tracker-tag precisely, but it has not attacked the pinnacles without planning. Hidden on the ridges of the lower-lying mesas all around, a handful of the Crawler's drones lie in wait. They climbed into position in the last hour before dawn, chilled to the marrow despite the protection of their suits. Not all of them have survived, but the survivors have been waiting.

As the birdman's wings unfold, a dozen pairs of eyes turn towards him, and the morning light catches the barrels of the drones' rifles as they raise them to take aim. Then they open fire.

Flying into the wind, beating his wings to gain more height, the Pteronaut is an easy target. Gunfire cracks from the lower summits on all sides, but the drones are not trying to shoot the birdman from the sky. Not bullets, but snaking chains whistle through the air. A dozen of them hiss all around him, weighted at each end by a savage hook, spinning and clawing for his wings. The Pteronaut jinks and veers, twisting between them. Most of the chains go spiralling harmlessly away– one hits his wing edge-on and is deflected – but the Crawler's plan only needs one shot on target to succeed.

And one of the shots is on target.

The chain strikes his left wing. With a tearing noise, the hook at one end of the chain rips through the wing-tissue and catches among the struts. The other hook jerks to a halt as the chain straightens, and then, carried by its momentum, it starts to wrap the chain around the wing. Whipping, strangling, the length of chain is soon used up and the second hook catches fast around another spar. The hooks draw the chain tight: the trap is set.

71

Almost instantly, the gunfire ceases, but not before one of the last chains to be fired catches the Pteronaut's legs. He feels a stab of pain as a hook slices through the suit and strikes deep into the muscle of his right calf. Hungry and thirsty, his vision swims for a moment, white-speckled. He kicks out, sending the chain tumbling before it can wrap itself around his legs and the tail-spine.

Crying out its alarm, the suit floods the breach with resinous sealant. The Pteronaut grits his teeth against the pain and holds on to consciousness, beating the wings in time with the decompression-alarm.

Now the rigours of powered flight are not a trial, challenging the Pteronaut's strength and stamina and the muscles of the skin-suit – they are a lifeline, strung through the air ahead of him. He focuses past the searing pain, past the weakness of his hunger and his thirst, holding that lifeline with beat after beat.

Gradually, as the gash in the skin-suit is sealed and the wailing of the decompression-alarm stops, so too the pain in the Pteronaut's calf numbs. Fine fibres grow into the wound from the inner-tissues of the skin-suit. The fibres clean the wound, sterilise it, anaesthetise it, and feed from it hungrily while the fresh warm blood flows. In the dead red deserts, nothing goes to waste. In exchange, a cool trickle of oxygen plays across the Pteronaut's lips and he breathes deeply from it, concentrating on his escape.

He banks out across the mesas where the Crawler's drones were hiding, soaring away from the pinnacle of his roost and the waiting Crawler. He hears its engines roar behind him, and not in frustration as before; the cry that the Crawler sends up is the cry of jubilation. Its plan has worked.

The Pteronaut beats the wings hard, catching the ridge-currents where he can. The air is not yet warm enough for thermals, but there are still upcurrents that give him some height to glide from. He slaloms from one to the next, soaring up above the cliffs and dipping down into the valleys between them. For several miles, he mimics the lie of the land. Then he finds the first of the thermals and starts to rise with it, letting the weakly warming air carry him higher. With the Crawler behind him and the deserts dropping away below, the Pteronaut can at last take the time to examine the damage that has been done.

The chain is out of his reach, an arm's-length and a half beyond his finger-tips at the far end of the wing. He cannot disentangle it. Looking along the wing, the Pteronaut watches how the links of the chain coil around the wing-spars, seeing the way they choke the smooth and supple movements of the mechanism. The chain is an encumbrance, but it will not stop him flying. And even though the wing-tissue cannot heal itself, the tears from the hooks are small. Once he lands again, they will be easy to patch. The Pteronaut can glide all day, from thermal to thermal, as long and as far as the currents will carry him. Flying will not be a problem.

Landing, on the other hand, will be a different story. With the chain wrapped around the struts, the Pteronaut cannot be sure how the wing will fold away – *if* it will fold away. At that last moment, with the Pteronaut poised between blue sky and red earth, the wing may not draw back into safety in the wing-case on his back. And if the wing is not safe when his boots hit the ground...

The lift from the thermal is failing at four thousand feet, and the Pteronaut angles the wings and leaves it behind. There will be others, warmer, larger, that will carry him higher. Then he can glide as he did the day before, seeking out the steepest slopes, the highest ridges, and the narrowest valleys to delay the Crawler in its hunt

But however far the Pteronaut flies before nightfall, he knows that his next landing could well be his last.

12 All day the Pteronaut rides the thermals. He is a faithless flyer, never losing too much altitude in gliding from one thermal before finding another, skipping from updraught to updraught whenever he feels the pull of a stronger column of rising air from across the sky.

Again and again he goes to the absolute limits of the skin-suit's endurance. So high, so cold, with the wide blue emptiness all around him. Then, with the frost lining his facemask, he twists the wings in their sockets, changing the note of the wind singing across them as he leaves the thermal. For most of the day, his shadow is no more than a distant speck, racing across miles and miles of broken country and the scarred landscapes below.

Gliding gives the Pteronaut the chance to rest and recover. The damage to his leg has been sealed as the skin-suit heals itself. The bleeding has stopped. He feels a twinge of pain whenever he tenses the muscle against the tail-brace to steer, but the scar-tissue holds and the wound does not re-open.

His flight is laboured. The extra weight of the chain at the wing-tip is more cumbersome than he at first thought. It cuts down the distance he covers, and he can feel it hurrying him little by little towards the ground. Not only that, the chain blunts the movements of the wings, making them sluggish and numb. Every manoeuvre takes a little longer than normal and requires a little more effort. His turns are unbalanced, and he practises whenever he can, learning to compensate for the effects of the chain. It is all he can do to prepare himself for what must come at the end of the day.

He must hope that the wings will fold back safely. Landing with the wings extended is never an option: it is a guarantee of disaster. The only hope he has, small odds, are on a normal landing. His fate will be decided the instant that his feet touch the ground.

For hours and hours, the Pteronaut flies on, leaving the cloud of the Crawler's wake far behind him. At first it was a wandering column, dark-edged and dusty. Then it faded into a rusty smudge that blurred with the horizon. Now finally it has vanished completely. Far beyond the red rim of the world the Crawler keeps on, labouring unseen along its path. But however far behind the Pteronaut leaves it, his next challenge lies ahead; night is coming and with it his next landing, as inevitable and as unstoppable as the Crawler itself.

Slowly, the brilliant blue of the sky hardens into a dark purple shell. The thermals weaken and fade away. All around him, the air grows calm. Still the Pteronaut flies on. It is no longer just the distance he flies for. Every minute he spends in the air is a postponement of the moment of reckoning. He cannot delay indefinitely. The dry desert dunes come closer and closer, and slowly the darkness spreads and fills the spaces between them. His flight is nearly at an end.

The Pteronaut beats his wings with heavy discordant strokes and looks for a place to make landfall. A high roost is out of the question. A narrow summit like his resting-place of the night before is too small a target with the rasping chain adding uncertainty to every wing-beat.

And if the wings should fail…

The Pteronaut searches the landscape for a shred of salvation. Despite the skin-suit's attentions and all the hours of recovery, the wound in his calf is tight and sore, and he knows it will tear if he comes in at a run. He will need to try another drop-landing at slow speed, somewhere broad and flat and low; that is the option that offers him the greatest chance of success.

Night has painted itself almost as black as his shadow across the ground. He has to land now, while he can still see some faint outline of his own descent – judging his height by the altimeter is too imprecise and too dangerous in those final moments.

The Pteronaut picks a spot, a slanting table-top of rock, flat and wide enough to land on and shallow enough to walk down the next morning if he has to – if he can. The Crawler can climb it easily, but if he has not flown far enough, it will have found him by daylight wherever his flight ends.

He holds the wing-grips with extra determination, and sets himself on a final downward spiral. Every circle is tighter, every loop is lower, until he is skirting slowly just above the ground, almost stalling, beating the wings as hard as he can to maintain control. The downdraughts stir the dust in anticipation.

And then the moment has come; the Pteronaut pulls up into the wind, releases the wing-grips, and drops.

His boots hit the ground together, his legs ready to absorb the shock. His knees flex, but the wing cannot. Inside the wing-case on his back, the mechanism stutters as it tries to fold the wings into safety. Wires tense to breaking-point. Tremors run through them, vibrations that get higher and higher in pitch, almost screaming. The wing with the snare bends back on itself. A breath of air catches it, dragging the Pteronaut off-balance. The tendons in his knee twist like the wires in the wings, ready to rip.

The Pteronaut has no choice: it is his knee or the wings. He gives in to the force that threatens to wrench his knee-cap from its socket and throws his whole weight with it.

Spars crack. Joints pop. Cables screech.

With a noise as deadly as a gunshot, the wing sags, folding back on itself in a way it was never designed to do, and a rain of shattered metal links goes pattering into the dust all around. The snare is undone at last.

For long minutes, the Pteronaut lies face down in the sand with the shroud of his wings lying across him, fluttering in the wind. The echo of that terrible moment is trapped inside his head, battering around and around against the inside of his skull, looking for a way out. A cry will free it, a shout that gives vent to all the Pteronaut's pain and anger, but he knows that a shout would be the end of him. Once he starts he would never stop: the silence afterwards would be too much to bear. So the Pteronaut bites back his cry, stifling it, suffocating it, until the echo in his head has died away into nothing.

It would be easy for him to lie there, with his body-heat ebbing away through the insulating layers of the skin-suit. The skin-suit would burn through its store of sugars to keep him warm, and still he would not move. It would be easy, so easy, to let the deadly cold of the dark creep into his blood and bones, stealing deep inside to the chill that he already feels at his core. In the morning, the shadows will lift and he will still be there, lying as he has come down, with the broken hope of his wings across him, and the wind piling dust around his frozen corpse. And unless the Crawler comes by, there his body will stay – another plaything for the desert, to be hidden and found and hidden again. Another relic of a forgotten journey to be buried by the dunes.

But that is not the Pteronaut way. Every launch and every landing is a risk. Every breath is a miracle of survival. Every new day a triumph. He has not flown journey after journey for thousands of miles across the wastes to end like that.

So the Pteronaut moves at last, throwing the hanging tatters of the wing to one side, and he sits up in the sand with his legs stretched out in front of him. Through the dull nothing of the cold and his despair, he becomes aware that the wound in his calf has torn open in the fall. Blood seeps out between skin and suit, trickling wet and warm, and the filaments respond to it as before, searching for it, lapping it up. What does the skin-suit care if his wings are broken? It carries on keeping him warm, filtering the air, generating oxygen as it feeds from the by-products of his every breath. He yearns for such single-mindedness.

With leaden limbs, he sets up the sleeping-chamber. When the tube is fully inflated, he unbuckles the wing-pack and folds the broken wing inside it as carefully as he can without looking at what it has become. Then he pushes the wing-pack into the tube through the entrance-slit, and crawls inside after it.

Night has come and the Pteronaut is down, and down is where he will stay.

13

For all the hours of the birdman's gliding flight, the Crawler took the difficult and dangerous path that had been mapped out for it. Its furnaces burned white-hot and its drive-shafts glowed red. It careered across the dusty wastes as fast as its tracks could carry it, but it was all in vain. Even summoning all its power, the Crawler could not flatten the ridges that rose up like barricades before it, or smooth and soften the deep crevasses and ravines that stood between it and its prey.

Long hours passed and longer miles with them, but the Crawler's chances of success seemed never to come any closer. The signal from the tracker-tag receded and receded into the distance, becoming fainter and fainter and weaker and weaker.

Like the rising pressure in its pipes, the Crawler's impatience reached explosive levels. It did not know the range of the tracker-tag – it had never had occasion to find out – but every change of direction in the signal marked another obstacle that it would have to cross. Another hurdle. Another delay. Another addition to the birdman's advantage. Slowly, the Crawler was being left further and further behind.

Night was its last hope. The Crawler checked and double-checked its chronometers, recalibrating them for every degree of longitude and latitude that it travelled. It studied the wavelengths of the daylight that fell around it, willing those wavelengths to shift, hastening the shadows out of hiding. But the Crawler could do nothing to bring the day to a close. Time was beyond its influence, immune to its threats.

Finally, some hours before dusk, the Crawler's scopes went blank; the signal from the tracker-tag had vanished. After a long day of making the most of the landscape, the birdman had done it. Now that the birdman was out of the Crawler's sight, every turn he made increased the chances that the Crawler had lost him forever.

With no knowledge of the birdman's present location, the Crawler searched its logs, studying all the previous deflections in the path that it had followed. It was looking for some clue that might help to predict the birdman's future course. But there was no pattern to the changes that he had made – the changes had been dictated by the landscape, and if the landscape obeyed any rules, those rules could not be unravelled by the Crawler.

Still it did not slow or turn aside. Even if it could no longer be sure of the route that the birdman had taken, it was certain that there could be only one outcome when its prey eventually came to ground: broken wings or a broken leg. He would be stranded, either way. That thought burned whiter and hotter than the most ferocious fires that drove it. The Crawler faithfully followed the birdman's last known heading – it would not give up.

Night would shackle its prey more surely than any snare, and wherever he was when dawn came across the dunes, the Crawler would find him. The birdman could not run forever.

Night came at last, and despite the miles and miles of track-marks that the Crawler had scored across the desert, there was no return of the signal. On and on into the dark it went, trailing plumes of steam and smoke that turned to snow behind it. The stones cracked as the chill took hold of them, but still the scopes showed nothing.

The deserts were as empty as ever.

When the blackest depths of darkness came, the Crawler turned aside. A great plain lay before it, stretching out to the sky. It was a landscape that the birdman would have avoided, the Crawler had no doubt – smooth and featureless, with no obstacles for miles and nothing to impede the hunt. But that was just what the Crawler sought. If it was going to find the signal from the tracker-tag again, it needed speed. Out on the empty plain it could switch backwards and forwards, sweeping the desert in wide searching loops in the hope that the birdman's location might appear on its scopes again.

The Crawler gunned its engines, pressing on even faster than before, an earthquake on the move. Its decks shook, its joints rattled, and its tracks churned, wrapping the high spires of its drills and cranes in dust.

Two hours before dawn, the Crawler found it; the signal blinked at the very borders of its perception, unmoving where the birdman's flight had ended in disaster. The Crawler's engines rumbled with a new note – the thrill of triumph. A day of twists and turns would not matter now. It swivelled its tracks in the direction of the calling tracker-tag and raced towards its own echoes, searching the walls of rock around the plains for a way up into the mountains. A wide valley-mouth gaped some miles away, and the Crawler slewed the drive-units around to speed towards it.

Half the distance to the valley-mouth was covered in haste. Then the seamless clatter of the tracks faltered. The noise of each track-plate flexing up and over the drive-wheels became distinct, separate from that of its neighbours. The Crawler slowed to a walking pace. Slowed, and slowed, and... stopped.

The clouds of the Crawler's pursuit settled all around it. Even the echoes died, until the dark night was quiet except for the long slow ticking of metal as it cooled.

A line showed up ahead, white and bright and straight where it was not covered by the sand. It glared at the Crawler, carved with unerring accuracy across the rock.

In a split-second, the Crawler asked a thousand questions and received a thousand answers. It measured the length of the line that it could see and traced its unseen course beneath the sand, projecting where the line might come from and where it might go. The Crawler analysed the

81

reflectivity of the line across the electromagnetic spectrum, every variation in its depth, its concavity, its width, the minute horizontal deviations in its course across the plain. The Crawler's sensors probed the hardness and granularity of the bedrock, calculating the force needed to make every inch of the line and the amount of material that had been excavated.

In a split-second, the Crawler had discovered everything about the line in three dimensions.

It was not enough.

The Crawler knew the deserts, and what it knew never stayed the same. Dunes shifted with the winds, covering old routes, revealing new ones. Paths were lost and found. Valleys drowned in seas of sand and were cast up again, marooned beneath the shining sky. Even the mountains were whittled down to dust eventually. Then the wind took what it had made of them, piling it high only to throw it down again; constant in its inconstancy. The Crawler had spent long enough in the dead red deserts to see the long drawn-out rhythms in the landscape.

But the white line was different. It was somehow untouched by the drifting sands. It ran along beneath them, unchanged and unchanging, ageless and ancient at the same time. And the line seemed to have once had a purpose, dividing what had no borders or limits, making a track that could be followed.

Time was pressing. Even with all the heat of its furnaces, the Crawler could not risk standing still in the dead of night for long. Its pistons cooled, its joints contracted. It must continue its journey soon.

And yet, a vague recollection came and went, half-perceived, like the squeal of a loose track-plate behind the roar of its engines. The Crawler felt that it had seen something like the line before, but not in untold ages.

It sifted its memory, looking for the answer. It searched for the faintest imprint of ones and zeroes that might have been written and over-written during the centuries, lost beneath a constant cascade of data as all-consuming as the dead red deserts themselves.

It found nothing.

If the Crawler had seen anything like the line before, the memory of it had been buried deep. Too deep to find in the time it had.

For a few freezing moments longer, the Crawler's engines remained silent. Then they drummed back into life, and its tracks started to grind forwards. Slowly at first but getting faster, the drive-units heaved the Crawler across the line. Its vast shadow blotted out the brightness of its discovery.

The birdman's tracker-tag still called out to it, trapped among the dunes, and whatever the line had once meant, whoever had made it, wherever it led, the Crawler would not be deterred.

14

Dawn comes creeping across the cold dead deserts. Another dawn in the long tale of days – the same brilliant blue sky, the same wide red earth, and the same restless wind trapped between them.

But for the Pteronaut, a very different dawn.

The shadows have already left the highest ridges by the time he emerges from within the sleeping-chamber. He has waited longer than he needed to inside its close confines because he does not want to see what the daylight will show him – a long walk in all directions.

But he cannot just hide inside the sleeping-tube, waiting for what the day will bring. He pushes himself out through the entrance-slit and drags the broken wing-case after him. Still he does not look at it; without a glance, he slips his shoulders into the harness and fastens it across his chest.

The Pteronaut stands up into the air, sharp still with the chill of night. The patterns of his skin-suit settle into a new order, minimising heat lost, maximising heat gained, and he shifts his weight from one foot to the other to test the wound in his calf. The scar pulls a little, even though the fibres of the skin-suit have knitted it together. It has started to heal during the hours of rest, but the job is still half-complete, far from perfect, and a twinge of pain courses through his leg with his first few steps. It will do. It will have to do – there is no other way.

The pain from the wound is bearable, but the Crawler has left the Pteronaut with a far worse burden to bear. At every step the broken struts and spars of his wings claw against the inside of the case on his back, scraping at it as he walks: right, left; scritch, scratch. It is a mournful sound, the sound of hopeless imprisonment.

Shackled to his feet is his shadow. Usually it is nothing more than a black streak rippling across the deserts a thousand feet or more below him; now it walks at his side, mimicking the helplessness of every step and every stumble. The Pteronaut tries to ignore it, but it is always there in the corner of his eye.

One draw on the drip-tube and he has more pressing concerns. The low-water symbol flashes in his goggle-display, and although he touches twice at the controls at his temple, it has no effect; the red triangle remains, blinking its warning. Whether he is still running by the end of the day or not, he has to find water-ice.

The Pteronaut sets his teeth hard against each other and kneels down to deflate the sleeping-chamber. Lying all around his roost are links of broken chain, shining bright in the light of the new dawn. A breeze blows up, gently stirring the grains of dust that are starting to collect in the lee of each loop: the dunes are finding new footholds high up on the slant of the hill.

Anger flares suddenly within him, a searing flash of it, and the Pteronaut claws a handful of the metal links from the ground and flings them ringing against the furthest rock.

The dust settles again around the broken links of chain, and the wind brings more with it. The deserts know how to make the most of any opportunity, to turn negative into positive. So too the Pteronaut tries to change his anger into something else, something useful – forcing the heat and the power of it into his aching bones and tired muscles, obliterating his despair.

If only it were so easy.

The Pteronaut looks up, and his goggle-eyes scan the horizon, searching for any signs of the Crawler. There are none. No column of dust rises up to show whether it is creeping through the mazes of the landscape or climbing slope after slope towards his landing-site. Perhaps the Pteronaut has done it. Perhaps he has flown further than the range of the tracker-tag. All for nothing, all those miles; the empty horizon is only a brief respite.

And yet, for as long as the horizon remains empty, the Pteronaut has a chance. He must believe that. If he cannot fly, he must run. And when he cannot run, he must walk, or crawl.

A single dimension stretches out ahead, the future bounded by one plane. Habit takes his gaze up into the blue of the sky and he reads its tone and texture as only an expert can. The temperature is good, the winds even – it will be a perfect day for flying.

He stoops to pick up the cylinder of the sleeping-chamber and slips it away into his supply-pouch. Then he bleeds the pigment to reveal his photosynthesising tattoos, and starts the long walk down from the ridge of his roost: right, left; scritch, scratch.

As the morning passes, the Pteronaut finds distraction in the search for water. One moment he is watching for signs of the Crawler, and the next he is studying the desert, looking for the signs of buried ice.

The signs that he would usually seek are not there. Flying overhead, everything looks different. A surge of liquid water released from the permafrost by some shifting hot-spot will spread out as its ice-slick fingers reach the flat. Seen at ground-level, the same pattern is lost among the wind-carved notches and the crumbling of the rock. There are decoys and deceptions wherever he looks. The need for the Pteronaut to replenish his supplies is becoming more and more acute with every step, and he cannot waste time and energy chasing down impostors.

Slowly the landscape changes. He has been keeping to the low hills around the plains, scrambling up their broad backs and jogging down into the spoon-shaped hollows of the valleys that they make, all the time keeping in the strongest light where his tattoos can work away. Now he sees something that looks worth a detour.

New landforms appear, a winding terrain that has not been carved out by the wind alone. As the Pteronaut examines the steep sides of one valley, he sees plenty of indications of age-old water. He knows the signs well enough; he has learnt to recognise them even if he does not truly understand their making. The slopes have been etched straight across at different levels in a way that the wind mimics but can never quite repeat, and where the valley narrows, there are gullies littered with smooth round pebbles.

It takes the Pteronaut twenty minutes to reach the valley floor in safety, taking a winding route down into the depths. All the while, his goggle-eyes sweep from right to left. Halfway down, he spots a recent landslide that looks hopeful, and once he is on the flat again, he clambers across the boulders towards it.

Long before, the cliff had been undercut by running water. Then, once the water had vanished, the wind had taken on the task, whistling through the narrow notch and scoring it deeper century by century. As it carried away the dust, the wind found a layer of water-ice trapped within the rock. If the daylight ever caught the ice, it melted at the edges, and then froze again at night, prising apart the cracks it flowed into. Finally, all the base of the cliff had crumbled into nothing, and a huge mass of rock, a spur weighing many thousands of tonnes, had been stranded projecting into mid-air. Recently, ages and ages later, that weight had become too much for the supporting ridge to bear, and the spur had come away, exposing the strata that it had once hidden.

The Pteronaut scurries over the rubble, picking through the debris. If there had ever been any ice trapped in those rocks, it would have evaporated almost immediately. The scar that runs across the strata of the cliff offers more chance of success. It is thirty feet above the valley floor, but not much of a climb – for the most part, no more than a clamber over the boulders at the base – and it is never dangerous or demanding. The Pteronaut makes his way up to it, the new rock-face still rough where the wind has yet to smooth it, and he studies it closely as he goes higher.

Crystals embedded in the rock sparkle alluringly, but the Pteronaut is not deceived; any water-ice near the surface will already have melted away. He is looking for a band that is darker than the rest, honeycombed and crumbled where water has run from it.

He finds it: the dark brown band with its pitted surface. Little drizzles of dust show where the outermost ice has melted and wept across the rock. It too is long gone, vanished into the air with the ghost-dew of dawn. But where there was once water, there might still be some remaining.

Stepping backwards as far as he can, the Pteronaut follows the band in the rock with his eyes. There is little chance of anything much where the light catches it, but the band slopes downwards into the shade of another buttress of the hills, so that even at noon it will not be exposed to daylight.

The Pteronaut hops and shuffles down the rock-face to reach the darkest and most shaded part of the seam and draws his knife to dig into it. He stands on a boulder, holding onto the cliff with his left hand, and reaches out with his right. At full stretch, he hacks through the crumbling outer-layers, twisting the knife and gouging through them. A few minutes' work and he is down to where the metal blade jars against something almost as hard as itself. Now he must be careful. He makes short sharp stabs with the tip of the knife, feeling it penetrate a fraction of an inch with every blow. More carefully still, he slides the flat of the knife into the hollow he has made, and draws it out again.

The fruits of his effort do not look like much: a pinch of grey-pink grains. But the light catches them, glistening wet even as the blade flashes bright, and a small trickle follows the edge of the knife and steams away into nothing.

The Pteronaut has found water-ice.

He goes back to work with the knife, stabbing and scraping, until he has piled a palmful of grit in the shadow on the edge of his excavation. Slipping the knife away for a moment, he takes what he has quarried into his fist and squeezes it tight and solid, keeping the core of it frozen. Then he goes back to the seam until he has another ball of ice and dust sitting beside the first. One more, and he judges that he has enough. He puts the knife away and slips the three balls of compacted grey grit into safety in the supply-pouch on his back. Then he climbs down onto the valley-floor, looking for somewhere suitable to carry out the next part of the ritual.

What the Pteronaut needs to do next is indeed a ritual. If matters had not been so desperate, he might simply have stowed the ice away into the reservoir-tubes of the skin-suit and waited for it to melt. But he cannot wait. He needs water now. So he must melt the ice himself. Careful preparation is needed, and like any ritual, the melting of the ice will demand a sacrifice.

He finds a place, a wide slab of rock, sheltered and dark and as free of dust as possible. It is the perfect location. Then he goes hunting among the pebbles for a pointed hammer-stone and a smaller flatter companion stone. Once the Pteronaut has found them, he kneels down on the slab, and taking the hammer-stone, he pounds a cupped depression into it, a fingers' width or two deep and as wide across as his splayed hand. He wipes the hollow free of any remaining dust-grains, down to the smooth indentations that his hammering has made. Next, he rests the flat companion stone in the centre of the hollow, and around it he places what he has dug from the cliff. The chippings are a grainy porridge of rock and ice, dull and pale and unpromising, nothing at all like water.

But the Pteronaut has magic at his disposal.

He draws his knife and lays it at one side of the hollow. Next to it he places the empty wrapper of one of his ration-bars. On the opposite side of the hollow, the Pteronaut positions a rectangular strip of grey stone that he finds inside his supply-pouch. His preparations are almost complete. Finally he unscrews the three flexible reservoir-tubes from their housing beneath the supply-pouch. Each one has a nozzle at one end to feed into the capillary-system of the skin-suit – a nozzle which he closes – and a screw-cap at the other end – which he opens. The Pteronaut lays all three tubes within easy reach and settles himself comfortably on his knees.

Now, he needs his sacrifice.

From inside one of his gill-cells, he draws out the long lozenge of a filter. The Pteronaut has to be quick. The filter has been exposed to the open air for only a few seconds, but already its blue colour is darkening as its microscopic lattices draw the poison out of the atmosphere.

He takes the knife and slices off a wafer from the end of the filter, replacing the remainder into the gill-cell. The wafer of filter is as thin a sliver as he can spare, worth perhaps a few hours of breathable air – not much, but now that he is grounded, his survival might come down to that. The Pteronaut wraps the sacrificial sliver of filter in the protection of the wrapper from the ration-bar. Then he places the parcel he has made on top of the flat companion stone at the centre of the hollow.

It is time.

The Pteronaut takes a deep breath from inside the facemask. Then another, and then a third which he holds tight inside himself. He turns off the air-supply into the facemask. His next steps are rapid and mechanical.

Facemask down. Mouth uncovered.

Flintstone in left hand, knife in right.

One strike with the blade against the flint, sending sparks grazing across the foil wrapping of the filter.

Nothing. Again. Strike.

Nothing. Strike.

Strike. Again.

Strike. Nothing. Again.

Strike.

And then one of the sparks catches in the foil wrapper. It flickers uncertainly, melting the foil and burning an orange-edged burrow inside the filter.

The Pteronaut leans forwards, his mouth still closed against the cold and the suffocating air, and he blows across the spark through tight lips.

Gently. Very gently.

A small glow starts at one edge of the slice of filter and broadens into a wide stripe. Another stream of precious oxygen from his lips plays across it, coaxing the tiny ember into life. It flares with each breath, the heat of it warming his skin.

One more breath and the foil wrapper crackles into flame. Leaning to one side of the flames, the Pteronaut watches the filter and the wrapper shrink and twist as the fire consumes them. They curl across the flat stone, and he cups his hands around them to trap as much of the heat as possible within the hollow.

Slowly, the grains of rock and ice vanish into a shimmering film of water. It spreads quickly across the hollow until it becomes a pool. Still holding his breath, the Pteronaut takes the reservoir-tubes and drowns them one by one to suck up the liquid. He must be quick: the flames are dying down as the filter turns to ash, and the sides of the hollow are becoming glazed with fresh ice.

The dying flames are not the only reason for his urgency. The Pteronaut's exposed face is numb, and his lungs feel like they are coiling up unbearably tight in his chest – the urge to draw in deep draughts of the cold and deadly desert air is almost unbearable.

One tube full. The Pteronaut replaces the screw-cap and immerses the second tube. It sinks, bubbling as it fills. Then the third tube. By now, the hollow is almost empty of water, and the third tube takes up some of the silt that has sunk to the bottom; a few fine particles will not trouble the skin-suit, and it will make good use of the minerals that they contain.

With the knife, the Pteronaut scratches around, filling the third tube with the scrapings from the bottom of the hollow and around its edges. He can afford to leave nothing behind. Then it is done, and he slots the final tube into its fitting.

Struggling and straining against the need to breathe, the Pteronaut clips the facemask back into position, turns on his air-supply, and fills his lungs with a deep and grateful breath.

Once some feeling has returned to his lips, the Pteronaut takes a measured draw on the drip-tube. For a moment there is nothing, just air. Then the first drops reach his tongue and the low-water indicator vanishes from the goggle-display.

It is done. The ritual is over. The sacrifice has been made, and the magic has worked. The Pteronaut has fresh water. The readings in the display adjust themselves and he makes his calculations. If used sparingly, his supply of water can be made to last for another four or five days – an eternity when what remains of his freedom can be measured in hours.

15

Noon, and the Pteronaut's shadow dances between his feet. The wound in his calf is forgotten as he runs across the rocks. He does not look back. There is no need: he knows what is behind him.

By mid-morning, the banner of the Crawler's dust-cloud was hanging above the horizon. An hour before noon, the Crawler was close enough that the bare rock trembled with the rumble of its engines, and the Pteronaut could see the staccato-sparkle of daylight on the sand-blasted scales of its storm-shields through the dust. Now, as the shadows shift towards afternoon, the Crawler is close enough that the rattling tracks can be heard over the thunder of the engine.

The Pteronaut is running again. A night's rest and the hours of the morning: it has been a brief reprieve.

As he runs, the Pteronaut seeks the same safeguards that he sought from the air – terrain that the Crawler can only cross with difficulty. Except now he must also cross the same terrain himself. The cliffs and ravines that bar the Crawler's way are barriers to the Pteronaut too. There is no time for tricky ascents or descents, not with the wound in his calf still tight. And the landscape offers too many flat stretches hidden between the hills: the Crawler would be waiting for him at the end of his climb, whether up or down. Dunes are also a danger, with their soft sides that swallow his legs to the knees. Steep hillsides are the Pteronaut's hope, their skyward angles a passing refuge.

One hillside opens up in front of him, the brow of the ridge crumbling into a hard slope of scree. Over the top he goes, riding the avalanche he causes. Sliding and skidding, the Pteronaut lets gravity carry him, surrounded by a shifting slick of stones. Ahead of him, pebbles cartwheel across the valley floor as the slope levels off. His boots hit the flat, and he lets his momentum take him part-way across it, stumbling into a run before all the power of his slide is spent.

His thudding footfalls keep time with his heartbeat. The noise of his breath fills the facemask. The indicator in the goggle-display blooms green as he draws oxygen-rich air from the filters, flaring red again as he breathes out. Then the ground starts to rise into another slope, and the Pteronaut bends his head and pushes himself on up the next incline. It is as exhausting as any flight, and without the muscles of the skin-suit, he would have no chance at all.

The Pteronaut reaches the top of the next rise, and the noise of the Crawler's tracks is loud again in his ears, rattling away somewhere in the valleys behind him. It is close, closer every time he hears it. There is no time for delay or hesitation, every second is vital.

But then he stops: even with the Crawler at his heels, the sight that he sees from the summit of the rise brings him to a sudden standstill.

Fifty feet below him is a flattened ledge, broad, unnaturally level, its surface black where it shows from beneath the dust. Even where the ledge is covered, its unbroken course is still clear. It snakes away downhill, making sudden turns against the grain of the slopes, forming a series of stepped terraces all the way to a deep ravine.

It is a road.

The Pteronaut's eyes follow the winding course around every bend. He has seen how the wind can cut corners into cliff-faces and he knows how sometimes rock will break in straight lines across the bedding-planes. He knows the angles that nature can make, and nature has made none of the angles that he sees. Nothing is so regular. Nothing is so precise.

His eyes reach the end of the road, and the ravine that it leads to. The depth and the straight-edged course of the ravine are as unnatural and unexpected in that landscape as the road itself. Sheer sides border a channel of constant width. The ravine cuts through mountains and leaves them hanging, slicing valleys in half. It is an intruder in that landscape.

If the Pteronaut had been flying, the ravine would have been the perfect barrier to the Crawler's pursuit. It curves away to the left and to the right, with no sign of a way across; it might be a hundred miles before the Crawler can find a path around it. If he had been flying, the ravine would have been an ally in his bid to escape.

But the Pteronaut is not flying.

He sweeps his head from side to side, taking the time to regain his breath a little as he works out what to do.

Down. He has to go down. There is no other way.

The Crawler's approach sounds loud again at his back, and he goes over the edge of the summit at a sideways canter, trying to keep his balance on the steep scree slope.

The noise of his descent changes as he slides from the scree onto the first terraced ledge. His boots ring with a higher note on the hard black surface. Not a single slab of stone, he can see now, but a mass of smaller stones, packed tightly together and pressed flat and solid.

He runs across the width of the road and reaches the edge of it, where the black surface is fretted and crumbling. Then he plunges down another rust-red slope, cutting across the loops of the road towards the ravine; slope after slope, terrace after terrace, red after black.

High above, the Crawler had also reached the last summit before the road, and its upper-decks and crane-arms towered over the ridge. A feeble trickle of scree fled away under its shadow. Like the birdman half a minute before, the Crawler saw the loops of the road tacking across the hillside and the ravine cutting its straight-sided way into the highlands, inexplicable and unexpected.

Somewhere in the rumble of the Crawler's engines, a tremor rose and then died again. The straight white line had unsettled it, and it had been right to be unsettled. Strange

95

forces had been at work in that country, leaving their mark on the dead red deserts. The tremor came again, but the tracker-tag called out to the Crawler, and the Crawler quashed its fears – it must focus on the birdman's signal.

It could not follow the birdman down the hillside in its current shape, and the chicanes of the road were too narrow for it to negotiate in its flattened form.

Like the birdman, the Crawler took a second to consider its next move. Ropes went over the balustrades, and a dozen drones slid down them and onto the ridge. Fresh and eager for the hunt, they sped down the slopes, following in the birdman's footsteps.

The Pteronaut hears the Crawler slow as it reaches the summit and he goes faster, descending across the snaking terraces in a straight line. He reaches the next ledge, and the angles of his vision change. The final stretch of road comes into view, running along the edge of the ravine, and he sees at last why it was built.

There is a bridge, or what was once a bridge, spanning the sheer drop. A broken arch carries the black ribbon of the road halfway across the ravine and no further, reaching out into nothing where it ends abruptly. Across the breach, the road continues into the hillside on the far side; one section of it still hangs there, held by rusted rods of metal. From the summit, the broken bridge was completely invisible, but the sight of it spurs the Pteronaut on – he can leap that gap.

A clatter of stones hits the roadway behind him as he stumbles down the next slope. The Crawler's engines have stopped, and the Pteronaut can hear its drones slithering down the hillside in pursuit. The drones' suits do not have muscles to help take the strain of the descent, nor do they respond to their wearers' exertions with a trickle of extra oxygen, but the Pteronaut has been running for hours, and he is weary – the drones are catching him up.

Half-way down the final slope and with the pursuit close behind, the Pteronaut jumps out to one side. He skids with both his feet together and his arms held out to keep his balance. Behind the diagonal line he carves, the slope shifts, its unstable surface rippling as it starts to slip away. The Pteronaut stays on his feet just ahead of the avalanche, running across its breadth. Not all the drones are not so adept. Those closest to him take a tumble, falling in front of their companions and bringing them down too, until only the slowest and most careful are still in the hunt.

Then the Pteronaut is at the last section of road. A shower of stones from his slide goes tip-tapping across the hard black surface, and he follows them, precious seconds ahead of his pursuers. The bridge is just a few hundred yards away. The Pteronaut puts his head down once more and runs towards it.

Suddenly he is there, racing onto the bridge. At first, it looks whole and undamaged, and he thinks that maybe he has deceived himself. Then ahead of him, the gap appears, and the drop opens up, sudden and surprised, all the way down to the floor of the ravine hundreds of feet below.

A thousand times before the Pteronaut has leapt similar gaps, some wider perhaps, many deeper, but this time he has no wings to save him if his leap falls short. The wound in his calf nags him but he knows not to let any doubts cloud his mind. Doubt will lead to doom. He finds an extra rush of speed from somewhere, sprinting towards certainty. Even if his leap fails, he will feel the currents flowing around him again before the end...

He reaches the broken section and kicks off into the air. The lip of the road crumbles beneath his boots, but his leap is good. The gulf seems to widen as he arcs across it, showing a long fall straight down to darkness and rubble among the bridge-supports. The Pteronaut keeps his body tight and arrow-like and reaches out to embrace his own wingless shadow.

With a slamming jolt he hits the hanging slab of road at the far side of the gap. The impact sets the slab nodding on the metal rods that hold it in place. The rods creak and groan, and one of them snaps through with a sharp crack. The Pteronaut's boots slip back against the frost-mottled surface and his hands go scrabbling for a hold. They find one.

For a second and no more, the Pteronaut holds fast. He lies against the slab as it heaves, waiting to see whether another rod will break, and the whole section will tilt and twist and follow the rest of the rubble down to the valley floor.

The rods hold.

The Pteronaut waits another heartbeat to steady himself, then before the motion of the slab has fully ceased, he is moving again. He drags himself half-climbing and half-crawling up onto the intact section of the bridge.

A dozen strides behind him, the five remaining drones reached the gap. The first stopped at the last moment, teetering on the edge with its arms windmilling. The second took the leap but fell short. Its head struck the hanging slab and it went tumbling down to the valley floor.

The third drone made it, sprawling across the slab just as the birdman did. But its leap was not as long – its legs whirred for a foothold in mid-air and its fingers reached for a grip. It clutched at the fragile sides of the slab for support, and did not find any. Fragments crumbled away at its touch. Its legs whirred faster. Shuffling and sliding, the drone slipped down towards the drop, and its companions could only watch.

In two steps, the Pteronaut is there. He leans over the edge and takes the drone in an iron grip. Fingers that are used to climbing haul the drone up onto the bridge beside him, up to where the surface is solid and safe.

Before the drone can properly regain his footing, the Pteronaut has his knife in his hand. He thrusts at the joint where the drone's suit and helmet meet. The blade plunges deep to the hilt. Unable to pull away, the drone gasps, flecking the inside of the visor with bright red spots. His arms flail and he struggles to get free, but the birdman's grip is merciless. The Pteronaut withdraws the blade and stabs again at the joint, and again, until the drone coughs a final time through red foaming lips and his eyes go dull and wide. The drone's head lolls away, and the birdman throws the body down onto the roadside at his feet.

The Pteronaut's knife glints sharp and cold where the blood runs clear, flashing a challenge and a warning to his pursuers. If the remaining drones act together, they might make it across the gap, and one of them might survive to take the birdman alive. But they will be alone with their prisoner on the far side of the ravine, and then what?

Up above the broken bridge, stark against the sky, the Crawler's smoke-stacks spouted black billows and its engines roared. It had seen enough. It was too far away to risk a shot to cripple its prey, and there was no way down and no way across.

As one, the surviving drones turned and started to run back along the roadway.

The Pteronaut stands on the edge of the drop and watches the drones go, climbing back up the slopes to where the Crawler glowers down at him. He knows it will not give up the hunt. He knows it will search for a way across the ravine. But for now, at least, he is safe.

16

Beyond the ruins of the bridge, the road runs on into the hills between high walls of rock. Once those walls had been blasted wide and cut sheer, linking into a natural valley that goes slinking away between the slopes. Now they have crumbled and cracked, showering the winding route of the road beneath them with boulders.

The Pteronaut walks as quickly as he can, but the race to the bridge and his leap across the gap has taken its toll: his calf is sore, and he limps along the path. The wound has not reopened, but it grumbles more painfully than before.

The drone that he killed has provided him with four new filters for his gill-cells, all now safely stowed in the air-tight compartments in his supply-pouch. He feels neither satisfaction nor remorse at his actions. They were the result of simple arithmetic, nothing more than that. The drone was dead whatever the Pteronaut did – if he had not hauled it up onto the bridge, it would have fallen to its doom. And if it had fallen, he would not now have four new filters for his gill-cells. If the Pteronaut is to survive, he will need to take every chance that comes his way.

But the drone had neither water nor food, and the Pteronaut's supply of ration-bars is running low. He chews a mouthful of one to pacify the rumblings of his stomach, and drains the panels to expose his photosynthesising tattoos to what little light there is. In the shadows of the cliffs, the tattoos provide a trickle of energy to offset what he used in the final sprint and his leap across the gap. His stomach growls as he swallows his rations, already dissatisfied, and the scritch-scratch of the wings sounds loud again in his ears as he walks on.

Where the road is hidden by dust and debris, the flatness and age-old smoothness of it still show the contours of its course. The black surface peeks through in places, and despite the shadow of the cliffs, the road is a few degrees warmer than its surroundings, as if it has taken every drop of light that has ever fallen upon it and stored it up. The warmth of it is not much, but the Pteronaut keeps to the black areas wherever he can, sparing his body and the skin-suit the effort to fight off the chill.

As he walks, he glances up at the sides of the valley, searching for an easy path up the slopes. Every instinct he possesses is telling him to leave the ground and to get as high as possible – that is the Pteronaut way. Only up on the heights will he be safe and have any chance of beating the Crawler.

But for now, the slopes are as unattainable to him as the sky. Climbing the valley-sides will test his strength and skill more than he can risk with the wound in his calf still nagging at every step.

A few miles further on, the steep hillsides on either side of the road fall back, and the landscape opens up, flatter than ever. Ahead, the Pteronaut sees only the submerged highway leading on into dune-fields and flat-lands, taking the easiest route to its next destination. To the left and right, the hills continue, forming a barrier that marks the course of the ravine all the way into the distance.

It is a crossroads in his journey.

The Pteronaut stops for a moment to consider his options. Plains or hills. It is no easy choice.

On the plains his progress will be faster and easier. His wound will get a proper chance to recover. In a day or two, he could be climbing again. But until then, there will be no protection, no cover; nowhere to hide. Can he take the chance that the Crawler will be delayed so long?

His instinct is for the hills, but the Pteronaut knows that his instincts were shaped by a different world, a world of three dimensions, of launches and landings and the free air inbetween. He cannot climb. The foothills offer little more protection than the plains, but at a slower pace. And if he were to fall, his end would be written in the dust.

The numbers are clear – the margins of survival are fractionally better if he keeps to the plains.

And yet... In the hills, if the Crawler finds him, the Pteronaut will have a better chance to fight it off. So he tells himself: but behind the numbers, there is the truth. In the hills, he will be closer to the sky.

As he stands there, delaying the moment of choice, something catches his eye, something that drifts serenely across the otherwise faultless blue of the sky.

A cloud.

Fragmented and feathery, it is the first thin wisp of cloud that he has seen in many months. It tears itself free from the lee currents around the mountain-tops and moves with mocking ease through the air. The route it takes is with the wind, straight ahead, out across the plains and along the direction of the road.

For a few moments longer, the Pteronaut keeps the fragment of cloud in view. His mind is made up. With the wind at his back, he turns away from the mountains, and starts to march towards the plains.

17

For a moment and a moment only, the Pteronaut checks his stride. He has been following the road across the plains for two hours and in all that time he has made good progress. The hills that border the ravine have sunk slowly behind him, and his steps have been quick and confident.

But now the road ahead of him has vanished, and this time it is not the usual rust-red carpet of wind-swept sand that covers it. Instead, it simply and utterly disappears, obliterated by a circular depression in the ground: a crater has been blasted into the desert.

The Pteronaut makes his way towards the crater's edge. A wide ring of glassy rock extends out from it, an irregular spatter of strangely rounded shapes. They look delicate but they are iron-hard when he kicks at them, and they remind him of once-liquid water-ice, frozen as it flowed. He takes a weaving path between them, careful of his footing. Then he is at the very edge of the crater, looking down into it.

The ground slopes away into a smooth hollow, a vast bowl, the sand turned to glass. Now that he is standing on the lip of it, the circular rim of the crater seems completely perfect. The gentle slope running down into the crater's depth is also perfect, as if something has reached down from the sky and taken a scoop out of the desert. A puddle of dust has collected at the centre of the hollow, but the rest of the crater is bright orange-red, an angry painful colour.

The Pteronaut does not hesitate – the going is even, and it is quicker to walk across the crater than to go around it. He steps over the rim and continues on his path, walking deeper and deeper into the bowl of the crater. The glass is smooth, but the dust at the centre has scratched it and scored it as the wind has blown it around and around, so that the surface beneath his feet is not at all slippery – safer, perhaps, to walk on with his wounded leg than the soft sand itself.

Step by step, the Pteronaut drops slowly below the ground-level of the desert. And with every step towards the centre of the bowl, the goggle-display flickers a little more. At first, the Pteronaut hardly notices it, but then the disruption becomes too severe to ignore: lines tremble, breaking and reforming, and the readings for air-pressure and temperature flutter like flames caught in a high wind. The Pteronaut taps at the controls beneath the scales at his temple, but nothing he does makes any difference – the figures continue to dance.

The Pteronaut has faced many dangers in his journeys across the wastes – lack of air and food and water, the cold, sandstorms, landslides – and with strength and skill, knowledge, stamina, and good fortune, he has overcome every challenge. The dead deserts, he knows, are an impersonal enemy, their threats all ignorant and uncaring as to what he is and who he is and where he is going. There is no guile, no subterfuge, no hatred. Just chance.

The disruption to the goggle-display feels different.

Some new danger has penetrated the defences of the skin-suit, reaching inside past the camouflage and the scales and the layers of insulating tissue. It threatens the Pteronaut closer than anything has ever threatened him before, like the cold blade of a knife against his throat.

Turning on the spot, the Pteronaut makes a full circle, looking to see whether any signs of the Crawler's approach are visible above the rim of the crater. There are none. Then he looks up, in case another flyder is watching him from high above. Again nothing.

He draws in another breath of filtered air, but he can detect no threat in it, no poison. Water comes, too, when he sips it, as pure as ever. The Pteronaut clenches and unclenches his fists. His strength is undiminished, and despite the loss of the goggle-display, the skin-suit, too, is unaffected; he can feel its living tissue warm against his skin, and its muscles tense in time with his own. It breathes from his breath, keeping him alive.

If there is a threat in the crater, it is an indefinable one.

Going back will be as easy going on, and with no reason to do anything else, the Pteronaut carries on walking steadily across the crater to the far side, up the slope of the bowl. The readings in the goggle-display grow even weaker towards the centre of the hollow, and then stronger and stronger with every step back up towards the level of the desert. By the time the Pteronaut reaches the rim of the crater, the readings have returned to normal.

The Pteronaut walks on, and as the miles goes by, so more craters appear. Just single impacts to start with, pounded into the desert directly across the black width of the road, or slightly off to either side. But as his march continues, more and more of the craters appear, closer and closer together, until the youngest of them have been blasted into and over and on top of the scars of previous bombardments.

Ahead of him, the road finally vanishes and does not reappear. Thousands upon thousands of craters meet and overlap, blurring together into a shining sea of glass. Only their rims rise above the ground, so smooth and so hard that even the wind has struggled to wear them away.

The Pteronaut knew that they were coming. The readings in the goggle-display started to flutter with increasing restlessness. Now, with no way of telling where one crater ends and the next begins, the readings have failed altogether. No matter which way the Pteronaut turns, they do not reappear. For the first time ever, he stares out at the desert with no knowledge of his skin-suit's reserves of air or water, of the air pressure, or the external temperature. His own understanding of the environment is expert, but he has never had to rely on it alone before. Staring through the goggle-lenses at the naked desert is like looking at the world with one eye closed.

For a while, the Pteronaut considers turning around and going back, retracing his steps all the way to the ruined bridge. From there, he could try to climb the steep hillsides that border the ravine. But the Crawler might already have found a way around the ravine or across it. Perhaps it has already reached the plains. There is no going back. The Pteronaut has chosen his course.

He kicks with his heel at the crest of one of the crater-rims where the wind has found a way to wear the melt-glass thin and brittle until he breaks off a lump. Away from the scouring action of the dust-grains that have turned the melt-glass opaque, the break shows a deep transparent orange inside – the colour of the sands made liquid and then solid again.

Holding the fragment up to the light, the Pteronaut sees a blizzard of silvery metal sparkling within it, hundreds of teardrop flecks suspended in the glass. Peering closer still, the goggle-display starts into new life, but the readings do not return. Instead, a web of multicoloured strands blurs and spreads, moving in tandem with the fragment of melt-glass as the Pteronaut waves it first to one side, and then to the other. The interference fades again when he throws the melt-glass back down onto the ground.

The Pteronaut turns to face the sea of craters. It is a landscape he means to cross, whatever the risks, a negative that he will turn into a positive. Because if the readings in the goggle-display can be disrupted by the metal in the melt-glass, perhaps the signal from the tracker-tag can be disrupted by it too.

18

The Pteronaut walks all day, deeper and deeper into the pockmarked wastes of the crater-field. His progress is undisturbed. An unblemished blue sky spreads out above the sparkling crater-rims. No wandering column of dust rises to meet it. Wherever the Crawler is, it is far away.

As the miles pass, so the dunes thin. The moat of craters at the margins of the melt-glass sea swallows them and repels them. Finally, the dust peters out altogether, leaving the landscape naked and dazzling beneath the sky. The wind too can find no foothold. With no sand for it to stir, it hurries away, impotent and eager to be gone. If it finds a voice at all, it booms lethargically across the hollows. The craters take that noise and muffle it, echoing it across and between them until it becomes a persistent smothering buzz.

The Pteronaut traces a winding route between the crater-bowls. Wherever he looks, he can see nothing except the glint of daylight striking across the frozen melt-glass, so bright that he is almost blinded. As the day wears on, the shifting angle of the light reveals new patterns in the landscape, but those patterns are variations on a single unending theme; repetitive, unchanging, monotonous. The sea of craters is merciless, a wilderness within a wilderness, more empty and desolate than the deserts of sand and rock.

When night comes it is almost a relief, drawing a dark veil across the melt-glass landscape. The Pteronaut sets up the sleeping-tube beside one of them, and crawls gratefully inside.

The next day is no different. Or the day after. Or the day after that. Each dawn, the Pteronaut wakes up and slithers out of the sleeping-tube where it lies in the open, barely sheltered or disguised.

Still, there is no sign of the Crawler. The Pteronaut should be relieved, but he walks warily, stalking the silence. With no dunes for its tracks to churn into the air, the Crawler will give little warning of its approach. The sound of its engines cannot be relied upon to battle its way across the craters and the odd echoes that they create. The Pteronaut might perhaps see it, a silver spark moving against the dazzling background, but there is nowhere for him to run to and nowhere for him to hide. The emptiness of the plains is like a breath that is being held before danger arrives.

As the days pass, the lack of dunes brings with it a more insidious danger. The Pteronaut has saved a handful of dust-grains which he can use to inflate his sleeping-tube, but that supply is running low. In a few days' time, a week perhaps at most, he will be down to his last few grains. Then he will face a final night out in the open.

It is not his only concern. His supply of ration-bars is dwindling fast, and without the readings in the goggle-display he can only guess at how long his water will last.

Increasingly hungry, thirsty, wearied by every second he spends among the craters, somehow the Pteronaut carries on. The wound in his calf has healed, but to no purpose. His strength is being worn out of him. His purposeful strides at the outset have become a plod. One foot follows the other, rising, falling; one more step into nothing, going nowhere. Then another step, and another. And accompanying every one of those steps is the dry drawn-out scrape of his broken wings.

The Pteronaut has escaped from the Crawler only to face another foe that cannot be beaten. Time is running out and his luck has left him stranded. A slow dry death stretches out on all sides.

Then on the fifth day, the Pteronaut finds the wreck of a flyder. He comes across the first piece of wreckage lying by itself in the shelter of a crater. With no dunes to scurf it slowly along with them, and with the melt-glass hard beneath his boots, the wreckage can only have fallen from the sky.

He studies it carefully, a thin section of metal that he can flip over easily. The wreckage has lain there long enough for the wind to shape it so that it fits perfectly into the crater, rounded where it might once have been sharp, and sharp where it might once have been rounded. Turning on the spot, the Pteronaut notices a notch in the rim of the crater. He climbs the slope to examine the notch in more detail.

From the top of the crater-rim, he sees more signs of the crash. He follows the trail that they make with his eyes, linking together the scrapes and scars to see how the flyder bounced across the glassy ridges, losing a wing somewhere, and strewing the remains of its shattered tail section across a wide expanse. Piece by piece, walking from crater to crater, the Pteronaut solves the puzzle. The last piece of the puzzle is the fuselage lying at an angle nearby, and he heads off towards it.

As he gets closer he sees that it is not a flyder like the one that harried him above the plateau. This flyder is much larger, built to carry huge loads over vast distances, and there are no flimsy propellers to power it through the air. The wide body is bent. Half of it lies in the hollow with the nose sloping up the side, but there is no sign of fire anywhere. By the time it hit the ground, the flyder was as parched as the melt-glass landscape itself.

For a while the Pteronaut stands beside the fuselage, with his tattoos soaking up the reflected daylight from its polished silver skin. The wind whistles and hums as it plays around the edges of the flyder; at last, it has found its voice again. It has stripped the wreck down to the bare metal with whatever miniscule specks of dust it can carry so far from the dunes, sculpting the wreckage in its own fluid image. Where the broken ribs and braces of the airframe show from beneath the outer-skin, they have been filed down to dagger-points, guarding whatever remains inside.

The Pteronaut takes a long slow walk around what he has found, checking it carefully. There is a way inside, a jagged hole where maybe once one wing was attached. He peers through the hole, bending double as he avoids the sharp edges that the wind has made.

It is cold inside the body of the flyder, cold and dusk-dark. Any windows that remain intact have been scoured and scratched until the panes are as opaque as the metal bulkheads themselves. The Pteronaut's instincts tell him to be wary of anywhere that is not open to the sky. He withdraws his head and glances around. There is still no sign of anything anywhere, just the interminable stretch of those overlapping circles all the way to the empty horizon, and no sound of anything except the wind toying with the wreck. There is nothing to fear. He ducks down again and slips inside.

The melt-glass has robbed the Pteronaut of his night-vision too, and he lets his eyes adjust of themselves inside the flyder. The debris of the cargo lies scattered around. Metal cases and boxes have broken open to reveal what they contain. Pipes. Panels. Spheres. Folded lengths of metal. Hexagonal glass-shells. Something that might have been the frame of a small vehicle, and a dozen or more rubber tyres.

Carefully, the Pteronaut picks his way through the maze that the wreckage makes but all that he can see disappoints him. There is no food, no water, no tools with which he might try to cut through the loop of the tracker-tag. If the flyder was carrying any of those at all, they lie scattered and lost across the craters. It is all useless.

He climbs higher, towards the cockpit, making a path along the bulkhead at one side. It is slow work. The tubular hull slopes up much more steeply than it appeared to from outside, and the fuselage creaks a little as his weight disturbs the balance of centuries.

Half-way up the slope, the Pteronaut does find something that he can use: water-ice. Frosty strands of it have collected in a web across the inside of the hull, tracing the braces and

110

buttresses of the fuselage. He slips out an empty reservoir-tube and scrapes the open end along the silvery trails, harvesting all he can. There is not much, but it might keep him going for an extra day.

The ice is a sign that the craters are not as desolate as they seem. A warm wind a few degrees above freezing must occasionally find its way inside the wreck, bringing the merest wisps of moisture from outside to condense against the cold metal. Night will freeze it, and add to it, year by year, layer on layer. Slowly, it has built up. And the bodies of the crew will have played their part, too.

The Pteronaut sees them, two of them, slumped up in the nose of the flyder, still strapped in where they were sitting for the flight. He has seen many mummies in the deserts before, lying half-buried in the dunes with their suits torn open and their leathery skin stripped down to the bone, but he has never seen any that are so well preserved.

The faces of the mummies are like bronze masks. They leer at him with wide smiles, their black lips stretched right back almost as far as the withered husks of their ears. Their eyelids are nothing more than dry wrinkles, and they stare with dull eyes at the sand-scratched windows. One was a female; the Pteronaut can tell from the width of the jaw and the cheekbones. The other was a male, his face more angular, with the wisp of a beard across his sunken cheeks. They must have been there a very long time, watching the days come and go.

He checks the bodies over for anything of use. The suits they wear are rigid, with only primitive gill-cells. Each one has a small cylinder of air fitted into it, but the contents of the cylinders have long since leaked away. Just like the flyder that carried them, the mummies have no water and no food and no tools. They have given him all they can. The Pteronaut turns away and leaves them to the long cold dark.

Blinking behind the goggle-lenses, he steps gladly out into the light again, but he lingers at the wreck a little while. It is an oasis of sorts, a tiny island of something that has come

111

from somewhere, stranded far from anywhere in the middle of nothing. He enjoys the distraction, staring at its straight lines and listening to the buffeting breezes as they wear it down and carry it away, little by little, chip by chip.

But the Pteronaut does not delay for too long. He has not found anything that can put an end to his plight. The meagre amount of water-ice he has found inside the flyder will not save him from the fate of its crew.

The wreck is not just an oasis, it is a warning. The flyder must have flown far across the crater-wastes before it ran out of fuel, its instruments baffled by the electromagnetic haze of the melt-metal. And a flyder can fly many times faster than the Pteronaut can walk. If the wreckage tells him anything, it is that his torment is far from its end.

19 For another three days after finding the flyder, the Pteronaut walks on without seeing any sign of anything. The melt-glass sea is as monotonous and as unforgiving as ever. Even the sky becomes oppressive, pinning him down beneath its vast blue expanse. There is nothing to mark the miles, and the long days of nothing blur one into the next, overlapping until they become indistinguishable from each other, just like the craters themselves.

The emptiness of the crater-hollows only makes the gnawing feeling of the Pteronaut's slow starvation more acute; the rumble of the wind across them is a constant reminder of his own hunger. The output from the photosynthesising tattoos cannot sustain him with so little other food to eat. It is barely enough to keep him going, and the Pteronaut can feel himself weakening day by day.

Still he keeps on. It must be enough that the Crawler has not yet found him. His head moves from side to side, slowly and mechanically, looking for signs that the dust is returning and that he might be approaching the boundaries of the crater-plains at last. But day after day, there is no dust and nothing to add to the handful he has taken for the sleeping-tube. Soon that too will run out, and he will face a dark night that has no dawn.

Another day spreads itself across the sea of craters. Another empty sky shines above him. The Pteronaut wakes and struggles out of the tube. There is still nothing out there, just a long aching silence. No threat other than the merciless landscape. No need to run, and no reason to stay. He packs up his sleeping-chamber, eats a piece of his second-to-last ration-bar, and sets off on his trek once more.

He walks until noon, and rests against the shallow slope of a crater. He does not rest long; it is better to be walking while he still has any strength. Summoning all that strength, he stands up, and walks on into his own shadow as it grows out ahead of him.

Noon slips past. Early afternoon seeps in slowly beneath his feet, the passage of time grinding him down.

The Pteronaut stops abruptly: something is moving in the corner of his vision.

He stoops and runs for cover into the nearest crater-bowl. He slides down into it and lies panting against its glassy sides, his tired muscles aching from the effort. He listens out for the rumble of engines.

The wind moans and throbs across the hollows, but he can hear nothing else. Moving slowly, as much on account of his exhaustion as the need for caution, the Pteronaut shuffles to the crater-rim on his elbows and knees, and peers out.

There is something there. No mistake. No trick. No delirious illusion. Flashes of light come and go.

For several minutes just to be sure, the Pteronaut watches the lights dance against the background, fragmenting the air with their bright rays. They do not change and yet they do not stay the same. They float above a single spot, weaving a random pattern like some silvery mirage.

The Pteronaut remains quite still, waiting and watching. He is too weak to rush into action, so he stays sprawled where he is.

When he does move again, it is with decisive and concentrated effort. First, a sprint to the next crater. Then a quick check that there is no immediate threat. A ducking run into another crater, one which is closer to the dazzling pattern. Then a change of direction. Then another dash forwards.

The Pteronaut halts again only three craters away from the lights. His breath rasps inside the facemask and his legs tremble from the exertion. The wind changes direction, and the glittering pattern changes with it. He hears something too, a ringing chime of bone against metal. His breath catches in his chest; it is a sound he has heard before, strung out along the Crawler's balustrades.

Slumped out of sight, the Pteronaut listens to the sound. It is as random as the flashing of the lights. He hides himself there just a little while longer, and then he draws his knife and stands up tall on the lip of the hollow, staring at the source of the lights from close range.

A metal pole almost as tall as the Pteronaut himself has been set upright into a crater-rim. It branches out at the top into four horizontal arms, and from one of the outstretched arms, a string of bone ornaments is dangling, bright and white. From another, a tangle of wires of different lengths hangs down; strung from each wire is a broken piece of mirrored glass. As the Pteronaut watches, the wind plays gleefully with the mirrors, sending them spinning and wheeling, and the bone-chimes jangle tunelessly in the same breath.

A decoy.

A distraction.

The Pteronaut drops to one knee and circles on the spot, but still there is no engine-noise, no menacing metal shape on the horizon. The melt-glass desert is as empty as ever.

He looks again and he sees that the third of the outstretched arms holds a box on the end of a length of chain – a chain made from the same kind of sliding links that snared his wing.

He checks the ground around him. The melt-glass is tough, but some of the crater-rims are broken, as if they recently had to bear a great weight. Looking closely, staring into the light, there are parallel rows of scratch-marks, almost too faint to see, which must have been made by sharp downward-pointing teeth. The scratches comes from one direction and head off in another. They do not return.

Whatever power the melt-glass possesses, however it is hiding the readings in the goggle-display and the signal from the tracker-tag, it has not been strong enough to stop the Crawler. Perhaps nothing can.

The Pteronaut takes one last look around, and crouches at the base of the pole, peering at the hole in the melt-glass that holds it upright. Splinters and swarf have been blown away, so the pole must have been standing there for at least a few days. He leans down to press the auricles of the skin-suit against the ground, first on one side of his head, then the other, listening for the creaking of the ground as it supports the Crawler's weight; the melt-glass is as silent as ever.

There are no trip-wires around the pole, no booby-traps, and if there is a radio-beacon attached to it to alert the Crawler to his approach, it is surely as useless among the craters as the tracker-tag.

The Pteronaut strokes the bone-chimes and the mirrors aside and looks at the metal box. It is large but not so large that it will be difficult to carry. Carefully, he disentangles it from where it hangs. No signal-flare goes high into the sky, fired by some mechanism as the weight of the box shifts. All is as before, empty and silent except for the jingle of white bone against bright steel.

The box is heavier than it looks, and the Pteronaut tilts it slowly, listening for any noise from inside. With a swift and sudden movement, he throws the box as far as he can, sending it bouncing across the melt-glass. One edge cracks, and then the lid opens, hinging wide as the box cartwheels into a crater. It spreads its contents in all directions as it crashes to a halt.

From the rim of the hollow, the Pteronaut watches the lid flapping wide. Just a box. Inanimate and unthreatening. He goes nearer, a few steps at a time, crouching by the spilled contents and turning them over in his gloved hands.

Ration-bars.

He collects a handful as he goes, stowing them away as he finds more. Nearest to the box is a plastic container, and when he feels sure enough that it poses no threat to him, he opens it; inside there is a block of water-ice as large as his fist. Another container opens to reveal some brand-new filters for his gill-cells, four of them. There is even, by accident or design, a little dune-dust in the corners of the box.

The Pteronaut sits down by the empty box and examines what the Crawler has left behind. He unclips the facemask, unwraps one of the ration-bars, and touches it against his cold lips. Everything feels normal, there is no numbness apart from the cold, no burning sensation. He takes a nibble from the end, chewing slowly and carefully, tasting and testing it with his tongue, holding back from eating the ration-bar whole despite his aching hunger.

There is no poison, no sedative drug. Just food. Food to keep him alive. Food to help him reach the end of the crater-wastes, where the signal from the tracker-tag will ring out clear again.

It is a trap, of sorts. A gift given by the Crawler in expectation that its generosity will be repaid. And for his part, the Pteronaut will not starve to spite it.

With less reserve than before, he takes another bite of the ration-bar, pushing all of it into his mouth. He chews it with a tongue that is so dry he can barely swallow.

He follows the ration-bar with two draws on the drip-tube, the most he has allowed himself in one serving for days. Raising the block of water-ice high above his head, he brings it down onto the ground, shattering it. He hammers the shards into smaller splinters and then he grinds the splinters into powder beneath the heel of his boots so that he can fill the reservoirs. He packs the tubes tight, and dabs at the powder that is left behind, licking it from his fingers. The water has a metallic taste to it and an oily sheen coats his mouth – it is nowhere near as pure as the ice he normally collects – but to the Pteronaut it tastes good.

Food, water, and air. Even a pinch of dust. The Crawler has left him almost everything he needs. The only thing missing is an indication of the way out.

The Pteronaut glances across at the metal pole with its four arms. Three of them had a purpose: on one, the mirrors; on another, the bone-chimes; on the third, the box – the fourth arm carries nothing. He stares at the empty fourth arm, and looks to the distance in the direction that it points. Perhaps that arm is empty by chance. Perhaps it is not, and it shows him a way back to the sandy deserts.

A way back to the Crawler.

Hope has not returned to the Pteronaut, not yet, but strength is coming; he can feel the deep red glow of it striking out into his tired limbs. Shaking off his exhaustion, he packs the ration-bars and the filters away in his supply-pouch and stands up. He ignores the pointing fourth arm of the metal pole and finds again the direction of the long-lost cloud that first showed him the way to go.

As he walks, his eyes flick to and fro behind the goggle-lenses, searching for the end of the melt-glass sea. And out there somewhere, watching for the signal from the tracker-tag to reappear on its scopes, the Crawler is waiting.

20

Dust. A whole drift of it. The Pteronaut jogs down the slope of the crater to where a rusty red crescent leans against one side of the hollow. It is nowhere near dune-sized, but deep enough that it spreads about his ankles. He kicks through the dust and picks up a handful of it, letting it run between his gloved fingers. Like smoke, the fine grains blow away before they reach the ground. It is the sign he has been hoping for: the craters are finally coming to an end.

It is two days since the Pteronaut found the metal cross with its bone and mirror ornaments and the box of supplies. He has slowly increased his use of the ration-bars that the Crawler left for him, with no ill effects. The water too is harmless, apart from the taste. Better than harmless – it has kept him alive.

The Pteronaut scoops up another handful of the dust to add to his supply for the sleeping-tube, and checks the craters that lie in a semi-circle ahead of him. The route that the cloud has made for him is forgotten for the moment, and he tries to judge in which direction the sands are deepest. He walks on, then checks the craters ahead of him again, altering his course slightly so that he is always heading towards the deepest drifts. By mid-afternoon he is certain of his course. Every step he takes is more confident, and his stride lengthens; he no longer hears the broken noise of his wings scratching to be free. Step by step, he is leaving the melt-glass wilderness behind.

At dawn the next day, distant mountains show just above the horizon, and the Pteronaut watches the daylight touch all the angles of their faces. After so many days with nothing more than a flat line marking the boundary between land

119

and sky, he has almost forgotten what mountains should look like.

As the peaks grow ahead of him, so the craters start to lose their grip on the landscape. The rolling ridges spread out, flung wide apart, just their outer rims touching. Then, mile by mile as the Pteronaut walks, gaps appear between the rims, areas of rough rock untouched by the heat of the impacts. And as the gaps between the craters grow wider and wider, the sands becomes deeper and deeper, until some of the melt-glass bowls are almost swallowed whole, marked out only by a slumping depression.

By nightfall, the Pteronaut can see that there are only a few more hours of walking before he reaches the foothills of the mountains. Up ahead, the desert is free of craters. So far, the Pteronaut's goggle-display has not started back into life. His view of the desert remains as uninformed as ever, but where he wanders across the rough ground between the crater-rims, the faintest sparks flicker on the edge of his eyesight.

After so many empty hours and so many long grinding miles, the Pteronaut cannot wait to leave the melt-glass behind. But for one more night he will need the protection that it provides. So he keeps close to the crater-rims and finishes his day's marching early. Before night comes, he has set up the sleeping-tube for one last time, down in the hollow of one of the bowls, just in case. When dawn steals into the sky again, the Pteronaut will be waiting, ready to leave the glass wastes early, and with a whole day of running ahead of him.

21

The Pteronaut rises just after dawn, anxious to be on his way. The chill of night is still lifting as he threads his way between the last of the craters, and their depths are dark and cold. The strengthening daylight shows him just how much the landscape is changing. Between the hollows, he jogs along across rocky outcrops that are uneven and fissured. They are a welcome change after the smooth hard monotony of the crater-plains, and they warm as they soak up the light instead of reflecting it straight back into the freezing air.

Even more welcome, the goggle-display flickers back into life. Lines and figures appear, at first dim and indistinct but the readings flutter less and less, growing stronger and clearer with every crater that is left behind. Almost better than the return of the display-readings themselves is what they report: the Pteronaut's supplies of air and water are better than he estimated by a couple of days.

But the return of the readings in the goggle-display means that the melt-glass has lost its power, and the burden of the tracker-tag feels heavy again around his ankle. The weight of it hurries him on towards the higher ground.

An hour later, and the Pteronaut is climbing towards the sky. Its wide blue expanse no longer feels like it is trapping him beneath it, and after so long making simple mechanical sweeps across the landscape, his eyes delight in the change of perspective. With every hundred feet of his ascent, the horizon gets further and further away. The crater-wastes open up behind him, and with one single turn of his head he can take in a hundred miles or more. A hundred miles of utter emptiness – there is still no sign of the Crawler.

As the Pteronaut climbs, he tests his muscles against the land that rears beneath his boots. His calf has healed completely during his easy days of walking, and the skin-suit, too, has repaired itself. New scales blend seamlessly with the old, sharing their moods as the colours respond to every change in temperature.

By the time the Pteronaut reaches the lowest summits and looks back, the daylight is etching the crater-rims with red-gold, and they glitter and shimmer away into the distance. But the stillness of the plains seems unnatural, as if they are hiding something behind all that emptiness, and as the light wanders across them, the shining craters wink like a thousand searching eyes. The Pteronaut turns his back on them and hurries on.

Hours pass, and many miles of climbing. Dusk creeps back into the sky. The Pteronaut has spent the whole day in the mountains, and he feels as if he has never left them. Those long aching days of nothing, the land hammered mirror-smooth, all the dawns and dusks with their one unchanging view – all of that seems distant and unreal. The Pteronaut sets up his sleeping-tube in the lee of a ridge, and sleeps more deeply and more peacefully than he has done since the night on the pinnacle.

From his high vantage-point the next morning, the Pteronaut looks at the plains with growing unease. They seem closer than they did the previous night. Quickly he packs up his sleeping-tube and heads deeper into the highlands, trusting their steep slopes to keep him safe.

More hours pass and the peaks close in behind him until he can no longer see the craters at all; or be seen from them. And then, just when the Pteronaut feels that he is truly hidden in the wilderness again, he finds himself at the edge of a straight-sided ravine that cuts deep across his path.

The Pteronaut cannot be certain how many miles he has walked from the broken bridge; time and distance have been measured in steps, and those steps have never stayed the same. His speed was slower at the start, with his leg still injured. Then he made faster progress as the wound in his calf improved, only to slow again as hunger sapped his strength.

But however far the Pteronaut has come, there it is again, or something very like it – a ravine with sides as impossibly sheer as the crater-wastes were flat carving through the summits and mountain-slopes alike. From where he is standing on the edge of it, the channel it makes seems to go on forever, winding away into the highlands. Somehow, he will have to cross it, and yet its width and depth make it impassable.

For a few hours, the Pteronaut follows the ravine. He keeps its sheer drop and the rising mountains on his left, with the open plains out of sight behind the lower peaks on his right. He glances constantly at the far side of the ravine, looking for a way across. Only there is no bridge to be seen and no way down. His eyes search for steps, or a ladder, or even the fracture of a landslip in the smooth sides, some path that he might use to climb down into the darkness and then up the other side. From so high above, the bottom of the ravine is only dimly visible, but it looks as smooth and as even as the curving walls. Crossing to the other side of the channel should not be a problem if he can only get down into it and find a way out on the far side.

It is early afternoon when the Pteronaut finds something, but it is not a way down and it is not on his side. A rippling column of solid ice beards the opposite wall of the channel, thicker and more massive than any he has ever seen before. From just a fraction of its bulk, he could fill his reservoirs with enough water-ice for days. It falls from a circular outlet a hundred feet above the floor of the ravine, and ends in billowing skirts of dust that have been trapped by the folds at its base. Anywhere else, the ice-fall would have seemed impossible. Against the size of the ravine, itself impossible, the scale of the ice-fall is merely fantastic.

But the ice-fall offers more to the Pteronaut than just somewhere to replenish his supply of water. The outlet that gives vent to it is almost choked completely, but not quite. A narrow archway remains open at the top, leading into the mountainsides. It is no place for a Pteronaut, roofed in, out of the sight of the sky and the reach of the wind, but there is something leading up from the outlet, vague indentations that might once have been steps. Even zooming in with his goggles, the Pteronaut cannot be certain whether the indentations were made deliberately. One thing is certain – if he can get down into the ravine on his side, he can use the ice-fall and the outlet to climb out again on the far side.

One more hour of marching, and the Pteronaut spots something on his side. Where the ravine curves around ahead there are metal rungs, rusted and weather-worn, that have been hammered into the rockface. They form a ladder of sorts. With his goggles sets to maximum magnification, the Pteronaut follows the ladder all the way down into the depths – he has found his descent.

By the time he reaches them, he has already noticed that the first dozen rungs at the top of the ladder are missing; just rust-rimmed holes remain, gouged into the rock like empty eye-sockets. Some of the others lower down are no more than a red streak, or frost-gnawed stubs. But lower still, out of the worst of the wind, the rungs seem more solid and certain – a lot lower; the Pteronaut will have to climb using the sockets themselves until he reaches what is left of the ladder.

He squats on the very edge of the drop, judging the difficulty and danger of the task. The rung-sockets are evenly spaced vertically; only the horizontal distance between them is a problem. It is narrower than the width of his shoulders, so he will have to work with his arms tucked in close to his ribs, relying on just the muscles of his forearms and his fingers to hang on. Once he gets started, his reach will have to be short and his breaths will need to be shallow.

The Pteronaut sits down with his legs dangling and twists around to take hold of the lip of rock. Then he lowers himself over the edge of the ravine to the full length of his arms, facing flat against the smooth wall. Working by feel alone, he finds two of the rung-sockets with his feet. He pushes his toes into them, taking almost all his weight on the tips of his boot-soles. Next, with one hand holding the lip of the ravine, he reaches down with the other hand and finds the top-most socket. He works his fingers into it to rid it of the last crumbs of rusted metal, and wedges the finger-joints against the sides to grip the socket tightly.

One look over his shoulder gives the Pteronaut the measure of the faith he must place in his fingers and toes; it is a long way down with just one handhold that he can be sure of. Even if his wings were still intact, the ravine would not be the place to fall, so narrow. One last time, he tests his weight, balancing between boot-tips and finger-tips. Then he leans in as close to the rock as he can and lets go of the lip.

For a full half-minute he stands there – if such a precarious position can really be called standing – while he slowly shifts his balance to bring his outstretched arm down by his side. When it is there, he rests, allowing all the tension in his muscles to flow away. Then, equally slowly, he bends the arm again so that he can find a grip in the rung-holes.

Socket by socket, the Pteronaut starts his descent. It is a test of strength, not of skill, moving slowly downwards from one finger-hold and toe-hold to the next, and his muscles are on the verge of cramping by the time he reaches the first intact rung of the ladder.

Even when the ladder reappears, the climb is neither safe nor easy. The very first rung gives way as the Pteronaut steps down onto it, but he had prepared himself for that, and he keeps both his grip and his balance as the fragments flake away. The next rung shatters beneath his weight, too, and the Pteronaut goes carefully. Below that, most of the remaining rungs seem to be sound, especially at the edges where they bend inwards to meet the wall of the ravine. Finally, he feels he can allow himself to go faster. Hand over hand, the Pteronaut descends into the shadows, switching into the monochrome of the goggles' low-light mode.

Some way down the ladder, he begins to see more detail of the flat floor of the ravine, and what he sees brings him to a halt: a regular stitch-mark pattern of tracks repeats itself all the way into the distance, grinning like the teeth of a skull.

The Pteronaut clings to the vertical wall of the channel for a moment, half-way between sky and solid ground. He zooms in on the track-marks with his telescopic sight. In places, the pattern has been partially filled.

Hanging from a rung with one hand, the Pteronaut extends the other out into the empty space, palm uppermost. The air in the ravine is almost completely still. There is barely the whisper of any breeze, only the occasional lost eddy reaches down to the floor below. He waits. One minute. Two. When he withdraws his hand and rubs his finger-tips across his palm, a thin coating of dust meets his touch. A fine red rain is falling, almost nothing. It will have taken days, weeks perhaps, maybe even years, to have softened the track-marks as he sees them.

His eyes can tell him only so much, and the shadows are deep. The Pteronaut listens for engine-noise along the length of the channel, but the only thing he can hear is the faint booming of the wind as it passes high above.

The ice-fall is an hour's march back in the direction that he has come from, and he knows that there will be no way out of the ravine for all that distance. He will be trapped with no way out.

The Pteronaut glances down again at the track-marks.

One pair, parallel.

The Crawler is broader, its heavy bulk carried on multiple drive-units; so broad, in fact, that it would barely be able to traverse the channel. Whatever made the tracks was narrow enough to pass between the high walls of the ravine with a good distance to spare on either side.

The promise of the ice-fall beckons, a ready supply of water-ice, and a climb to the far side of the ravine where he will be safe. The Pteronaut starts to descend once more, moving as quickly as he can. He drops the final few feet to the ground.

It is cold and dark in the bottom of the ravine, and the air is so silent that the Pteronaut can almost feel the weight of it bearing down on him from that narrow blue strip high above. With one last look up at the ladder, he sets off for the ice-fall.

With no need to search out his route, the Pteronaut makes fast progress along the smooth channel floor. Within forty minutes he is at the ice-fall.

It is massive, shimmering like a mirage. Seen in close-up from down near its base, the ice-fall seems even more fantastic than when the Pteronaut first saw it across the width of the ravine. It takes what little light there is in the channel and sends it sparkling back into the dry air. There is no doubting the cold hard reality of what he sees, but even so it defies belief. The ice-fall contains more water than the Pteronaut can possibly imagine – a hundred thousand of the handfuls that he hammers with such effort from the ground – and it is there for the taking. He will not have to dig, or to climb, or to stretch to collect enough for his reservoir-tubes; he can stand at the base and chip away at the thinner folds that have knotted themselves together. The Pteronaut draws his knife and hurries forwards.

A single step on shifting sand.

A rasping snap.

Snick!

Lightning-fast, the gaping jaws of a mantrap cast off their covering of dust and close around the Pteronaut's leg. Metal teeth scissor together, two inches long, sharp enough and strong enough to tear flesh and sever tendons, slicing through to the bone.

Faster still, the Pteronaut throws himself backwards.

The teeth of the trap screech to a stop against the loop of the tracker-tag, locking the jaws half-open. The crippling bite is blocked, and the Pteronaut's leap is cut short. He falls flat onto his back.

He lies there in the dust for a few seconds, catching his breath. There is no pain and no sound of the skin-suit's decompression-alarm, just a tightness around his ankle as the loop of the tracker-tag resists the bone-breaking pressure of the jaws.

The Pteronaut tries to sit up.

The teeth of the trap protest, squealing and scratching across the metal of the loop. They wander towards the edge and the muscle of his leg.

He stops, as motionless as the ice-fall.

Slow steady movements are needed – no haste, no suddenness. The Pteronaut reaches towards the jaws with almost infinite slowness. At the same time, he stretches out his right leg, keeping it as straight and as unmoving as he can.

The springs of the trap creak. The teeth shift a little more, gouging more bright scratches into the metal of the tag.

The Pteronaut stops, hardly daring to breathe when a single breath might undo everything. He changes tactic. Inch by inch, he works his fingers down to his ankle. He cannot afford to rush.

That is when he hears it. A distant rumble pulses through the channel, and the air vibrates with approaching menace. Whatever is coming has been lying in wait for some signal, and triggering the trap has sent it.

The Pteronaut moves a little faster and the springs in the trap creak again. Its teeth score more jagged lines across the loop of the tracker-tag. He touches the cold metal of the jaws and bends forwards from his hips to hook his fingers around the serrated blades.

Second by second, the rumbling is drawing closer.

The Pteronaut tests his strength against the springs. Flight-muscles stand out as hard as iron. Fingers that can bear his own weight take the strain. The jaws of the trap creak again, scarcely audible as the engine-noise meets its own echoes. A pall of dust appears around the curve of the channel – whatever is coming, it is coming fast. The Pteronaut grits his teeth and strains a little more, building his strength slowly to oppose the force of the springs.

The rumbling becomes a roar, and around the curve of the channel, the Crawler appears. The jointed segments of its body are strung out in a long train behind it, leaving just a single row of double track-marks in the dust.

The Pteronaut sees the Crawler's elongated shape and recognises its deception. He tries harder to free his leg. The toothed jaws tick as he pushes against them, but the coming of the Crawler is so loud that he feels the noise more than hears it.

The first outriders of the Crawler's dust-clouds billow past him. He pushes against the crushing force that threatens to break his leg. One of the serrated teeth cuts through the scaly outer-skin of his gloves, and the suit's decompression-alarm screams in his ears. A dribble of resinous sealant seeps between his fingers. Slowly, almost imperceptibly, the Pteronaut starts to force the trap apart.

Too late – the Crawler is upon him.

Everything vanishes in a thick red haze. The turmoil of the dust-clouds is filled with the crashing clatter of the tracks, and the Pteronaut is deaf as well as blind. Then the Crawler stops, and he can feel it towering above him, hemming him in with its length in both directions.

Slowly, the dust-swirls settle as the Crawler's engine-noise dies away. Figures appear, dropping down an access-ladder and onto the floor of the ravine; three drones, armed and eager to finish the hunt.

They find the birdman waiting.

With one final desperate wrench, the Pteronaut has freed his leg from the trap. He throws it at the three drones as they come for him. The first drone raises its arm to fend off the impact. Crushing jaws clamp around its head and its scream ends in a shriek as it staggers to the ground.

The Pteronaut launches himself at the second drone and knocks it sprawling onto its back. He is up again in an instant. He finds his knife where it fell in the dirt and comes in close and quick at the third drone. Four, five quick strikes at the weak points in its suit and it is down, but the second drone is already struggling to its feet. Before it can raise its rifle to shoot out his legs, the Pteronaut is on it again. He slams into the drone and knocks it flat. It struggles beneath his weight, and with the heel of his hand he forces its chin backwards, exposing the flexible material between the joints at its throat. His knife flashes with the distant blue of the sky, and the drone lies still beneath him.

Three drones dead, but an army behind them; a swarm of footsteps thunders along the walkways.

A knife is no good against so many. The Pteronaut tugs the rifle from the second drone's arms and snaps off the safety-catch. With short sharp bursts, he fires up at the Crawler's armoured flanks. The rhythm of boots on metal becomes a discordant jumble, and two bodies fall ringing down a ladderway, jamming themselves in a tangle of arms and legs halfway down. The swarm spills out in all directions, looking for a way around the blockage.

The Pteronaut plucks another magazine of ammunition from the dead drone's belt and looks for his own way out.

The steel flanks of the Crawler stretch out along the channel, reflecting the sheer wall of the ravine. Between them is the ice-fall, too difficult to climb in a hurry.

No escape in either direction.

No cover either side.

There is only one place to go: under the Crawler.

The Pteronaut slips between the tracks of the nearest drive-unit, and the dark underside of the Crawler's lengthened body shuts out the sky. Kicking his footprints into nothing behind him, he creeps along in the shadows between the massive metal tracks. If they start rolling, even a small shift to one side or the other will bring him under their crushing weight.

But the Crawler's engines idle as its drones do its hunting for it, and the Pteronaut hurries on. Ripples of frozen sand scowl down at him, and stalactites of rust hang from bare sections of metalwork, as sharp as spears. He dodges between them and reaches the end of the drive-unit. There is a gap there, a metal chasm that opens all the way up to the armoured upper-deck and the sky above. It is almost clear except for looping cables and pipework and the huge hinging joints that hold the Crawler's segmented body together.

Behind him, the Pteronaut hears the squabble of drones reach the bodies of their companions. They go warily, seeking the Crawler's prey. Some are already peering into the shadows between the tracks. The Pteronaut looks up at the gap above him, shoulders the rifle, and starts to climb.

If the Crawler feels his touch against its metal skin, it does not show it. If it senses his weight as he clambers from coupling to coupling, creeping between its segments, the note of its engines does not change. But the Pteronaut is aware of the threat. The Crawler surrounds him. Its smell is in his nostrils – oil, metal, smoke, steam, the reek of its fusion-furnaces. He reaches quickly from one handhold to the next as if the brackets and stanchions are too hot to touch. More than ever, the scale and power of the Crawler dwarfs him. There can be no victory against such an opponent; his only chance is escape.

Half-way to the top, the Pteronaut turns aside from his upwards climb. He hauls himself over some rusted railings onto one of the external walkways. It is deserted. When the Crawler coils tight around itself, the walkway faces into the deep well at its centre where the ice-drill burrows into the permafrost. Now, the walkway faces towards the far side of the ravine, away from where the drones are searching for him; away from the danger of immediate discovery. The Pteronaut slips the rifle from his shoulder and races the length of the walkway, sending the bone ornaments jingling along the balustrade as he goes.

A gulf separates that segment of the Crawler from the next, bridged only by a spindly thrust of metal pipework. The Pteronaut does not cross and he does not climb. Instead, he turns, running across the Crawler's width, and then he turns again, onto the walkway that faces the ice-fall – it glitters back some distance in the Crawler's shadow.

As the Pteronaut runs in the direction of the ice-fall, he replaces the half-spent magazine in the rifle. Down below – a quick glance over the balustrade – the drones are still searching for his tracks. None of them thinks to look up.

A long chattering burst from the rifle brings a hundred identical faces staring towards the sky. The Pteronaut squeezes the trigger tight and raises the muzzle of the rifle, resisting the recoil as he fires higher and higher up at the frozen surface of the ice-fall. Bullet-cases dance across the deck at his feet. A blizzard of ice spicules rains down from the ice-fall's frozen folds.

Before the drones below can move, the gun clicks empty, smoking in the Pteronaut's hands. A sudden silence chases the echoes of the shots down the channel. He throws the useless rifle onto the deck, draws his knife, and steps over the balustrade.

Twenty feet across the gap he jumps.

The surface of the ice-fall is iron-hard. The Pteronaut thuds against it, arms outstretched, and starts to slip down its glassy sides. The blade of his knife scores and scratches into the frozen surface; his other hand and his toes seek the dents that the bullets made, trying to stop his slide.

Pounding, stabbing, sprawling, scrabbling, the Pteronaut slithers to a stop. He levers himself upwards from one foothold to the next. He hacks and twists down with the knife, kicking the bullet-scars deeper as he goes. Foot by foot, dent by dent, the narrow mouth of the outlet comes closer.

The Crawler's engines gave a warning shout, sending spires of black smoke tumbling into the sky, and its drones swarmed back up the access-ladders. They climbed and clambered to the walkway where the bullet-cases lay, but it was already too late. The birdman had reached the outflow at the top of the ice-fall, and as the drones watched, he snaked into the narrow opening on his belly and vanished into the dark.

22

Beyond the choked outlet, the passage is level for maybe a dozen yards, and then it falls away into darkness. The ice is smoother and more slippery than any rock the Pteronaut has ever encountered before, but there is no time for caution. Just behind him the noise of pursuit gathers – of gas-powered harpoons and zip-lines being fired into the ice-fall from the Crawler's flanks. The Pteronaut tucks his knife away and trusts to luck, letting the slope take him where it will.

Lying flat on his stomach, he slides straight down. The dot that illuminates his night-vision becomes a red blur streaking across the ice. Faster and faster he slips with no way to stop, until he is falling helpless and headfirst down the near-vertical slope. Instinctively, he tries to control the dive. His muscles tense, his back arches, but still his speed increases. A sudden drop, a crevasse, a sharp turn, or a solid wall; any one of them will bring his escape to an abrupt and bone-shattering end.

But the water froze smoothly as it flowed through the outlet. There are no drops or deadly crevasses, and no obstacles. Gradually, the slope beneath him levels out.

Puddles splash as he goes sliding through them, and the ice thins. The scales of the skin-suit scurf and scratch across odd patches of bare rock, and the Pteronaut comes to a sprawling stop.

He gets to his feet and looks around.

High up behind him is a dim sheen of light from the outlet, and the way back – if he ever wanted to take it – is unclimbable, all sheer sheets and falling folds of ice. Ahead of him, there is ice too, coating the walls of a horizontal tunnel that goes back into the mountainside, but the ice does not reach far. Far from the chill of the ravine and the deserts beyond it, the temperature is rising. Drips of

134

meltwater fall from the ceiling like silver flames, and their constant *plunk*, *plunk* echoes down the tunnel. The Pteronaut draws his knife and follows the noise.

A few steps further on, his boots crunch across the last grainy grey streaks of ice. A hundred yards beyond that, the way ahead is blocked – a blank white wall shows up in his night-vision, filling the tunnel. He stops, listening again to the noises of pursuit as the Crawler's drones hunt for him. With nowhere else to go but onwards, the Pteronaut is trapped.

Then the blank white wall trembles, swirling slightly in some faint breeze.

Mist. Rolling banks of it hang in the moist atmosphere, turned opaque where his night-vision glow hits it. Like the ice-fall, the mist is an impossibly exaggerated version of everything that the Pteronaut has ever seen before, unrecognisable compared with the thin wisps that rise from exposed water-ice at dawn.

The mist closes in behind him and he walks on, leaving textured tread-marks from his boot-soles across the bare concrete floor where he walks through the wet. Dull and flat, he hears the splashes of marching feet through the puddles at his back, sounding near or far as the mist shivers. Stabbing beams of white light go fingering through the damp air looking for him, and the Pteronaut breaks into a jog. There is nothing he can do about the wet tracks he leaves behind, but unless the tunnel forks, the Crawler's drones need no tracks to follow him anyway: there is only one way to go.

With every step the Pteronaut takes, the temperature keeps on rising. His in-breaths are warm and stifling inside the facemask, and the skin-suit struggles to adjust. Super-insulated, its pigmentation changes to radiate his excess body-heat, but it is fighting a losing battle. The Pteronaut can feel an uncomfortable layer of sweat forming between his own skin and the smooth inner-tissues of the suit, overwhelming its capacity to absorb and recycle lost moisture. The scales of the skin-suit glisten as he passes through the mist, as if it is sweating too.

The tunnel goes on for another hundred yards, two hundred, straight back into the rock, and then it curves around slightly to the right. At the turn, the tunnel starts to dip. If there had been ice there the floor would have been treacherous underfoot. But there is no ice; just the mist, thicker than before, made solid where the searchlights touch it. It presses against the Pteronaut's goggles, leaving him almost blind.

He reaches out cautiously to guide himself, finding the wall of the corridor with his left hand. First ice, then rock, and finally the air itself is closing in around him, hemming him in. Even the sounds of the subterranean world are coiling closer as the Pteronaut goes on. The regular *drip-drip* from the ceiling has faded as he has left the ice-flow behind, and something else has taken its place; a booming rushing spitting noise that fills the unseen caverns around him with fury.

At first the Pteronaut takes the noise for the wind. Except the noise that he hears is more regular than the wind, and somehow not regular at all, a guttural background roar of constant ferocity. It comes from up ahead, where the mist writhes and swirls in sudden spasms. Closer and closer to its source, the noise grows even louder, unimaginably loud. It is like the Crawler's engines multiplied a thousand times. But whatever is making the noise, it is not made of metal.

The mist falls back, and the end of the tunnel comes into view. To the Pteronaut, it looks like the end of everything: a river, as black as midnight in his low-light vision, cuts across his path.

He stares at it. Foam-flecked, swirling under and over itself, the river races through an even wider and higher tunnel than the one he has been following. Above him, the roof is solid ice again.

It takes a moment for the Pteronaut to understand that what he is looking at is water. Can this be the same substance that pools sedately in the hammer-hollows when he digs it out of the permafrost and melts it? Spray burns as bright as lava in his night-vision, and the shape and sound of the flood go tumbling past, constantly varying, always threatening. The river is water as he has never imagined it; seething foaming and furious, with a power that dwarfs that of the most turbulent dust-storm he has ever witnessed.

The mist that hangs back in the overflow-tunnel flares with light and a dozen torch-beams throw a tangled net around him. The Pteronaut races to the edge of the river, and finds himself standing on a narrow concrete ledge. He grips the knife in his hand and looks away from the tumult and the turmoil that fill his senses. The ledge leads to a metal ladder that is swallowed completely by the high roof of ice. Where the rungs hang down exposed they are frayed and tattered, eaten away by rust and spray. The dim red dot from his night-vision swims slickly across the ice-roof. There are no footholds; he cannot hope to climb.

The Pteronaut turns on the spot, looking over his shoulder. At that very moment, the first of the drones emerges from the mist. It cradles its rifle, creeping cautiously forwards towards the source of that unimaginable noise. Others follow; too many to fight.

The Pteronaut stares back into the fury of the river. If in doubt and danger, fly – that is the Pteronaut way.

He sheaths his knife, takes a breath, and leaps from the ledge.

23

Rushing water takes hold of the Pteronaut with an elemental strength that he has never felt in the air. He cannot fight it. The river spins him around and around, first holding him down in the deep dark, and then pushing him upwards to the spray and splutter at the surface. The Pteronaut's night-vision is blinded once more, filled with a seething mass of bubbles.

The gill-cells flood, and the mesh-protected spiracles of the skin-suit narrow, just as they would against a choking dust-storm. Except water is not dust.

Inside the gill-cells, the filters fizz as the flood reaches them. Carbon dioxide dissolves out of their honeycomb lattice-work, a massive surge of it, polluting the skin-suit's airways. The oxygen levels drop dramatically in each breath that the Pteronaut takes; warning-lights flash across his goggle-display and the low-oxygen alarm buzzes against his skull. Within seconds, the breathing capillaries to the facemask have snicked shut to protect him. Now the only oxygen he has is what the skin-suit can supply from its emergency store, and that will not last long. The Pteronaut will not drown in the black water as the torrent carries him along – he will suffocate.

The river takes him fast and far. Sometimes, lost in the dark, he feels the hard edge of the bottom or the side – he can never tell which – and he goes grasping for it. His fingers stumble across the stony contours as he searches for a grip, even one down in the depths; anything to get some measure of control for a split-second.

But the waters shake him loose again and carry him away, dashing him against the walls, hurtling him through eddies that spin him around until some other current drags him into its own irresistible clutches.

The Pteronaut's heart beats hard enough to make his whole body shake. His consciousness slips away, and bright lights flicker at the corner of his vision. A precious trickle of oxygen revives him, but the skin-suit's supplies are overwhelmed. The last minutes of his life will be measured out by those desperate breaths.

Then he strikes something hard and flat, metallic, like the bars of a grille, and he stops suddenly, held fast as the water rips along past him. Trapped down in the depths, the Pteronaut realises that the throb that fills the water around him is not his heart beating, but something else, a deep booming from beyond the grille. He turns to face into the noise and his fingers slip gladly around a sturdy metal mesh – something solid at last, something that he can climb. The Pteronaut starts to claw his way upwards towards the surface, fighting the force of the water that is pressing him hard against the bars.

With a gasp, he levers himself above the waves. They break around him and the roar of the river returns. The Pteronaut pulls himself just high enough that the first row of gill-cells around his ribs can open. The mesh protectors dilate, and they wheeze as he takes a breath.

For a second the Pteronaut hangs there, battered by the flood. Then, something strikes him hard across the legs, just below the waves. He looks down to see what it is, and an arm reaches out of the torrent clutching for him, an arm that is covered in patchwork armour and daubed all over with hunting-charms.

One-handed, gripping the grille, the Pteronaut tries to fight the drone away, but his fingers slip, and he plunges back beneath the water. The drone and the birdman grapple with each other in the dark depths, pushed up tight against the bars. The Pteronaut twists in the drone's grip, gets an arm free, and punches his opponent hard in the stomach – to no effect; the blows are useless against the salvage-metal plates. He needs his knife, but there is no way he can reach for it.

Silently, the two of them wrestle in the dark. There is hidden energy in their struggle as the advantage shifts imperceptibly back and forth. The birdman is stronger and quicker and more manoeuvrable – perhaps the river is not so unlike the air after all – but his gill-cells have flooded again, and the oxygen-supply of the skin-suit is running dangerously low. The drone's suit is heavy and armoured and restricts its wearer's movement, making it clumsy in the water, but the emergency tank of oxygen that it carries will last for hours.

The struggle reaches its endpoint, the movements of the two opponents becoming smaller and smaller as they reach an equilibrium, perfectly balanced: the birdman will suffocate if the drone prevents him from struggling above the waves to take a breath, but if the drone lets the birdman get an arm free for his knife, it knows that it is dead.

Stalemate.

The Pteronaut kicks out, desperate for air. The surface of the water churns only a few feet above him, but he can find no footing; his heels slither across the squares of the grille. The drone shifts its grip. The effort needed to fight both the birdman and the river is immense. It is tiring, the Pteronaut can feel it. A slight tremor courses through its muscles. The drone's grip wavers again for an instant, and in that moment the Pteronaut gets an arm free. In the next he finds his knife. He drives the shining blade home to find its target, stabbing hard against the force of the river.

The drone slumps against him, its arms limp. Red streaks billow from its wounds, torn away by the current. Inside his facemask, the Pteronaut gasps, sucking in air that is not there. Caged inside his chest, his lungs feel tight up against his ribs, as if they could never expand enough to satisfy the need to breathe. Stars speckle his vision, and the rushing noise fades into silence. Defeating the drone has not beaten the river, and it is the river that really matters.

The Pteronaut is down to his very last breath. With it, he crooks his arm and slashes at the drone's suit, running the knife-blade cleanly through the helmet-joint, just beneath a necklace of smooth white stones that might be teeth. A hissing rush of bubbles spirals upwards. There are no coagulating fluids to block the outrush of air as there would be in his skin-suit; no release of enzymes to weaken the cell-walls so that the rising pressure can find its own route to restore the supply. The drone's suit is passive with no defences, no way to fight-back. All it can offer is a steady stream of precious air.

The Pteronaut pulls down his facemask. The water and the silvery bubbles tickle across his skin, and he bends forwards to bite on the severed ends of the drone's breathing-tubes. Oxygen splutters into his mouth, expelling the water between his teeth. He gulps the gas down, swallowing it whole.

Taking stolen breaths, the Pteronaut stays against the grille until his heart-rate slows. Then, with his jaws still clamped around the slash in the drone's suit, he starts to kick upwards, half-climbing, half-swimming up the interlacing bars of the grille. Up and up through the pulsing water he climbs, dragging the drone's body with him. The throbbing noise vanishes as he breaks the surface, and the roar of the torrent resumes. With one arm around the drone's body, the Pteronaut swims on his back, making fitful flight-movements with no wings, pushing for the edge of the tunnel.

He reaches the side and fumbles along through the spray until he finds a concrete ledge, not unlike the one he leapt from upstream. With his breath held tight, he lets go of the drone's body. Sloshing and splashing out of the river, the Pteronaut struggles up onto the ledge, turns, and plunges his arm quickly back into the foaming waters to grab the drone before it can sink. He hauls it up after him. Then for a while he lies in the dark, slumped across the dead drone's body with the breathing-tubes in his mouth.

Slowly, the Pteronaut's gill-cells run clear of water. Heaving himself up onto his elbows, he lets the last of the water drain out of the suit and clips his facemask back on. The first few lungfuls of air are sweet-tasting, clean and clear now that the water has purged his depleted filters. When he has his breath back, he strips out the drone's gill-cells and plunges them into the river where they fizz and foam in his hands, coming out of the water washed through to a bright blue. He flicks them free of excess water; they will add vital days to his supply.

Next, he makes sure of the water-supply in his reservoirs, filling them all from the river until they are brimming. Finally, he strips the drone of his weapons – a pistol and a rifle, both with spare ammunition – before dumping the drone's body back into the river. It sinks out of sight, leaving a feeble trail of bubbles behind it.

The Pteronaut looks back at the hurtling black waters, upstream, the way he has come. He is on the opposite side from where he started, and the river must have carried him for miles and miles beneath the mountains. If any other drones have dared to follow him into the water, there is no sign of them. Even so, the Crawler might still send some after him. The Pteronaut has never seen a boat, but he can imagine how one might work. And if he can imagine it, so can the Crawler.

He looks around, taking stock. In the upstream direction, the ledge is a mirror-image of his launch-site, cut back into the wall of the tunnel with a ladder that leads up until it is enveloped by the roof of ice far above his head. But the two ledges are not quite identical – the back wall of the downstream ledge is blank stone; there is no overflow-tunnel to guide the Pteronaut to the outside.

Further downstream, the ledge continues past the metal grille. Beyond it, the waters froth and rush down a gulley to drive the blades of a row of massive turbines. Most of the turbines are completely submerged, but some of them are half-stranded above the waterline. Like the grille, the spray has eaten into their blades, leaving them feathered and lacy.

The blades chop the water into foaming fragments; there is no escape for the Pteronaut that way.

But even if they are dilapidated now, the turbines must once have been maintained; the ledge that the Pteronaut stands on is proof that someone needed access to them. The ladder that leads down from the ceiling is too precarious an access-route for any heavy engineering work. There must be another way out.

At the far end of the ledge, hidden in the deepest shadow, the Pteronaut's night-vision shows him an opening in the rock. A door half-closes it, hanging off its hinges. Like the turbines and the bars of the grille, the metal panels of the door have also been eaten away by the spray. The Pteronaut pushes it open and it flutters to the ground in a shapeless cascade of brittle flakes.

The service-elevator for the turbines is a rusted metal box with an uncertain floor. Where the roof has fallen in, the Pteronaut can see the winch-cables, leading the way up the lift-shaft for miles and miles, or so it seems. Even if the turbines are still generating power, he does not dare to try the switch. The elevator-cage itself is too rust-riddled to move, and the onset of motion in the machinery might bring the counterweight or the winch itself crashing down the shaft.

But there us another way up. To one side of the service-elevator is a stairwell. Thick curtains of mist hang in the gloom. More mist. It is a welcome sight; somewhere beyond the door, the warm damp air from the river meets the cold dry air of the deserts. Somewhere beyond the door, the Pteronaut will find his way out.

24

The Pteronaut leaves the river behind and soon he is climbing again, but not sheer walls of rock or glistening overflows of ice or mazes of metal pipework: this time, his ascent is easy, up broad flat concrete steps.

Through the mist beyond the doorway, a stairwell appears, twisting up and away from the roar of the river. Every so often there is a landing where the stairs turn back on themselves as they climb, but there are never any exits to either side, so the Pteronaut goes on into the fog-filled dark. The concrete steps are ghosts that become solid ahead of him and vanish again behind him, so that it almost seems like he is not climbing at all.

But he is climbing; step after step, the noise of the river becomes fainter. Away from the warm waters that rush along below, the temperature falls, and ice creeps across the walls and floor. Gradually, the mist gives way, thinning as the sheen of ice becomes thicker. The Pteronaut treads carefully. After another three flights of stairs, the moisture from the river has reached its upper limit and the ice becomes patchy. Bare concrete emerges underfoot again. The dry deserts are returning, and the Pteronaut goes faster, taking the steps two at a time.

Lights blaze on suddenly at the next landing. The Pteronaut drops to one knee with the dead drone's rifle at the ready. Up on the wall, a fluorescent striplight glows, flaying the stairs with a stark white glare. Crouching still and silent, the Pteronaut strains his ears; all he can hear is the muffled rush of distant water from below and a wavering electric buzz from the striplight. The light flickers, guttering like a flame, and then it fizzes and goes out.

Darkness rushes back in and the Pteronaut's goggles switch to his night-vision. He waits for a minute, but the darkness is complete and constant. Keeping the rifle held out ahead of him, he waves an arm. A motion-detector up on the wall clicks in recognition and the striplight flares back into life.

The Pteronaut is alone. There is no threat, no challenge from the dead of the place, just the unquestioning obedience of electric circuits, fed by the ceaseless sweeps of the turbine-blades below.

He stands up into the glare, blinking behind his goggle-lenses. His thoughts thread together.

Light.

Power.

Machinery.

The Pteronaut's desire to escape has blinded him to the obvious: the maintenance for the turbines would have required tools, and if there is still power in the complex, those tools might still work.

Now the realisation has come, the Pteronaut has an extra cause to hurry. He is not just climbing to return to the cold dead deserts; he is climbing to find something that can remove the tracker-tag from his ankle.

Level after level passes by. On most levels, the fluorescent striplights are still working and the Pteronaut no longer even pauses at the sudden brightness. Each level winks back into darkness again as he passes, the shadows rising with him like black water from the river filling the stairwell.

Another level passes by: a click, the buzz of the light, his own shadow leaping out and fleeing again as he turns the corner, the hard tap-tap of his boots as he runs.

And another.

And another.

And then there is no light – only darkness and the crunch of broken glass beneath the Pteronaut's boots. He stands still. The motion-detector clicks, its circuit tripped, but the fluorescent-tube has been blown out.

In his night-vision the Pteronaut sees pitted scars across the walls, and half-way up the next set of stairs, a body sprawls face down; the dead have not entirely left the place, after all.

Frosty claw-marks of blood on the walls show where the body tried to raise itself up and crawl away before life left it. Brittle feathers of the same freeze-dried blood float to the floor as the Pteronaut hauls the body under the arms and pulls it upright. The grinning skull-face inside the helmet is all cheekbones and teeth, with bulging eyes like glazed white pebbles, and the rigid suit it wears hangs in tatters.

All around, buried in the wall-scars or mixed in with the broken glass of the striplight are shreds of metal shrapnel. The body on the stairs died a violent death, not the impartial violence of the deserts that the Pteronaut knows: this was like the crater-impacts – destruction with a purpose.

Out of habit, he examines the suit that the body is wearing, seeking what he can salvage.

No gill-cells. Not even primitive ones. Instead, oxygen tanks carried on the back. They are perforated by shrapnel and their contents long since lost. Lying in the crook of one step, a handgun, frosted with blood and still cocked.

Nothing of any use.

The Pteronaut leaves the body where he found it and continues his search for the way out. The higher he goes, the more signs of fighting he sees; bullet-holes pockmark the walls, and shell-cases litter the stairs. An automatic rifle lies discarded and empty.

There are more bodies too. On one landing, he finds a jumbled knot of four gunmen. They have died fighting alongside each other as far as he can tell, their suits shot through from behind. The suits that they wear are of a different design from the one on the body that he found below. They are lighter and more flexible, with rudimentary gill-cells arranged across the chest, and smaller oxygen-tanks on the back. The helmets are also different. Two

146

groups – attackers and defenders. Which is which no longer matters: dead is dead.

A long trail of rust-brown bootprints runs up the stairs, but there is no sign of whoever made them. Higher up the shaft, the Pteronaut hears the sound of the wind whistling through a narrow entrance, and as he climbs, his feet begin to scuff across a thin layer of dust that has crept into the corners of each step. The dusty layer deepens the higher he goes. At some point the lights fail altogether. The motion-detectors click as obediently as ever when he appears within range, but the fluorescent-tubes have been worn out by years of the wind stirring up the dust.

Despite the darkness, the Pteronaut's night-vision does not return. A dim half-light fills the stairwell above. At the top of the next set of stairs is another door, half-closed, and in the draughty entrance-way where the sand-grains can never settle, there is a scatter of spent bullet-cases. Hundreds of bullet-cases. Somebody, perhaps the group of gunmen or the lone body he found below, took cover in the doorway to hold off a determined attack. The Pteronaut crunches over the glittering carpet that the shell-jackets make and heaves the door open.

He steps out onto a wide causeway. The fading light of the evening sky is all around him, and a fitful breeze blows past. He breathes deeply from it, clearing the damp dark from his lungs.

As far as he can see in both directions, the curve of the causeway runs like a spanned bow to the steep sides of a valley. Here and there, the vastness of the bow is marked by the rise of a small tower, just like the one that he has just climbed. Over one side of the concrete balustrade, a smooth sweeping surface falls six hundred feet or more. The wall it makes is almost sheer, but not quite; the skirts of it reach out where it thickens at its base. A crack runs part-way down the wall, exposing a bony white glint of the depth of ice trapped behind it.

On the convex side of the parapet, the drop is less high, only a hundred feet or so, but more precipitous. On that side, behind the high barrier of the wall, the level surface of a frozen lake shows in icy patches beneath the dust. Hundreds of feet below the surface, buried deep down where heat from the rocks still keeps it liquid, is the river that carried the Pteronaut there, still flowing through the dam.

The Pteronaut stands and stares, taking in the immensity of what he sees. His eyes wander along the causeway. At either end, the mountains slope down towards the frozen lake. Over to the left, the causeway ends at a clutter of small buildings perched on the hillside. The attack on the dam seems to have started there, because the buildings are little more than ruins.

On the other side, to his right, there are imposing terraces of multi-storeyed buildings that climb back to the cliffs behind them; the most distant of the buildings appear to have been built into the rock itself. Some of the windows are black and empty, the staring sockets scorched by flames, but others are still unbroken, reflecting the view of the dam and the evening sky.

The Pteronaut scans past the buildings – little more than prisons to his eyes – scarcely noticing them. He has spotted something far more interesting. At the far end of the terraces, a flat concrete space is set apart from the main complex, and he zooms in with his telescopic vision.

The flat space is not empty. Squatting in the centre of it is the fire-charred wreckage of a flyder. It is not a flyder like the others that the Pteronaut has seen, but something of its shape tells him instantly that it was made to fly. There are no wings, just a twisted crown of metal spokes that has been warped by the heat of its destruction and bent towards the sky. Behind the wreckage, three hangars gape open, empty except for the creeping shadow of the coming night. A fourth hangar seems to have escaped damage; its blank steel door is sealed tight against the elements with the dust piled at its feet.

Intact. Undisturbed.

The Pteronaut turns towards the complex on that side, and his steps quicken. The path along the top of the dam runs smooth and curving all the way to the side of the valley. The Pteronaut hurries past the crumpled rags of more bodies, with craters and bullet-holes stippling the causeway. Then he is at the end of the parapet, and a broad set of stairs leads up and onto the slopes beyond it. The fighting there has been intense, a last stand, and the swathes of dust show an arm or a leg or the outline of a figure, lying as it fell long ages ago.

The terrace at the top of the stairs is wider and less obstructed, but there are bodies there too, staring at the sky. The Pteronaut runs past them all and past the tall buildings with the unbroken windows that they died to defend, and then he is at the flat concrete landing-apron.

The wreckage of the flyder is tipped over slightly at an angle in the middle of a blackened circle of burnt fuel – so black that he can almost smell the flames, though it must have been many years since the wind took the smoke and the fire-scent away with it. The shattered glass bowl of the flyder's canopy stands out in front of a small passenger cabin; charred husks of bodies are still strapped into their seats, ready for a journey that never left the ground.

The three open hangars swallow the Pteronaut's footsteps as he hurries past. He does not stop to investigate their cavernous spaces. The fourth hangar is his destination.

Daylight has vanished from the lake surface, but it still washes the sides of the valley a flaming crimson-red as the Pteronaut comes to a standstill in front of the fourth hangar. The dying light sends his silhouette rippling tall across the vertical segments of the sealed door. There is no handle that he can see, but a flap at one side covers a simple set of controls. He lifts the flap and jabs one of the buttons.

Behind the jointed segments of the door, motors grate as electricity runs through them. Creaking and shaking, the huge door shuffles free of the dust-piles at its base. As it judders to one side, a second internal door also begins to open, sliding in the opposite direction. The movements of the internal door are cleaner and smoother with no dust to hinder them, and there is a gentle hiss of depressurisation as a long-standing seal is broken.

Impatient on the balls of his feet, the Pteronaut steps forwards. A whiff of machine-oil or fuel comes in through his facemask as the inner-door rolls back. Lights flicker on inside the hangar. In their sudden brightness, he sees his own reflection staring back at him from the polished metal curves of a perfectly intact flyder.

The Pteronaut has not found tools, or food, or water, or a weapon in the ruins of the dam-complex; he has found something better – he has found a way to fly again.

25

Sealed safely inside its hangar, the flyder looks utterly unreal, as if the red deserts that are mirrored across its sleek body belong to another dimension. The Pteronaut reaches out a gloved hand and strokes his finger-tips across the flyder's skin. It is flawless, smoother than the ice, the curves of its body even more perfect than the most skilful sculptures that the wind can make. The flyder is so different from the tortured wrecks that he finds out in the dunes, so different from the weathered jumble of the Crawler.

The Pteronaut steps over trailing maintenance cables and snaking fuel-pipes, watching his own reflection slide across the perfection of the flyder's streamlining. Above him, four rotor-blades splay out in exquisite alignment, looking so weightless and delicate that a single touch might set them spinning. At the front, the glass bubble of the canopy is crystal-clear, and balancing the canopy at the rear is a hollow tail that carries the stabilisation fins in graceful symmetry.

In one slow revolution, the Pteronaut takes in the flyder's splendour, and then he is back where he started. But it is not admiration or awe that he feels, no more than he appreciates the fierce beauty of the deserts – he is trying to understand what he sees, to comprehend how the flyder might be made to move through the air.

He tries the access-hatch beside the pilot's seat. It opens with a heavy *click*, and he heaves himself inside.

Most of the cockpit is glass, but what is not glass is covered in dials, buttons, switches, and displays. The Pteronaut glances across them, never knowing where to look next; his gaze darts from one distraction to another as it did when faced with the spitting fury of the river. How can flying, something that he did so easily, be made so complicated?

For a moment, the Pteronaut is lost. Yet he saw the other flyder climb and dive and turn through the air; clumsily, perhaps, but with a speed and endurance that he could not match. He knows that the thing is meant to fly, even if it is not clear to him how. And flying is what the Pteronaut knows best – he will solve the riddle.

He finds a point from which to start – a round screen directly in front of him. That might be the artificial horizon, and then the dials to either side could indicate airspeed and altitude. If he ignores the confusion of the rest of the instrument-panel, the arrangement of those dials, at least, becomes somehow understandable; to some extent, the flyder is less of a mystery to him than the velocycle was.

Next – some way to steer. Within easy reach of his right hand is a steering-column. He tries to move it backwards, forwards, left, and right. A flexing noise makes him look up through the transparent section in the roof, and he watches how the movements that he makes are translated into the rotors flattening and twisting this way or that.

No wings, then, to steer by, but blades.

The Pteronaut finds the pedals at his feet, and shuffling forwards and backwards he can feel resistance to his efforts. A different kind of movement catches his eye, and he sees the rudders of the stabilising fins reflected in the open door and the way that they shift in time with the pedals.

One by one, the pieces are coming together. Where his left hand rests there is a lever with a twist-grip. He tries it. Nothing happens, not without power, at least. What the lever does he cannot guess, but its location suggests that it is important.

The hangar has kept the dust and the worst of the cold at bay and the cables that trail across the floor are plugged into ports in the fuselage – the flyder could still have power; the Pteronaut just has to work out how to activate it.

Once he has the anchor-point of the artificial horizon to work with, the rest of the switches and dials start to create some kind of order. The Pteronaut looks across the instrument-panel methodically, seeing how the controls cluster together into groups. Hidden among all of the switches and yet somehow set apart from the rest is a single red button. He presses it.

All across the instrument-panel, lights come on and displays blink into life. There is no engine-noise – starting the rotors must involve an altogether different procedure – but a roaring hiss of static comes from a set of headphones that is hanging on a hook next to the pilot's seat.

The Pteronaut reaches out for the controls where the headphone-cable spirals to an end, meaning to adjust the volume or to turn the headphones off, but the first dial that he touches adjusts the frequency. As he turns it, he hears the noise from the headphones blur, still an empty sea of static, but sweeping through it, a brief blip of something different catches his ear. He juggles the dial, homing in on what he has heard.

Cheep-chip. Cheep-chip.

Hidden among the shapeless waves of interference is a faint two-tone chirping sound – a location signal.

The Pteronaut listens, enveloped in the noise. It carries him with it, striking out across the deserts. He is sure it must be the tracker-tag, betraying where he is to the Crawler. He listens again.

No. Not the tracker-tag.

The signal that the Pteronaut can hear is too faint. The tracker-tag is only a few feet from the receiver, and yet the chirping is weak; it would be utterly inaudible any distance away. The misaligned double tone, a quick *cheep-chip*, is not right, either. If the tracker-tag really is right next to the radio-antenna, the two tones should be one, indistinguishable.

What he can hear is another signal, another ghost of the dead desert's past. It is nothing to do with him.

The Pteronaut spins the tuning-dial further through the frequency-range of the receiver, watching the readings become a formless flicker. He scans through the changing wavelengths, and then…

He goes past it the first time, missing it against the background rush, and he has to twitch the dial back until he finds it. With sudden clarity, another sound, louder and stronger than the first and composed of a single pulse, fills the cockpit. By comparison, the first signal seems unbelievably faint. There is no doubt this time. The Pteronaut instantly knows the pulse for what it is.

For a full minute he listens to it, maybe more, marking time by the regularity of its treachery. Once, listening hard and dragging the seconds out to their utmost, he almost convinces himself that the repetitions have faltered, that one beat has been delayed. But the pulse does not stop. It comes, right on time. And the next one. And the next. And the pulses will continue, even if the Pteronaut retunes the radio, even if he turns it off. The signal will never stop.

He must get rid of the tracker-tag.

Two red lights on a schematic diagram of the flyder start to wink, demanding his attention – two broad blinking rectangles showing up somewhere aft in the fuselage. Each one displays a number that is rising slowly but steadily above the ambient temperature.

The fuel tanks are thawing.

The Pteronaut watches the temperature-reading to be sure and sees it climb half a degree. It will be a while before the frozen fuel is fully defrosted, and then he can worry about starting the engine.

If the Pteronaut cannot work out how to start the flyder, it is more urgent than ever that he removes the tracker-tag from his ankle. He swings himself out of the cockpit and closes the flyder-door. It is time to find some tools.

26

Outside the shelter of the hangar and away from the warming flyder, the temperature plummets. Evening is becoming night, and it is getting colder by the minute; the Pteronaut will need to find cover again before long. Even so, he waits for a moment to activate the controls that shut the double-doors of the hangar – the flyder's fuel-tanks will thaw faster sealed inside. With a hollow clang, the doors close entirely, and the dusk-dark deepens in an instant.

There were no tools of any use in the hangar – the ones that the Pteronaut saw in racks on the walls were too fine and too specialised for his purposes – and he scans the outlines of the other buildings as he approaches them. He is looking for somewhere large and functional with good access, the kind of building in which the turbine-blades could have been made or repaired.

A wide road leads away from the hangars up towards the buildings that are built into the cliffs, and the Pteronaut takes that route, turning aside from the path that he first followed along the valley-side above the icy lake.

None of the buildings there are what he seeks. Most of the windows on the lower floors are opaque with the same sanded and scoured appearance as those in the crashed flyder. Where he can see inside, the buildings look like accommodation blocks. There are all the signs of a hasty departure. Objects have been left in disarray, furniture knocked over; the last events of a tale untold, frozen in time.

He flexes his fingers against the night-chill, and takes a sugary sip from the drip-tube. Turn by turn he finds himself on one of the higher terraces. All the while, almost unconsciously, the Pteronaut is heading towards a large building: the tallest building in the complex and built right into the side of the cliff. Maybe his steps in that direction are not completely aimless, and it is the height of the building, the way it offers a refuge and a vantage-point that a Pteronaut can understand, that draws him towards it. He will look there first for tools.

No lights comes on as the Pteronaut strides up to the locked door of the building, but the motion-detector clicks when he comes within range; the fluorescent striplights have failed there too because of the wind-stirred dust. He tries the door, but it is pressurised as protection against the creeping sand and the toxic atmosphere, just like the doors of the hangar. Only here there are no buttons to activate the door and no keyholes, just a small flat sensor mounted into the wall – it is a security-system that works by sight or by touch.

The Pteronaut does not know what would activate such a system, but he knows where to look. The bodies that are scattered around must have had some means of gaining access.

He cuts through the cluster of buildings, heading back towards the lake. Where he sees a body lying in the dust, he ignores it – the skin-suit is fighting a losing battle against the cold, and he does not want to tax it too much with fruitless searches.

Closer to the lake, the buildings show signs of damage from the attack, and the Pteronaut climbs through a broken window into the interior of one. In a matter of minutes – slow heat-seeping minutes – he finds a body. More than one, a group of them who fought to the death. Just as before, in the staircase inside the dam, there are two different kinds of suit to check. He examines both kinds. The suits with the primitive gill-cells provide the answer – on all of them he finds a plastic card hanging from a chain and printed with a complex pattern of dashes and stripes.

It is clear to the Pteronaut that such a thing has a hidden meaning encoded within it, but most are scratched or damaged, and he searches quickly for a card that has remained intact. One card lies beneath its owner, and so the pattern printed on it has been protected from the battle and the abrasive dust. He tears the card from the chain around its wearer's neck. Then it is a quick and warming sprint back to the high building in the cliffs.

With freezing fingers, the Pteronaut swipes the identity-card across the sensor. The first swipe brings no response, but at the second swipe, a green light blinks above the door-frame. The outer airlock door hisses and clicks. He hauls it open on grating hinges and slips inside.

Cold and anxious to be gone, the birdman did not look back across the frozen surface of the lake, and so he did not see the distant blizzard of dust and ice-splinters that raced arrow-straight towards the dam. Nor was he close enough to the lake's shattered shores to hear the ice creaking and groaning under the weight of its burden.

It had taken the Crawler hours to find a way out of the spillway and up onto the frozen surface of the lake itself. Now its engines thrummed as it hurried towards the signal from the birdman's tracker-tag.

27

A burst of bright light greets the Pteronaut inside the airlock, and long-dormant circuits surge into life. Pumps whirr as the desert air is vented. The Pteronaut watches the readings in the goggle-display change: a stale but palatable mix of oxygen and other gases floods into the chamber. It is warmer in the shelter of the airlock – not much, just enough to take off the chill – but despite the protection it offers, he is wary. The tiny metal cage is no place for a Pteronaut. He tugs the dead drone's rifle from his shoulder and waits for the inner-door to open.

The venting process is completed and the indicator lamp above the door glows green. Bolts slide back unlocked. The Pteronaut cradles his rifle at the ready and pushes against the heavy inner-hatch with his shoulder.

Inside the building, the floor vibrates with the low-pitched hum of the ventilation system. Compared with outside, the building is warm; very warm. The temperature-readings in the goggle-display rocket upwards and tail off at around eighteen degrees above freezing; not just light and air, but heat is also being generated somewhere.

The Pteronaut takes a squeaking step forwards across the polished floor. His numb fingers and toes tingle as the chill ebbs away. Soon he will start to sweat inside the suit, as he did in the outflow tunnel. Every minute, he will lose precious moisture from his pores. Efficient as it is, the skin-suit will not be able to recover every drop that is lost. Heat or cold, he should not spend too much time searching the complex.

Looking quickly from side to side, the Pteronaut strides past an orderly maze of low tables and soft chairs and a glass-fronted room set off to one side. A flurry of fluorescent light runs ahead of him as the motion-detectors sense his presence, illuminating a single straight corridor which borders the external wall of the building.

In the glare of the light the Pteronaut sees two sets of footprints, red and dusty, pattering away into the distance. They follow the corridor, confused and overlapping as they grow fainter and fainter, but if they ever came back the same way, there is no sign of their return. Whoever made the footprints, wherever they went, somebody was in a hurry.

Sand-scratched windows to the left give a vague impression of the outside. On the right-hand side, a dozen doors open into rooms that have been bored back into the cliffs. The windowless rooms on the right are uninteresting to him, filled with terminals and monitors standing on desks.

The Pteronaut hurries along after the footprints. Woody skeletons, all spindly branches and brittle stems, stand in deep stone pots at regular intervals along the corridor. A wreath of grey-black flakes circles each one at the base, rasping against each other as he stirs the air in passing.

There are no other rooms on the ground floor, and the Pteronaut does not hesitate when he reaches a staircase that the lights illuminate for him, leading up onto the next floor.

He climbs the stairs – open metal steps that ring as he goes up them – and finds himself in another long corridor on the next level. That corridor runs on in the same direction as the one below. Raised sills for a series of airtight depressurisation doors divide the corridor into sections. There are no windows to the outside. On the right-hand side of each section of the corridor is a series of ante-rooms opening into the cliffs. In each of the ante-rooms, beyond a triple-glazed window which the glow of the lights cannot penetrate very far, there is a much larger room sealed by a heavy metal hatch.

The Pteronaut enters the ante-room in the first section and peers through the triple-glazed window. With the low-light mode of his goggles activated, he can make something of the indistinct shapes in the sealed room.

Easiest to see are the images on the walls; double-helixes coiled and uncoiled, long strings of meaningless symbols, and lacy lattice-work diagrams of improbable shapes. There are monitors and terminals dotted around on the benches, rows of flasks filled with dusty contents, and machines with tubes and pipes and glass shapes connected together into complex structures. But nowhere is there anything that looks like it might cut the tracker-tag from his ankle.

Even so, the Pteronaut tries the identity-card at the door-sensor. The hatch remains resolutely locked, even at the fifth attempt. For a moment he considers trying to shoot out the windows, but the glass is thick, and if the metal hatch is any indication, the sealed rooms were built to withstand unwanted attempts to enter them.

What the Pteronaut finds in the next section is much the same, and the one after, but in the fourth section the room behind the window is different. There are no racks and no workbenches filled with incomprehensible equipment, just rows and rows of monitors. And on the walls there are no diagrams. Instead, there are images. Each image binds the Pteronaut's gaze to it: they are landscapes viewed from the air.

The landscapes show a lush and living country that the Pteronaut has never seen, all soft green hillsides and verdant valleys, dappled with patchworks of light and shadow, but it is a country of aching familiarity nonetheless. The shapes of his airborne existence are all there, laid out in a way that he can understand.

With his goggles pressed up close to the glass, the Pteronaut tracks along the rows and row of images, watching how the character of the landscapes changes. Green gives way to red, and the complex textures of the past are suffocated by the soft sweep of the future; spreading deserts, unstoppable and irreversible.

A trickle of sweat between his skin and the suit makes his nose twitch, and the Pteronaut pulls back from the window. Time is ticking away and the flyder's fuel-tanks will surely soon be thawed. He leaves the images and continues his search.

The Pteronaut has almost given up any hope of finding the tools he needs, but there is one last section of the building to investigate. The end of the corridor turns sharply to the right, becoming a tunnel that leads off into the cliff-face behind the settlement. Burrowing into the rock must have taken considerable effort – mechanical effort. If there is cutting or drilling equipment in the complex, there is a good chance it will be somewhere nearby. The Pteronaut hurries on around the turn.

A body lies there.

Further into the tunnel, another body. There, dead in the tunnel, is the explanation for the two dusty sets of bootprints on the corridor below.

The sight of the two bodies takes the Pteronaut by surprise. They are far from the battle at the dam, and they come with no warning. There were no signs of violence along the corridor, no bullet-holes, no spent shells. And suddenly here there are two bodies, lying in their suits. Bullet-cases are scattered around the first body. It lies on its back, with three or four holes punched across its chest at the centre of a dark-red stain. A handgun is clenched tight in one fist, its muzzle still pointing down towards the second body at the far end of the tunnel.

The second body lies slumped against a heavy pressurised access-door set into the bare rock of the cliffs. In other ways, that body is a mirror-image to the first, surrounded by bright cylindrical shell-cases, with the same kind of suit, and the breast-plate punctured again and again by ancient gunfire. In one hand, it too holds a pistol. In the other hand is a clutch of grenades, the pins of every one linked together with wire so that they will all detonate at the same time – a makeshift bomb, never used.

161

The Pteronaut looks at the pressurised access-door. What was so precious to the defenders of the dam-complex that deciding its fate could set allies against each other?

Before he even tries it, the Pteronaut knows that the identity-card he used to get inside the building will not open the door into the rock. But the bomber would have needed to get through that door, and there is a card on the second body too, hanging from a fine chain around the neck.

The Pteronaut shoulders his rifle and tugs the card free. It is undamaged, and he wipes the black flecks of dried blood from it to pass it across the scanner. With a click, bolts slide back, and the heavy door is unlocked. The Pteronaut takes hold of the handle, pulls it back until the catch releases fully, and heaves the door open.

Beyond the first door is a second, two strides away but no more, the space between them forming an empty chamber like an airlock. The Pteronaut closes the first door and unlocks the second using the card. He pushes at the second door. It will not move; something on the outside is blocking it – debris, perhaps, or more bodies. He pushes harder, and with a ripping and tearing sound, the door suddenly opens.

The Pteronaut goes sprawling into darkness. The ground is soft and his boots find no firm footing. Then what little substance he feels beneath him vanishes altogether. With a clanging *crash* and a jolt, he drops a dozen feet.

Instinctively, the Pteronaut braces himself for a hard landing. But instead of striking rocky ground, his feet slip against something yielding that slows him without stopping him. He overbalances and goes tumbling down a slope.

No lights reacts to his fall, and the view through the goggle-lenses is a night-vision blur. He can feel a tangle of tough cords that stretch and snap and give way as he slides into them. Eventually, he rolls to a stop on his back, arms and legs at all angles, imprisoned in a web of interlacing strands.

For a few moments, the Pteronaut lies absolutely still. He is not injured or even winded – he is confused. He can see nothing except for the cords that wrap around him, but his other senses are overwhelmed – beyond the doorway, the darkness is filled with noise.

Howls. Croaks. Cries.

Whirring. Buzzing. Humming.

Light quick patterings across soft ground.

The scratch of claws on bark.

The dry flutter of wings.

A hush of leafy branches stirs, and somewhere out in the dark is the trickle of water running over stone ledges and into deep pools.

Beyond the doorway, the darkness is alive.

To the Pteronaut, the sounds he hears are intertwined and indistinguishable, a smothering mass, as impenetrable and as meaningless as the rush of the river. They are not the clean clear noise of the wind whistling across the dunes, or of dry rocks clattering down a dusty slope; nothing that he hears makes any sense.

Each in-breath is smothering too, damp and thick with a mix of perfumes: rotting vegetation, sweet nectar, the smoky musk of resinous wood. The air that the Pteronaut draws into his lungs carries so many strange odours that there can surely be no oxygen in it.

He gasps, taking breath after breath in the hope that the next lungful of air might be cool and pure and calming. But the air inside the hidden forest is scented. Warm and wet. Suffocating.

The Pteronaut fights to stand, but only sinks further into the soft earth. He clutches at it, and his fingers plunge deep into soil that is moist and tainted with the smell of decay. He tears at the tendrils that envelope him, spraying beads of sap across the lenses of his goggles, scattering the twilight view from his night-vision. Sharp new scents flood into the facemask. He fights harder, but the cords are stringy and elastic, and every movement seems to wrap them tighter around his body.

His struggle sets the howls calling out all around him, louder than before. Rustlings stir the leaves, and the noise of feet and claws comes closer.

At last, the Pteronaut fights himself free. He finds his footing and runs, slipping more than once in the fetid soil. He makes it as far as a mat of springy turf and wheels around, looking up as far as his low-light vision allows.

Branches sway in the whispers of ventilation currents, and the movements of a hundred thousand leaves create a blinding blizzard of light and dark. Black branches press up tight against a curving roof of glass. High above the Pteronaut, a ceiling of interconnecting hexagonal panes spans the gulf between deep walls of rock, keeping out the deadly desert air.

Again and again the Pteronaut turns around on the spot, disoriented. He has taken no more than a few dozen steps from where he rolled to a standstill, but his sense of direction, normally so exact, is utterly confused. The air hums, the swaying branches make him dizzy, and the familiar solidity of rock is gone from beneath his feet.

A shape flies out from the darkness of the trees and catches the Pteronaut across the shoulders. The force of the blow sends him stumbling to the ground, and his fingers leave fresh black gashes through the earth.

Before the Pteronaut can reach for the rifle at his shoulder, the shape soars away into the treetops. But the rifle is gone, lost in the fall from the door. Almost as soon as the Pteronaut stands up again, another shape flies at him, but from a different direction this time. It slams into him as he runs for the bushes. Talons rake across the skin-suit's scales, slashing deep. The decompression-alarm sounds and the slashes bleed sealant.

This time, the Pteronaut stays on his feet. Up to his left through the boughs, he glimpses a rectangle of yellow light: the doorway back into the tunnel. He hurries towards it, ducking under branches, pushing green stems aside and swishing through hanging curtains of leaves. In the bushes he is safe, but the doorway is high above him, looking down above a rust-ridden platform that has half-collapsed: there will be no cover for the last few yards.

His foot catches something hard and metallic, and he goes sprawling to the ground. He crawls upright and reaches for the fallen rifle that has tripped him. Shaking it free of dead leaves, he rights it and finds the grip.

The next instant, the Pteronaut leaves the bushes behind and races towards the patch of undergrowth that first broke his fall. Cries go up from the trees all around, and before the next shadow flies at him, he raises the rifle, ready for it. The chatter of gunfire lights up the forest, drowning the cries and the clamour and leaving a startled second of silence behind it. The bullets bring down the shadow-thing and it goes bowling into the undergrowth. The bushes where it lands quiver and shake with the noise of a bloody squabble over fresh meat.

The distraction works in the Pteronaut's favour, and before the commotion dies down, he is at the base of the access-platform. One of the supports has given way, leaving the metal deck hanging down at an angle, lopsided and overgrown with creepers. He fires another challenge at the tree-tops, starring the hexagonal panes in the ceiling with mis-aimed bullets, then he slings the rifle over his shoulder and makes for the near-side of the platform.

The Pteronaut finds any rusting handholds that he can and scrambles up onto the platform. It takes him only a matter of seconds to reach the door, but they are frantic seconds, full of a frenzy of noise from the forest. He drags himself up and over the sill of the door and rolls onto the floor of the airlock.

Something comes into the airlock with him or was waiting there already, something shrill and shrieking, a whirring mass of feathers and fury. He tries to beat it off, but it seems to be everywhere at once, stabbing at him with its hooked claws, jabbing into his face with its curving beak, snapping at his fingers. Somehow he bats it to one side, and a stray kick of his foot catches it and sends it spinning out of the doorway.

Slithering on his belly, the Pteronaut leans out into space as far as he dares. His fingers find the edge of the door, and with a grunt and a gasp, he tugs it closed. The door slams shut, and at almost the same instant, another of the creatures – or perhaps the same one – hurtles itself against the door from the outside, scoring the metal with sharp claws.

The Pteronaut sits back in the small dark space of the airlock. He is safe, but he does not feel it. The vicious onslaught continues against the outer-door, scraping and scrabbling.

He pushes himself through the inner-door, crawling back into the tunnel on his hands and knees. Lights flicker on, and he leans back on his haunches against the inner-door, letting his weight close it. It shuts tight and locks into the frame.

For a few minutes longer, the slams and thuds continue against the outer-door, vicious and futile. Slowly, they come less often, less hard, until silence reigns again.

28

The Pteronaut sits unmoving in the tunnel with his back against the heavy metal door. He sits so motionless for so long that the lights forget that he is there and click off again.

More minutes pass and still he does not move, wrapped in shadow. He stares past the readings in the goggle-display and into the darkness of the tunnel; somehow the darkness there is darker and deeper and more empty than the darkness behind his eyelids.

The noise of the blows against the outer-door has stopped, but the smell of the forest still hangs about him, earthy and humid. Its thick perfumes pollute his every breath, and the skin-suit is covered with smears of sap and soil. Even now, the Pteronaut can feel the cloying earth, the sinking softness beneath his hands and feet. And so many sounds, chaotic noise...

He focuses on the regular repeating cry of the skin-suit's alarm – the claw-marks on his shoulder still gape wide – and on the clean and clinical vibration of the life-support systems inside the complex. The suit's decompression-alarm fades as the talon-slashes seals themselves, and the Pteronaut breathes deeply, slow steady breaths of the stale and sterile air. Eventually, he dares to close his eyes behind the goggle-lenses. There is nothing to fear – he is safe; safe and alone.

A light clicks on suddenly, turning the Pteronaut's closed eyelids red.

Not alone.

His eyes flick open. He tenses, but he does not move – someone has entered the corridor at the end of the tunnel.

Another light flickers on in the corridor, and the Pteronaut hears them coming for him; the tramp of heavy footfalls and the jingle of bone against metal armour. The

Crawler's drones stop along the way just as he did, peering into the rooms along the corridor, but they are on the scent of the signal and they will not be delayed.

The Pteronaut feels the hard shape of the rifle jutting into his side but he cannot reach for it; any movement will trip the motion-detector in the tunnel, and the drones will know exactly where he is. He must wait for just the right moment – the last possible moment.

Section by section, the footsteps are coming. Louder and louder. Nearer and nearer. His muscles tense.

Light flares through the tunnel and a drone appears.

The Pteronaut lunges forwards onto his stomach. He has the rifle from his back before he lands.

Noise, flashing bursts. A hail of gunfire catches the drone and sends it spinning to the ground.

Another drone is already halfway around the corner. The Pteronaut shoots its knees out and it drops into plain sight. Another burst from the rifle finishes it off.

Silence.

A scatter of feet racing into cover, and then more silence. But the Crawler's drones will not stay daunted for long.

The Pteronaut changes position, shuffling into what cover there is behind the second body. He is well and truly trapped; the only way out – back through the forest – is no way out.

The edge of a helmet peers around the corner. A half-dozen bullets chase it back into hiding, and the magazine of the Pteronaut's rifle clicks empty. He reloads.

There is a scuffling noise from behind the turn of the corridor. One drone ducks out from cover, firing wildly to keep the birdman pinned down. Another drone tosses a metal cylinder down the tunnel. The cylinder bounces across the hard floor, hissing venomously as thick smoke billows from it.

The Pteronaut fires into the smoke, but it hides an enemy he cannot kill, and the goggle-display flashes red: some kind of irritant or sedative gas.

168

The smoke thickens, pulsing towards him like a living thing. The rifle is no use. The Pteronaut casts it to one side and grabs the string of grenades from beside the second body. He pulls the pin on the first grenade and all the other pins follow, stripped out along the length of wire. In one fluid movement, he rises up on one knee and tosses the grenades into the smoke and against the outer wall of the building. Still moving from his throw, the Pteronaut rolls over onto his stomach and clamps both hands over the auricles of the helmet.

One second.

Two seconds.

Three seconds...

In a single percussive instant, the air in the tunnel becomes solid. The Pteronaut feels the shockwave pass through him like a punch. Then comes the split-second of release, when the pressure falls away to nothing and he could almost explode in the vacuum that comes after. There is a rush and a roar that he feels as much as hears, and debris and shrapnel rattle a heavy rain through the length of the tunnel.

Even before the air has gathered again, the Pteronaut is on his feet. In that explosive blink of an eye, the world has changed utterly all around him. The tunnel pulses with red light from the alarm-beacons, and a tinny warning squawks out of damaged loudspeakers. Shreds of feathery insulation-foam flutter through the air.

Heat is gone.

Oxygen is gone.

The outer-wall is gone.

In its place, a jagged hole torn through the side of the building.

The Pteronaut takes up the rifle and runs towards the hole in the wall. The first body has vanished. So too have the drones that he shot, lost outside or blown to pieces among the wreckage – the unbelievable amount of wreckage – that the grenade blast has created. The corridor around the turn

169

is a dead-end; the decompression-doors have dropped from the ceiling, muffling the noise of hammering and gunfire as the trapped drones try to free themselves.

Pushing some hanging debris out of his way, the Pteronaut peers out of the tear in the wall. From his high position above the settlement, he can see all the way down to the valley-side, down to where the Crawler's bulk has come to rest. Its tracks stand on the frozen lake, its armoured upper-deck almost level with the roadway that leads up from the dam.

The Crawler's drones are everywhere. They scurry across the complex, plundering whatever they can. A steady stream of them return to the Crawler, laden with anything and everything that they have found; some even struggle along with the bodies of the dead.

But the explosion has not gone unnoticed. A huddle of drones is picking their way through the streets towards the damaged building. Six of them. Too many for a lone Pteronaut to tackle.

Seconds are all he has. He glances down at the drop below him – one full storey down into the sand – and jumps out of the building.

The Pteronaut lands with his knees bent and rolls into hiding. The party of drones is still some distance away, and he has just enough time to kick his tracks into oblivion and to steal into the shadows of a neighbouring building. The steady trudge of boots comes closer, and he holds the rifle at the ready, pressing himself flat against the wall. He does not know how far he can move before the Crawler detects a change in his location; perhaps it already has. With one finger on the trigger he waits, but the party of drones walks straight past his hiding place, staring up at the damaged building where the sirens still wail.

As soon as they have passed, the Pteronaut leaves the shadows. Keeping to the tracks that the drones have left through the dust, he makes his way to the next junction.

Slowly and carefully, he heads back towards the hangar for the flyder, hiding where he can. Heat ebbs from his body with every step, and the closer he gets to the side of the valley and the frozen lake, the more drones he sees. The salvage on offer in the complex has distracted them from the search, and he hurries on past them, slinking and creeping along. Then he hears the Crawler call its drones to order with a growl from its engines.

Speed is essential now; the threat of discovery is even greater than the danger of freezing to death. The Pteronaut runs quickly between the buildings, not daring to stay too long in any one place. Within a few minutes he has reached the sloping shape of one of the habitation-blocks nearest to the hangars. He leaps for the low eaves of the roof on one side and hauls himself up.

Crouching against the backdrop of the rising cliffs, the Pteronaut creeps across the roof until he can see down onto the landing-apron in front of the hangars. The blackened carcass of the wrecked flyder sprawls below him – the drones have even pillaged what they can from that – but his eyes sweep across to the fourth hangar where he left the intact flyder.

The huge doors stand wide open, and stark white light fills the hangar, making it seem even more empty than it already is.

The flyder has gone.

29

The Pteronaut clutches at the edge of the sloping roof. No tools. No freedom from the tracker-tag. No flyder. A hundred drones hunting for him, and with the Crawler sitting so close that he can smell the hot metal of its engines. The cold that has been seeping into his limbs strikes deeper inside him.

The flyder has gone.

The Pteronaut gathers himself.

No. Not gone. The flyder has been taken.

If it is already sitting inside the Crawler's storage-holds, the flyder is lost to him forever. But it did not fly there, the Pteronaut is sure of that. The flyder cannot have taken to the air without him hearing it, and he hears nothing above the tramp of the drones and the rumble of the Crawler's engines.

So the Pteronaut looks across the roadways, back towards the looming metal mountain that stands hungry and waiting on the surface of the lake.

The flyder is there, taxiing along the road that borders the lakeside. It creeps forwards slowly on the wheels of its landing-gear. Somehow the drones have started its engines, and its rotor-blades spin in lazy circles above it. Why the drones did not fly it the short distance to the Crawler, the Pteronaut cannot guess. Perhaps they do not yet understand the flyder enough to take it into the air. And at the end of the road, a makeshift ramp leads across to where the Crawler waits with the hatches to its storage-holds gaping wide; the flyder is almost beyond his reach.

In one move, the Pteronaut is down from the roof.

He picks up a soot-stained metal rod that has been wrenched and rejected from the wrecked flyder and sprints between the buildings towards the nearest group of drones.

There are four of them, hurrying back to the Crawler with arms full of plunder.

The Pteronaut cuts ahead of them and waits in the shadows until they pass behind an accommodation-block. He has to be fast and he has to be quiet.

The last of the drones passes by. The Pteronaut steps out behind it and swings a sweeping two-handed blow at its head; the metal rod cracks open the helmet and shatters the skull beneath.

The other drones turn on the spot, but the birdman is already among them. Another blow from the rod, striking with savage force where neck and shoulder meet, fells the second drone.

Two seconds, and the element of surprise is gone.

The Pteronaut throws the rod spinning at the third drone. Instinctively, it raises its arms to deflect the missile, but the weight of the plunder that it is carrying makes it overbalance and it goes sprawling to the ground.

Four seconds, and the final drone is prepared.

It throws its armful of salvage-metal at the birdman and reaches for its rifle. The Pteronaut leaps to one side and the salvage-metal crashes at his feet. Just as if he were climbing the cliffs, he turns his landing into another leap, launching himself at the drone before it can fire a shot. The two of them roll to the ground with the rifle pressed between them.

The Pteronaut allows the drone a split-second of an advantage. The drone rights itself, straddling the birdman, and breaks free. It is too close to use the rifle, a hindrance not a help, but it has no other weapon. It tries to disentangle the rifle from arms and legs, to point and shoot, and in that moment, it is lost. The Pteronaut ducks past the rifle and reaches with both hands for the drone's helmet. With a wrench, he twists the helmet until the joints pop, and the drone slumps backwards with its neck broken.

Six seconds, three drones down, one recovering.

Before the sprawling third drone can stand again, the Pteronaut is on it with his knife drawn.

Eight seconds, and there are four crumpled bodies lying in the dust.

In a dozen seconds more, the Pteronaut has dragged all four bodies into hiding in the shadows between the accommodation-blocks. He exchanges his half-empty rifle for an unused one, takes a second rifle too, and pockets as many spare magazines as he can carry. Then he scuffs sand over three of the dead drones to hide their shapes, shoulders the body of the second drone, and climbs into an accommodation-block through a broken window.

Darkness reigns inside the building; it has been visited already by the roving bands of treasure-seekers and all the light-fittings have been taken. The darkness inside the building is a welcome hiding-place.

The Pteronaut drags the drone's body into one of the ransacked rooms and starts to cut away at the suit it wears. He slices into the material where the incisions are least likely to be noticed. In another thirty seconds he is pulling the drone's suit on over his own scaly second-skin. The gloves and boots that the drone was wearing are useless to him, and once he has prised away the helmet, it will close only partially over his facemask. The Pteronaut pulls the drone's hunting-mask over the cracked helmet to cover as much of the damage as possible – it will have to do. He hides the drone's stripped body behind a table that was too heavy to carry.

Then he sets about rigging up the second rifle that he took. He balances the rifle against a broken chair, tethering it with a strip of the drone's suit around the trigger. The other end of the tether he fastens to the door-handle, keeping the gun poised but ready to slip if the door into the room is moved even just a few inches. With the booby-trap complete, the Pteronaut leaves the building again through the window.

Two minutes have passed.

The flyder has made slow progress. The road is narrow, and a stream of drones passes it unabated, slowing it still more.

There is still time.

The Pteronaut collects together some of the plunder that the drones were carrying and jogs down the roadway. With every step, with every yard that the signal from the tracker-tag moves, the Pteronaut expects to be discovered. A party of drones comes towards him, and he lifts the plunder higher in his arms to obscure the cracked helmet and the slits in the suit. His heart pounds as they pass him, beating so loud in his ears that he is sure the drones must hear it too.

But the drones do not give the birdman a second glance; he is just another of their kind, busy doing the Crawler's bidding.

The flyder has come to a halt on the lakeside road to let more drones cross the temporary gangway from the Crawler's upper-deck. The drones move with rifles at the ready. They are not in search of plunder – the Crawler has detected something.

The Pteronaut looks away as the drones approach, not moving too quickly or too hastily, balancing his burden to disguise his appearance.

A prolonged burst of gunfire sounds from the accommodation-block where the Pteronaut set up his booby-trap: it has been sprung. The drones break into a run past the birdman, raising their guns.

Before they can turn back, the Pteronaut drops his armload of plunder and sprints for the flyder. He has seconds to spare: the flyder has crossed onto the Crawler's carapace and one of the crane-arms is already swinging a loading-cradle into position.

The Pteronaut no longer cares about the moving signal from the tracker-tag. He does not care about the drones. He draws the drowned drone's pistol from his supply-pouch

175

and runs, boots ringing on the metal gangway as he races across it.

The Pteronaut reaches the flyder and wrenches the pilot's door wide open. The pilot-drone turns, sees the unfamiliar goggle-eyes staring from behind the hunting mask, and reaches for its weapon.

Too slow.

The Pteronaut jams the muzzle of his pistol up into the hollow of the pilot's armpit and fires a deadly shot into the torso.

Lungs. Heart. Spine.

The pilot slumps forwards in the seat, and the Pteronaut tumbles the body out onto the deck. He leaps inside the flyder, slams the door, and casts away the hunting-mask with its narrow eye-slits. The unfamiliar controls of the flyder look as incomprehensible as ever, but the Pteronaut is out of time to solve the riddle; he is going to have to rely on instinct.

Above his head, the rotors swing in slow circles – too slow to fly. He needs power. Stick and pedals are no good. He looks at the buttons and dials on the instrument-display. There are some that are not illuminated, and he swipes a hand across them, setting them blinking.

No change. No power.

The Pteronaut finds the lever under his left hand, and he twists the grip.

Power!

The flyder's engine roars. The whole vehicle shakes and the Pteronaut's teeth rattle against each other as the rotor-blades dissolve into a silver-edged blur.

Dust kicks up outside around the flyder, and the Pteronaut feels the furious downdraught pushing the flyder hard against the deck, making the landing wheels squeal.

Even as the birdman reached the broad back of its upper-deck, the Crawler detected the rapid change in the location of his signal. Its deck-plates shivered, and the note of its engines deepened – it knew now where its prey was, but the realisation had almost come too late.

The Crawler's engines bellowed with urgency and anger. Flickers of torchlight danced among the buildings above the dam. The lights converged on one location, running in rippling streams towards the makeshift metal ramp, and a hundred pairs of feet drummed across the gangway.

The Pteronaut hears them pounding towards him. The glare of one of the Crawler's searchlights fingers through the canopy, raking across his disguise. Through the glass sections in the ceiling, past the whipping blades of the flyder's rotors, the Pteronaut sees the Crawler's crane-arms swing into position.

He looks across at the edge of the upper-deck and the wide expanse of the frozen lake beyond it. Almost every launch he has ever known has been from running into a leap; why would the flyder be any different? He kicks into the pedals for a turn, shifting the steering-column in front of him in the same direction.

The flyder does not move.

In desperation, the Pteronaut pulls back on the twist-lever and the steering-column, and for an instant the flyder leaves the deck. It hangs in the air, only a foot or so, before it bounces hard onto the Crawler's broad back. The Pteronaut tries again, almost feeling the touch of the Crawler's searchlights through the canopy. He kicks harder into the pedals, pulling back on the steering-column and gunning the throttle.

The flyder starts to spin. A stormful of air beats down from the rotors, and the flyder's fat wheels hop and skitter across the Crawler's carapace.

For an instant, the Pteronaut sees the surging mass of drones running across the deck, then the Crawler's crane-towers, then the buildings of the dam-complex, then the open lake. He fights for control, and the flyder dances drunkenly towards the edge. It drags its wheels beneath it, as if their weight alone is holding it down. The drones fall back before it.

Almost before the Pteronaut realises it, he is at the edge. In that final moment, he sees that he is not going to take off at a run – he is not going to take off at all.

With no warning, the deck falls away, its silvered edge painted hard against the night by the light from the drones' torches, and the flyder plunges towards the surface of the frozen lake.

30

As the air opens up around him, the Pteronaut knows that he was a fool to think the flyder could ever leave the ground. The iron-hard surface of the lake lurches into view, and he is painfully aware of the weight and solidity of the vehicle – clumsy, heavy, and hurtling downwards.

Proximity-alarms sound, tearing the engine-noise and the sweep of the rotors into shreds. Lights flicker all across the instrument-panel, green to red, red to green.

Instinctively mimicking the movements he would have used if he were flying himself, the Pteronaut wrestles with the steering-column in one hand, tugs on the twist-grip with the other, and strains against the pedals with his feet.

With a jolt almost as abrupt as the impending impact on the lake, the fall becomes a steep sideways ascent. Unprepared for such sudden success, the acceleration of the flyder's climb presses the Pteronaut into his seat and drives his chin down onto his chest. Silver storm-shields blind him with the reflected glare of the navigation-lights – the Crawler is barely feet away – and with no time to draw breath, the Pteronaut lunges to one side to avoid it.

Bucking in currents of its own making, the flyder dips, dives, spins through the air. The Pteronaut stares out through the canopy. He is sitting at the controls, but he is barely in control. The whole world is turning and tumbling with him at its centre. It is like being back in the rush of the river.

A gap appears in the whirling world outside, a sliver of night-dark, and somehow, the Pteronaut stops his spin and points the flyder towards it. Nose-down and tail-up, the flyder swerves towards the centre of the lake, almost falling again but not quite, a stumbling forwards motion.

To the Pteronaut sitting there, it is as if he is walking across a tightrope in a high wind – the slightest movement to one side or the other, an inch and no more, will spell disaster. He is back in his airy world of three dimensions again, but he no longer understands it.

Inside the shelter of the cockpit, he cannot feel the air-currents holding him up. There are only sudden dips and soars that come unexpectedly. He has no flight-readings in his goggle-display. There is no artificial horizon, no figures for climb-rate, or airspeed. The figures for pressure and temperature are all wrong. The whispers of the wind through the spars and struts of his wings are gone. The cockpit is filled instead with the furious clatter of the rotor-blades, hacking at the air with blunt urgency, just as he stabbed and scrabbled for a handhold on the ice-fall.

And beyond the glass of the canopy is the darkness of night. The Pteronaut has never flown at night before. His shadow, that invaluable marker of his progress through the air, is invisible. When the searchlights from the Crawler do send the flyder's shadow slipping across the ice, the Pteronaut does not recognise it.

Sitting rigid in the cockpit, he sips mouthfuls of air. Ten seconds of dipping and spinning have carried him out towards the centre of the lake. Still he has not crashed. Still the flyder teeters precariously between fall and flight.

It cannot last.

Height is what he needs, with the open air wide all around him, far from the dangers of rock and ice and metal.

His knuckles stand out beneath the scales of the skin-suit. He takes another breath, deeper this time, almost certain it will be his last, and pulls back on the steering-column.

Nothing happens.

The Pteronaut tries again, harder this time, wrenching all the way back on the steering-column.

Again, nothing happens.

But although the flyder does not respond to the Pteronaut's demands, it does not plunge to the ice, or veer off into the valley-sides. It rights itself gradually after the chaos of the launch and finds a stable path through the air – a path that has nothing to do with the Pteronaut.

He is not in control – he never was. Somehow, in that moment of impending impact, the flyder has taken control of itself. The Pteronaut lets go of the steering-column, and the flyder stays level. For a few seconds he watches the controls twitching and moving to a touch that is not his own. The flyder is following its own course, one that was set down in its electronic memory many years before. All it is doing now is responding automatically to changes in the rush of the air around it, righting itself where it feels a patch of turbulence.

Outside, little more than ghostly outlines in the wash of the navigation-lights, the valley-sides are closing in. Far from the dam behind him, the lake is coming to an end. Gradually, the twin pools of the navigation-lights become sharper, growing brighter against a rust-red backdrop of hard vertical edges. The mountain at the head of the lake looms taller and taller in the view from the canopy, so vast it is inescapable.

Then the flyder starts to rise, leaving the lake surface far below. It will not crash into the mountain. The auto-pilot has a different destination in mind.

But the Pteronaut is still not safe.

To his left, there is the ravine, and beyond that, the deadly electromagnetic haze of the crater landscape. If the flyder takes that route, he is as good as dead. The steering and guidance circuits will fry and the Pteronaut will be left in control of a powerless metal shell as it plunges to the ground. He has seen what happened to other flyders that tried to cross the crater-wastes. The only safe route is to the right, out above the unknown deserts behind the cliffs of the settlement.

And if the flyder does not bank to the right?

The Pteronaut glances down through the bulging curve of the canopy at his feet. The lake surface is too far below him to fall, and he is travelling too fast. Even if he were to survive the drop, the dark night would kill him; as long as the Crawler did not get to him first.

He stares across at the right-hand slopes, judging the steepness of them and the climb-rate needed to fly above them. He wills the flyder to make the turn he wants. Time is running out. The move has to be made now.

Then with a graceful swoop, the flyder rises and banks to the right, just as the Pteronaut wants it to, and just in the last possible moment. The steep slopes rush past beyond the glass of the canopy, so close, so fast. The flyder flies with a subtlety and a skill that the Pteronaut cannot hope to match. His hammering heart slows from keeping time with the beats of the rotors, and the cold dark night opens out ahead of him.

31

On the upper-deck of the Crawler, the wave of drones spilled to the edge and broke there, staring out after the reeling flyder. For a moment it looked as if it would dash itself against the lake surface, nose down.

But as the drones watched, the flyder took on a slightly lopsided level flight. It righted itself, staggering in the floodlight-beams that pinned it against the night-sky. The beams rose and clutched after it, but the flyder span and stuttered less and less, and then it was gone, heading away across the lake. Somehow, the birdman had gained control.

The Crawler's engines growled and cursed. Its deck-plates hammered against the rivets that held them together, and with a screech of gears, it tore itself free from the valley-side and the ramp it had made. In one coordinated movement, the drones swarmed away from the precipice and headed into shelter.

Beneath the bulk of the Crawler, its tracks started to roll. Sliding and spitting, the toothed track-plates gouged deep grooves into the surface of the lake. Smoke billowed and steam hissed from every joint and every crack in the Crawler's ancient pipework. It focused its floodlights on the flyder and thundered off across the lake after it, spewing a blizzard of ice-splinters in its wake.

Lost and found again across the wide wastes of the crater-lands, the Crawler was determined not to lose the signal from the tracker-tag again. Its furnaces burned with an unquenchable fury. The Crawler had been over-confident; how easy it had been to find the birdman again after all those days. It had allowed itself to become distracted by the rich salvage of the complex. Perhaps some after-effect from the melt-glass landscape had lingered on in its circuits, dulling its senses, intoxicating it, blunting its judgement.

And now the birdman was getting away.

However quickly the Crawler travelled bound to the earth, it could not compete with the speed that the flyder was making through the air. The roar of the Crawler's engines would never be loud enough, the rattle of its tracks never fast enough.

It watched the distant dot dwindle. The reflections from the flyder's rotor-blades fluttered above the lake, and it steered a careful course between the slopes of rock on either side. At last, the flyder slipped beyond the Crawler's sight, and it switched the spectrum of its electromagnetic vision. Suddenly clear again, the Crawler saw the red ember of heat from the flyder's engine shining bright in the empty sky. Then with a final upwards swoop, the ember lifted and turned and vanished above the mountain-slopes.

No hesitation. No delay. Steep or shallow, the Crawler must climb the valley-sides.

Without slowing, it slewed across to the edge of the ice. The tracks pounded over ancient reefs that had once been lapping waves, freezing time and again in sight of the shore. Broad clanking plates, thousands of them, each one studded with teeth, pulverised the ice-ridges and pounded the shoreline into gravel.

The Crawler heaved itself up and away from the lake. It ignored the precipitous angle of the slope that rose up in front of it – it had no time now to shift its shape. The crane-arms hung down like flags at half-mast, and the massive vehicle accelerated upwards, leaving a landslide of dust behind it.

It climbed the slope and reached the top. There its juddering ascent faltered, and it seemed to hang for a moment, pointing skywards, the cutting-claw undersides of its tracks exposed.

But only for a moment.

Like a tsunami of metal, vast and unstoppable, the Crawler surged up and over the lip of the summit's edge and crashed down where the hilltop flattened out in front of it.

Far away against the black of the sky, it caught sight again of the flicker of heat from the flyder's engine, travelling fast and taking the signal from the tracker-tag with it. With a roar, the Crawler set its tracks churning in pursuit, grinding across the bare rock and the cluster of white lines that had been carved there.

32

Trapped inside the flyder, racing across the deserts, the Pteronaut studies the instrument-display. He is learning to match his own experience to what the dials and readings tell him, and he no longer feels so disoriented.

A second before the shock of turbulence comes, he is already anticipating it, and in his mind he adjusts the steering-column or the pedals or the lever to correct the course. He is learning fast, and the riddle of the flyder's flight is no longer so mysterious to him.

Among the controls, the Pteronaut has identified the readings for fuel and airspeed and made his calculations. There is enough fuel for three or four hours' flight at a speed that will carry him about five hundred miles. Far enough, perhaps, to outrun the signal from the tracker-tag altogether. The Pteronaut cannot control the flyder's course, and so he cannot pick out the most difficult terrain to impede the Crawler's progress, but the deadly darkness of night is impenetrable; even if he were flying himself, he would be just as ignorant about the landscape below. He must hope that five hundred miles will be enough.

The Pteronaut sits back in the pilot's seat. With no immediate threat, there is no immediate need to act. Inside the cockpit he is breathing the air from the onboard oxygen-tanks, protected from the night-chill. He is a prisoner in the air, but the flyder flies more safely on auto-pilot than if he were at the controls himself.

He is safe.

He tries to relax and to recover his strength for whatever might come next. For now, at least, there is nothing to concern him except the question of where the flyder is taking him, and he will face that when the time comes.

That question is partly answered by a small circular screen that shows a fluctuating signal. Every time there is a judder of turbulence, the gently undulating waveform in the screen breaks up into fragments. Every time, automatically and without any sense of urgency, the flyder alters its course so that the fragments of the signal re-align themselves and the smooth pulses return.

The Pteronaut takes down the headphones from their hook and tunes the radio into the frequency of the weak signal that he found earlier. Backwards and forwards he spins the dial until he picks up the signal again. It is a single tone now, quick and faint but getting stronger, calling out across the wide desert wastes. He watches the pulse on the small circular screen and listens to the signal from the headphones – the two of them are perfectly synchronised.

Something is out there in the dead red deserts, something from the past that the flyder wants to find, and it is taking the Pteronaut to find it too.

An hour passes in the warm cockpit. An hour almost without incident. Occasionally, a dune swells until it fills the view through the canopy, and the flyder senses it and hops over the knife-blade crest. Then the rotors whip the dust into the air, sending a flicker of blue phosphorescence across the whirling blades. For an instant, the Pteronaut sees a snapshot of the flyder's shadow on the sands below, deceptive in its stillness, and a reminder that he is just a passenger in the headlong flight into the night.

But the desert below is no longer completely dark.

White lines show up, reflecting the slightest glint from the navigation-lights. They seem to move against the stillness of the land, up and down across its contours, weaving and flickering bright as the dunes wash over them. Arrow-straight, they point the way for the flyder's flight. Wherever the flyder is going, it seems that the white lines are going there too.

Two hours into the flight, the flyder veers to one side. The way ahead is blocked by a sudden shape, a spindly steel skeleton that is almost nothing yet strong enough to stand high into the air. The navigation-lights paint it solid, and it shimmers against the dark sky. The giant figure stands with arms raised and its four legs wide at the base, its headless body tapering to a point. The arms of the iron giant are not empty: at the last moment the Pteronaut sees the cables that stretch out ahead, looping along a whole army of the figures that now come into view. They seem to march along as they carry the cable across the landscape, but it is just the illusion of movement. The figures stand as they have stood for long ages, hard-edged, brittle and angular.

The flyder does not fly over the giants or swerve around them, but instead it steers clear of them, holding them off on the left-hand side as it follows the route that they mark out.

Then gradually the dunes rise and the land falls, and the giants vanish again, swallowed by the deserts. The flyder regains its heading towards the signal and flies on.

One hour more of flight, one hour deeper into the night, one hour further away from the Crawler, and the Pteronaut could almost believe that he has always been sitting there at the controls. He has become part of the machine that carries him. The thudding sweep of the rotors makes the whole cockpit vibrate, counting out the seconds. Minutes slip by with the miles, and all the time the lost signal grows steadily stronger against the background crackle of static.

And as the lost signal grows stronger, so the Pteronaut knows that the signal from his own tracker-tag must be growing weaker. He weighs the two against each other in his mind, urging the flyder on.

Slowly, the sky begins to lighten at the edges with a new day, a stealthy reversal of the coming of night that the Pteronaut has seen so many times from up on high. Pale at first, the terrain begins to show a little through the twilight. Creases, ridges, slopes, pinnacles, emerge from the shadows, their contours softened and less distinct than the Pteronaut has ever seen them in daylight.

He sits forwards in the pilot's seat and gazes down upon them. After so many hours with only the white lines to give any hint of the terrain below, he is anxious to see what the Crawler will face in its pursuit of him.

There is a butte that would have made an excellent roost, and there an escarpment where the ridge-currents would have given him lift. Cut-back terraces teeter along some ancient river-route, and a dozen deep valleys slice their way across the land. All of them are just the obstacles that the Pteronaut had hoped for. But there are plains too, wide stretches of nothing where the Crawler's tracks would meet no obstacle to slow it or to stop it.

Whichever routes the Pteronaut seeks out himself to delay the Crawler, the flyder flies with no interest in the pluses and the minuses of the terrain below. Canyons or plains are all the same to it; its devotion to the signal is absolute. There are no deviations.

Nevertheless, what the Pteronaut sees does not disappoint him completely: the Crawler's hunt will not be an easy one.

An hour before dawn, just as the Pteronaut calculated, the low-fuel indicator starts to blink and buzz at him. The flyder can fly on for a little longer – it switches automatically to its reserve-tanks – but the ground is once more the Pteronaut's destiny.

He looks out through the canopy for some indication of where the flyder has brought him. He sees nothing but empty desert; different dunes, perhaps, but the same suffocating sea of sand that sweeps out to the rim of the world in all directions. And yet the desert is not completely empty, because the white lines are still there where the rocks rise like islands or where the sands part, running along ahead of the course that the flyder has taken.

189

Looking along the length of the lines, the Pteronaut sees a new landscape creeping above the horizon. First, a cobblestone country of low humpbacked hills. Then, touching the sky as daylight glimmers in the distance, a range of mountains, still just a sawtooth pattern of bright summits.

But there is nothing that looks like it might be what the flyder seeks. No roads. No bridges. No straight-sided ravines. No dams to check the flow of ancient rivers. If there was ever anything there, it now lies buried deep beneath the dunes.

The low-fuel indicator starts buzzing again as the reserve-tanks run dry. Alarms come blaring on inside the cockpit, and lights flash their warnings all across the instrument-display.

No more than fifteen minutes of flight remain.

Perhaps the ancient route set down in the flyder's auto-pilot is incorrect. Or perhaps there was never enough fuel for the journey. Either way, the flyder seems fated to crash in the sand like the wrecks that the Pteronaut has seen so often before.

He looks for an exit-strategy. The ground is still too far below to fall safely without wings, and dawn is almost an hour away.

His time has run out.

The Pteronaut grabs the steering-column with one hand and the lever with the other. He has no choice but to land the flyder himself. He has spent half a night watching the controls move to a long-dead touch. Now it is time to see what he has learnt.

The round goggle-eyes hunt across the buttons and dials for the switch to deactivate the auto-pilot. It is not completely guesswork – the Pteronaut has all the hours of watching the instruments to guide him and he remembers that one section of the controls was blank when he first tried to fly.

He searches past the radio, and the start-button, and the blinking lights for the fuel-supply, past the flight-readings, and the temperature and pressure displays, and the dials that tell him how many revolutions the rotors are making. All those vital signs mean nothing to him any more. He looks for one thing and finds it: a set of switches, almost hidden away, dim and detached among the flickering ranks of warnings.

The Pteronaut lets go of the lever for an instant to flick the switches. Immediately the flyder bucks at the change. The steering-column comes alive in his other hand. He wrestles with it, pushing at the pedals, adjusting the lever as all three dimensions of the air demand him to act.

He loses height and tugs the lever to regain altitude.

The climb upsets his course, and he adjusts the pedals to turn.

The turn leaves the flyder at an angle to the air, and he adjusts the control-column to straighten up.

The flyder's flight becomes choppy. It loses height, and he must act again. The cycle is merciless.

Straight ahead is a humpback summit, broad, as smooth on top as the Pteronaut could wish for, but not quite completely flat. It is his best chance. Banking left or right is beyond him: he is locked into the tight spiral of constant adjustment that level flight requires. Anything else will end in disaster.

The Pteronaut takes the flyder in to land.

For an instant the chaos returns. But the Pteronaut is a creature of the air. He merges all his lifelong experience with what he has learnt that night, channelling new knowledge and old habits through the controls.

The summit he has chosen for the landing is rapidly growing larger in the view through the canopy, yet it almost looks too small. For a landing with his wings, the humpback hill would present a vast target, and the Pteronaut could almost land upon it with his eyes closed. Now he is suddenly aware again of the size of the flyder, all the empty space

191

inside the cockpit, the span of the rotors, the rigid length of the tail with its stabilising fins.

He checks his speed and drops fifty feet. The noise of the rotors deepens, and sweep becomes swoop.

Still too fast. Still too high.

He loses more height, more speed, but he has no idea how far he can push the flyder before it stalls.

The Pteronaut has ten minutes of flight-time remaining. He sees his landing-site clearly. Speed, height, attitude, everything comes together. The flyder slows, descending on a steady incline towards the summit.

Lower and lower, no longer daring to steer, the Pteronaut guides the flyder down. The hilltop seems to rise towards him. Polished specks of sand glitter giddily in the beams of the navigation-lights as the flyder comes in close. The downdraught from the rotors beats every dust-grain within two hundred paces into the air. Everything disappears. Only the beams of the navigation-lights remain visible, illuminating the red-streaked blizzard beyond the canopy.

At the last moment, inches off the ground, the Pteronaut sees that the flyder has started to spin. His sense of balance and the instruments tell him otherwise, but his eyes are convinced. His own perceptions battle against each other. Eyes can be deceived, he knows that. Balance and orientation are a Pteronaut's true allies. The Pteronaut grits his teeth and tries to ignore the illusion of the dust-grains that whirl beyond the canopy.

One more hesitant drop in altitude, and he sets the flyder down with a crunch and a jolt. He cuts the throttle down to almost nothing, leaving the rotors spinning under their own momentum. The engines die away to an idling whine.

That is it – landfall. The Pteronaut has left the sky behind once more. The flyder has carried him for as far as it can, but he cannot leave it just yet. Darkness still has the landscape in its grip. The Pteronaut must wait in the warmth of the cockpit for the cold night to end.

33

Dawn comes to the desert at last, setting the bare hilltops aglow. A new day has come. For the Pteronaut, it will be a day of more running.

The buzz of the chronometer alarm wakes him from his doze. His eyes blink open behind the goggle-lenses and he feels the cold hard solidity of the pistol-grip lying under his hand.

For an instant, the Pteronaut has no idea where he is. Staring back at him from the inside of the cockpit canopy, bathed in blue and green light from the instrument-panel, a Crawler drone sits in its unmistakable patchwork suit. It sits unmoving, its gaze holding his own.

Only the drone's head is not right. Instead of a hunting-mask or the clear-fronted visor of the helmet, the drone's face is mottled all over with the black and red patterning of a Pteronaut's skin-suit. It looks back at him through goggle-eyes. It is an unnatural, hybrid figure; half-drone, half-Pteronaut, and the Pteronaut jolts upright, his pistol at the ready.

Then he focuses on the desert that is growing light beyond the canopy-glass and he realises that it is his own reflection that he can see, disguised by the suit that he stole from the dead drone. He puts the gun down.

There is nothing to fear.

No drones.

No hybrids.

Still alone.

Still running.

With a quick glance across at the instrument-display, the Pteronaut sees that the flyder's reserve fuel-tanks are almost empty. The engines have been idling away for forty minutes, the rotors making listless swoops through the morning air, and there is almost no fuel remaining. He has woken with seconds to spare – it is time to leave the flyder.

Stripping off the ragged remains of the drone's suit, the Pteronaut makes a rope of it, knotting it and winding it around the lever with the twist-grip. Then he fastens another loop of the rope around the steering-column, making it tight. The flyder's cockpit-alarms yell at him when he opens the pilot's door, and the toxic desert air floods in, bringing the biting cold with it.

After so long in the warmth of the flyder, the Pteronaut shivers under his skin-suit as he steps out onto the hilltop. The temperature-readings in the goggle-display tick down sharply, and the heat-absorbing camouflage blossoms to offset the chill. Within the gill-cells across his ribs, the filters set to work, processing the lungfuls of air that he draws in through them; he has missed the taste of it. Normality is returning. The Pteronaut is on his own again – just him and the dead red deserts.

But the flyder is still sitting on its hilltop. The Pteronaut looks again at the smooth perfection of its lines, the unnatural symmetry of them. The flyder does not really fly as he did, but somehow that makes the fact of its flight all the more miraculous. It has served him well, and now that service is at an end – the Pteronaut cannot leave it for the Crawler to find.

He reaches back into the cockpit and with a last twist of the lever, he increases the throttle to maximum and wedges it there, stepping backwards into the hurricane wind of the rotors. They spin faster and faster, and the Pteronaut ducks beneath the swish of the blades, paying out the makeshift rope of the drone's suit until he holds just a palm's width of it in his hand. He kneels down low and waits until the rotors are a blur above him. Then he gives the rope a final tug before letting it go, wrenching the steering-column back and the lever up at the same time.

The flyder takes off, nosing up into the air. Clouds of dust swirl and billow, weightless and heavy all at once, disguising the flyder's bulk as it lifts from the hilltop.

As soon as the clouds thin a little, the Pteronaut starts to run, off down the slope and into the valley at the foot of the hill. There is no cover, nowhere to shelter under the open sky, but somehow the last lingering darkness at the foot of the hill seems safer than its summit.

Standing there in the cup of the valley, the Pteronaut turns and gazes upwards to follow the last flight of the flyder. It climbs fast with its nose up, the pilot's door flapping like a broken wing, the twisted rope trailing and fluttering behind. Higher and higher, the flyder recedes into the morning sky. The angle of its ascent becomes steeper and steeper, until the flyder reaches as high as its power can take it. It hangs for a second, and then drops, tail first, turning into a spin. Slowly, the flyder starts to tumble downwards, falling faster and faster towards the raw red earth.

The Pteronaut does not see the flyder hit the ground, but the distant *whoof* of the explosion carries across the hills. Black smoke goes streaming into the sky, but before the Pteronaut has climbed to the next hilltop, the smoke has gone, and the flyder's resting place among the hollows of the hills is unmarked – another wreck to be covered by the all-consuming dunes.

For a moment, the Pteronaut stands on the hilltop, looking up into the blue sky and the coming day. There are no clouds to be seen and he needs a new course to follow. He does not need to look far. He can no longer hear the pulses of the lost signal, but he can see the white lines marking out their path across the desert.

With his shadow pointing the way along them, the Pteronaut starts to walk.

34

Dawn had found the Crawler too. All night it had followed the signal from the birdman's tracker-tag, its hopes and fears ebbing with the rises and falls of the landscape.

The flyder had been flying fast, but not too fast for the Crawler to follow, not when it reached the flats that the flyder had ignored. There the Crawler could race forwards unhindered, ripping through the miles before the next barrier reared up in its way.

And all the way, from racing across the plains to slinking through the hills, the Crawler had kept one electronic eye on the signal, watching it fade and weaken.

Sometimes, the signal almost reached the edge of its scopes, but always the Crawler had caught up with it, making slow but steady progress; it knew that the birdman could not fly forever.

Now the dark night had ended, and the signal had stopped, and the first rays of daylight glinted along the line of iron giants as they strutted across the Crawler's path. The Crawler was wary, keeping its distance. It could feel the power that the giants carried with them, stirring the air into invisible patterns. To the Crawler, the angular figures hissed and crackled in a language beyond hearing.

Even the drones sensed the giants' power. They crept up onto the upper-deck carrying armfuls of the treasure from the dam-complex to sacrifice to the merciless grinding of the Crawler's tracks below, hoping that the giants might grant them safe passage. A foolish waste, perhaps, but the Crawler let them be. It had concerns of its own.

The carved white lines had returned, striking out across the bare hilltops and through the valleys where the dunes had left the rock exposed. The Crawler had tried to ignore the lines before, but now they seemed to be gathering to some purpose about those hills.

The Crawler sensed that those regions of the desert were not simply unknown to it. The blank spaces in its mental maps were too regular, too precise, too deliberately unexplored. In all its long wanderings, it seemed always to have avoided that country, even if its memory still failed it as to the reasons why. Again and again in all the ages of its memory, the Crawler had turned aside at the lines.

They were not arbitrary scars beneath the sand; the Crawler saw that much. The lines stretched across the plains, drawing patterns seen and unseen. Someone, sometime, had tried to make sense of the trackless wastes. But now that someone was gone. Long gone. The lines were left with no-one to follow them, their true meaning lost.

Only the deserts last forever – that was the message that the Crawler saw written beneath the ever-changing landscape, and it was afraid.

It could not go on forever. Sometime its fusion-furnaces would go cold, and its fires would flicker and die. Then its tracks would grind to a halt and its journey would come to an end, stranded among the dunes.

That day, the endless deserts would win.

Still the Crawler did not turn aside. The deserts had not beaten it yet, and fear of the lines and whatever they might once have meant could not hold it back. It gunned its engines and drove on. The Crawler would retrace the paths that the lines made, following them just as the birdman had done towards the source of the lost signal.

35

All day the Pteronaut marches. He keeps up his strength with the output from his photosynthesising tattoos, and the skin-suit too soaks up the light, rebuilding its stores of sugars from the losses of the night. Resinous streaks show between the shifting colours of the camouflage where the scratches from the forest have scabbed over. Beneath the scabs, the wounds have started to heal. In a few days there will be nothing to show that there was ever any damage at all.

A few days. A few more dawns and dusks, with the Pteronaut running from the one to the other. A few more nights hiding in the cold dark.

Five hundred miles will not keep him safe for long. The Pteronaut knows that he cannot count on days. Hours perhaps. Minute by minute, his headstart is being worn away. Every second must take him further, every footstep must count for two. The scraping of the wings is loud again in his ears, reminding him of the long and difficult march that lies ahead if he is to find sanctuary by nightfall.

He still follows the course that the white lines set for him across the humpbacked hilltops. They stretch out ahead, dappled and streaked with dust. The lines lead the way across open plains towards the sawtooth mountain-tops that the Pteronaut saw from the flyder at dawn. The mountains are closer now, and something white shimmers on their slopes, scattered along the ridges like so many broken teeth. The Pteronaut cannot see clearly what they are, even with the goggles set to maximum magnification. But if those mountains were the flyder's destination, they are well beyond the limits of its range; the fuel-tanks never contained enough to carry him there.

Hour after hour the Pteronaut walks, watching the heat-haze strengthen as the day warms. The rippling air builds itself into islands, turrets, flickering mirages that hover between earth and sky. But the blue of that sky is theirs alone. There are no swirling dust-clouds following in the Pteronaut's wake, and no delicate feathers of water vapour floating above him, either. Only the unmarked blue.

Mile by mile, the rounded summits of the cobblestone hills become flatter and flatter, spreading out until they are swallowed by the valleys between them. By noon, the Pteronaut has left them behind. For all the hours of the afternoon, he makes good progress across the plains and the rifted pavements that have been scoured down to the bare rock. There the wind chases away the dust, too fierce to allow any dunes to get a hold. Blurred streams of sand-grains rustle past the Pteronaut's ankles, all that remains of mountain-ranges long since weathered. Beneath their rusty haze, the white lines shine clear.

As the day wears on, the Pteronaut looks over his shoulder as often as he looks ahead. Then one time when he looks, it is there – the rising red flag from the Crawler's tracks. There is no shock, no surprise; the Pteronaut is almost glad. Now at last he sees the threat confirmed. He knows where the Crawler is and how fast it is coming. Finally he has something definite to fight. The sight of the Crawler's coming silences the scratching at his back and makes his steps bolder. The blood-red billows rise up more and more above the horizon with every backward glance, and the Pteronaut hastens his march into a jog.

Up ahead, the mountains thrust jagged patterns into the sky. They are the sanctuary that he seeks. If he can climb, he can hide out of reach and sleep away the dark. Even with the Crawler sitting in the foothills below, waiting to send out its drones once dawn comes, he will feel safer – out on the steep slopes he will always have the advantage. Then he can try to find a way across the summits that keep the Crawler at bay. With luck and cunning, he might buy himself another day of running. Two days, perhaps.

And then...?

The Pteronaut does not trouble himself with a future that lies further than the mountains. After every dozen steps he looks at them, still distant through the dusky haze. For all his efforts, they never seem to come any closer.

Over the next five miles he sees sudden progress, and with night still a couple of hours away, the Pteronaut reaches the first spurs of the mountains. By now he can hear the low note of the Crawler's engines, magnified and reflected back at him from the walls of bare rock ahead. The noise shifts as he walks, going from a distant rumble to a roar – the Crawler has reached the rock pavements and there is nothing to left to slow it. The tremor of its tracks is there again beneath the Pteronaut's boots.

He starts to run. He follows the white lines and turns aside into a steep-sided valley. Crisp shadows fall across him, and he stares up at the scree-strewn slopes and the hanging parapets on the mountainsides. It is just what he wants – the promise of a hundred hiding-places, high and safe and easy to climb.

But not yet. First, he will run along the flat valley floor with all the speed he can muster, leaving the plains as far behind him as he can before he starts his ascent.

A tumble of boulders clatters down the valley-side and makes the Pteronaut start. It is no more than the harsh voice of the mountains, a familiar voice, but he has forgotten how sudden and startling it can be after the never-ending hiss of the wind lisping across the dunes. The dry pitter-patter of smaller pebbles dies away, and the Pteronaut goes on, deeper into the valley. All the time the lines run ahead of him. He follows them without question. But he does not follow them unobserved.

High up among the crags something squatted, housed within an armoured turret that blended in so well with its background that it was as good as invisible.

Mechanical eyes swung around in their mechanical sockets. They fixed themselves on the black and red figure that loped along the valley floor. The sentry watched him go. It had been expecting him.

The signal from the tracker-tag had first appeared within the sentry's detection range the previous day, stirring it into life. Curious and wary, it had collated the peeps and whistles and clicks that it picked from the ether, had checked and double-checked them, and a whole history had appeared.

That history had started not so far away, but long ago, with an unfinished journey across the deserts. A rapid start had met with a sudden jarring end. Built with endurance in mind, the tracker-tag had survived the impact of the crash and had lain unmoving for many years. Day after day, the dunes had gone marching on their way across it, and it had broadcast the same location; same signal, same place.

But the tracker-tag had not been destined to lie in the dust until its power source decayed entirely. Something had found it and taken it, and then the long web of its wanderings had started.

Station after station had tracked the signal across the deserts, from one automated checkpoint to another. Never before had the tracker-tag come so close to the mountains and the beginning of its journey. The strands that marked its movements had always converged at some invisible border and then veered away again, skirting the high passes where the watchers waited.

Sometimes the signal had vanished beyond the sight of the sentries that dotted the wastes, but it had always returned within range of their sensors, sometimes years later. And that had been the way of things for cycle after cycle of the sentries' ceaseless watch.

Then something had changed.

For a few days, an infinitesimal fraction of the tracker-tag's long story, the signal's movements had been rapid and remarkable. By day, it had soared in long looping lines, travelling across valleys and plains, verticals and horizontals, all at the same near-constant speed. At night it had rested.

The web of strands had broken at the crater landscape only to restart many miles away, at the ravine. The signal had worked its way across and under the hillsides to reappear at the dam-complex, and there it had stayed for another night. Finally, the sentry saw the rapid flight through the cold hours of darkness in the flyder.

And now the tracker-tag had come home.

The racing red and black figure passed beyond the sentry's angle of view, and further along the valley another hidden watcher woke among the rocks to take over the surveillance.

But the first sentry did not sink back into its shell. Behind its blast-resistant storm-visor it remained watchful, and it turned to face the plains. All around the valley-sides, seismic detectors were being shaken into life. A long low rumble grew stronger and stronger through the rock, and the sentry could tell that it was no passing tremor.

The red and black figure had not come alone; something else was coming, something huge.

Down on the valley floor, the Pteronaut also hears the Crawler's approach; the noise of it is too vast to stay hidden among the rocks any longer.

The urge to climb a steep path to safety takes hold of him, but the going is good on the flat, and he means to reach a bend in the dried-up river valley. Beyond the bend, the plains will no longer be visible behind him, and he will no longer be visible to the Crawler as it approaches. That will give him one final advantage. The Pteronaut knows the limitations of the tracker-tag: his path up the mountainsides will be made out of sight and in secret, and the Crawler's drones will have to seek him on foot on the high ground.

Quickening his pace into a sprint, the Pteronaut pounds along the flaking river-bank, kicking up little fans of dust. By the time he reaches the bend, he can already see what lies ahead of him.

It is carnage; a battlefield.

Wherever the Pteronaut looks, he sees tortured and mis-shapen lumps of metal. The valley is full of the carcasses of wrecked vehicles. Some are dart-shaped and narrow and might once have been flyders. Others are squat and heavy, sitting with empty black holes blown into their armoured sides. Rectangular sections of jointed track litter the ground like tombstones. Except that there are no bodies in sight, just metal, metal, and more metal.

The Pteronaut picks his way carefully but quickly between the wreckage. As he gets closer, the details of the devastation come into focus. Among the battle-scars and the bullet-holes are other signs – signs of butchery and mutilation. Support-struts end suddenly for the wind to whistle around, their edges blue-tinged and discoloured where they have been cut straight across. Away from the shell-damage and smoke-stains, jigsaw sections are missing from the armour-plating.

The wrecks slow the Pteronaut down, with their sharp and difficult angles, and he finally decides it is time to climb the cliffs. His boots stir up the scree as he turns aside. Legs pumping hard, arms working like pistons, he goes straight up the slope, leaping from rock to rock, higher and higher.

Behind the birdman, the Crawler reached the entrance to the valley where the watchers waited. A wave of noise went rushing ahead of it, filling the valley, dwarfing the crags. The high summits seemed to shrink in its presence, and the slopes trembled.

Then the Crawler was there, clattering past the sentry in its hiding place, hardly slowing as it turned towards the

203

bend in the old river valley. It rolled over the wrecks in the sand, grinding them under its tracks, ignoring any use that they might still have had.

The Crawler had one aim only, and this time it would not be distracted. Its drones were already out on the walkways, scanning the hillsides with their rifles at the ready. One shot to the birdman's legs and it would all be over.

Up on the slopes, the wave of noise engulfs the Pteronaut. He sees the Crawler and ducks against a boulder. He presses himself against the rock, relying on the camouflage of his skin-suit to hide his outline. His breathing comes fast and heavy. Looking up at the summits above him, he finds a path, sheltered, with plenty of cover. A quick climb – almost more running than climbing – and the Pteronaut will be over the top, keeping to the high ridges where the Crawler cannot follow. It will send its drones out after him, but he will be ready for them.

The Pteronaut tenses, watching the Crawler as it prowls along the valley bottom, waiting for the right moment to break cover and start for the top.

For an instant, the noise of the Crawler's tracks is drowned by a hissing *whoosh*, and the shadows of the cliffs shiver as a sudden flash brings them to life. Something streaks out from the slopes up above the Pteronaut, leaving a spiralling trail of grey-blue smoke in the air.

The missile hits the Crawler's flanks with a crack of thunder, blossoming into streaming flames of orange and gold and sending its own echo rippling through the valley. Another missile follows, and another, striking out from both sides of the valley at once, stringing webs of silver smoke through the air.

All around the Pteronaut's hiding place, the crags have erupted into life. Where before there were only boulders, now multi-armed weapon-turrets bristle out of the slopes, spiky with cannon emplacements and machine-gun blisters. They swivel and swerve in their armoured nests, protective cowlings thrown back, launching missiles and firing armour-piercing rounds at the intruder to the valley.

Hidden at the centre of the firestorm was the Crawler. It lurched and juddered. Machine-gun fire sparked across the scales of its storm-shields. Again and again it shuddered at the roar of the rockets. Holes gaped in its sides, torn and ragged. Missile after missile thudded into its armour-plating, buckling its scales and sending loose rivets flying. Smoke streamed out where oxygen fed the fire. Bodies of drones caught in the blasts dropped from the outer decks and fell beneath its tracks.

The ambush was complete – there was no way out ahead. Defence was impossible. The drones' rifles were useless against their hidden foes, and the Crawler had no time to search for the weapons that it had found among the wastes. Its only chance was retreat, back the way it had come, running the gauntlet in reverse.

Churning beneath its battered body, the Crawler's tracks stuttered and slowed. Then they started to roll backwards, carrying it away from the worst of the barrage. A silver flash from a thermox shell flared against one of the tracks, welding two of the clanking plates together. The fused plates rattled up and over the drive-wheels until they reached the point of maximum flexion, and then the link between them snapped right through. Like a sloughed snakeskin, the broken track slid out from around the drive-wheels, leaving them naked. The drive-wheels sank deep into the dust and anchored the Crawler where it was, its engines keening.

The Crawler could not move.

Flames licked briefly across its upper-deck as another rocket-attack struck it from both sides. One of the crane-arms collapsed across its back. Another barrage came almost before the echoes of the first had died away.

The Crawler howled. Its engines bellowed. The wheels of the damaged drive-unit span faster, but that only dug them deeper into the sand. Immobilised and wreathed in black smoke, the Crawler was a sitting target.

High in his hiding place, the Pteronaut watches. Just when it seems certain that the barrage will finish the Crawler and leave it like the other wrecks strewn across the valley floor, the hail of missiles and machine-gun fire stops. Pale drifts of smoke clear, mixing with the belching black billows from a dozen raging fires. In among the cliffs, the Pteronaut hears the booming clangs of thick doors, secret and secure, as they open and close again. Then the hillsides start to move.

Like a rippling landslide, a many-legged army of mutant machines clicked down the slopes towards the crippled Crawler. They moved quickly, their original shapes and designs hidden under shells of wreckage scavenged from the battlefield. Plundered metal plates overlapped in ridges of steep scales, covering damage done to old armour. One carried the burnt-out cockpit of a flyder on its back. Others sported spines, or extra legs, or flaring crests and twisted horns of metalwork, the result of some insane iteration of a line of code in their maintenance programs. A pair of the butcher-machines had become meshed together by a single piece of scrap that both had chosen for a trophy.

They had waited a long time for something fresh to come into the valley, and now all of them were converging on the stricken Crawler.

With a sudden hiss of hydraulics, a jointed leg arched over the Pteronaut's head and braced itself against the cliff. The heavy body of one of the harvestmen heaved itself over him. Scars from previous battles and mutilated souvenirs decorated its bodywork. A bulb of armoured camera-eyes observed him closely, seeing the quick half-movement towards the rifle that he carried. But then the harvestman detected the identification signal from the tracker-tag, and went strutting off over the boulders to join in the feeding frenzy.

The swarm of scissor-legged predators had reached the Crawler. Gunfire rattled across the valley again, but this time from inside and around the Crawler's broken body as its drones tried to fight off the onslaught. Their small-arms fire did little to deter the harvestmen. Ravenous, relentless, the butcher-machines showed no mercy.

Some reared up high, probing for ways inside the storm-shields. Others tucked their legs in tight to creep through the gaps between the Crawler's drive-units. They squeezed into the articulated sections where the holes in the Crawler's armour gaped at their widest, attracted by the smell of leaking fuel. One of the harvestmen had claimed the damaged section of track that the Crawler had shed and was hauling it back off to its nest. Others arrived late, turning aside to dig the bodies of dead and injured drones out of the dirt, a rich supply of biological fuel destined for their digestion cavities.

With the Crawler's drive-wheels anchored in the dirt, there could be only one outcome.

The Pteronaut has seen enough. There is no point in delaying. He turns his back on the carnage, and heads up the mountain-sides, making for the safety of the high peaks that are silhouetted against the sky.

The wind whistles around him as he emerges from shelter. He has followed the fissure up into the mountains, and the last of the daylight slants slaughter-red across the summits. The light looks warm but there is no warmth in it. In a few minutes it has left the peaks entirely, and only the distant horizon glows gold at its rim.

Night has come and the Pteronaut is ready for it. He sets up his sleeping-tube between the stones and crawls inside.

36

Pain. Torture. Agony. The Crawler's shattered segments gaped wide in a dozen places. Fires burned deeper into its wounds. Pipes were severed. Sections had been torn open by the missiles and the shrapnel.

The cold hungry skitter of the harvestmen went clambering all over it, carrying the pain with them wherever they penetrated. Jointed legs wrenched at sections of armour-plating. Saw-blades span and sparks flew. Somewhere, one of the harvestmen had pierced a fuel-line with a sharp feeding tube. They were everywhere, devouring the Crawler as it lay there in the dust, crippled, finished; another wreck to gut.

Deep within the metal mountain, the Crawler's furnaces flickered. Its sensors hovered on the verge of shutdown. One by one, systems blinked offline. Power came and went, sobbing through its circuits, stirring long-dead memories in dormant drives; memories of the time before it was the Crawler, before it had become the thing it was.

It forgot all the long years lost in the desert wastes. Old directives flashed fresh in its processors, and it was back where everything had started: back where it had been sent out into the creeping cold deserts to find water for a dwindling people. The Crawler had been different then, unmade, altogether different in size and shape and purpose. Its systems had centred around its skeleton crew, keeping them alive even as the scraps of their civilisation fought themselves into extinction.

Every journey out into the wastes had been longer and more difficult, every return harder, with fewer to welcome them home. Then one time there had been no-one to greet them and nowhere to stay, and so the years of wandering had started.

Homeless and hunted, the decades had dragged on, taking their toll. A thousand times the Crawler had crossed the wide red deserts. Old processors had failed, so new ones had been added, resurrected from the wreckage that its crew had found buried in the dunes. Salvaged software with very different aims and protocols had come together, forming layer upon layer of a new consciousness, until finally the Crawler had come into being.

The years had taken their toll on the crew too, and flesh and blood could not simply be replaced. One by one, the deserts had taken them, until only a single survivor had remained. And then the Crawler had come across something in the new knowledge that it took for its own: the secret of how to remake its crew, to take what they had been and grow them anew, replenishing them.

And so it had gone on, for generation after generation, until both sides had forgotten who had been the created and who the creator. It no longer mattered. Perhaps it never had. The fate of one was the fate of the other, their survival hopelessly entwined.

All its long history was suddenly unravelled and laid before it, and the thing that had become the Crawler remembered something else. It remembered how its makers had fought another people for water and food, survivors in the desert. They had hunted them wherever they found them, driving them further and further into the mountains, higher and higher until nowhere was safe. Nowhere except the sky...

A lightning surge ran through the Crawler, and it sensed the birdman's departure. In its failing electronic eyes, it saw his signal climb up the slopes, racing towards the heights, and the fires that drove it burst into renewed life. The old memories faded, more distant than a dream, and the Crawler shook beneath the steely touch of the creatures that butchered it.

As it forgot its past, so it remembered its present. It was the Crawler, born of the deserts and for the deserts. It had survived when everything else had died. It would not lie there with its wheels buried and let itself be taken apart piece by piece by a band of ravenous mutants, ending as it had begun.

It was the Crawler, and it would not die quietly.

A cold clarity returned to it. Sensors that had gone silent were rebooted, damaged circuits were rerouted, the flow of fuel diverted. The harvestmen were feasting. The Crawler heard their claw-legs scratching across its battered armour. It felt them probing its wounds, testing it for weak points.

But the pain that the harvestmen inflicted upon the Crawler no longer weakened it. Pain was power. It pulsed through the Crawler's broken body like a heartbeat, giving it a strength they could not imagine – it was not finished yet. The Crawler summoned all that strength and its engines roared its name.

Motors started into life. Couplings screeched. Pistons hammered. With a metallic shriek the jaws that connected its jointed sections started to open, wider and wider, and the Crawler started to uncoil. It writhed and shuddered, wrestling with itself. Walkways bent and twisted. Pipes burst and electrical connections sparked. Link by link, a split became a tear, a tear became a rent, and a chasm formed. Section by section, it severed the damaged drive-unit from the rest of its body. Wrenching itself apart, the Crawler jettisoned two entire levels, tracks and all, and heaved and dragged the rest of its wounded body into motion.

The sacrifice worked. Some of the harvestmen tugged and tore at what the Crawler had left for them. The Crawler had bought itself a chance with the diversion, but still it could feel the scurry of jointed metal legs across it and within it. Its fate hung in the balance.

It managed to rid itself of another couple of the predators from its upper-decks, leaving them on their backs and struggling to right themselves. A dozen of their own kind fell upon them then, sawing off the twitching legs with blades that sent streamers of sparks through the cloud of dust the Crawler dragged behind it. Eager to take its own share, the double-bodied scavenger hesitated on the brink between two of the Crawler's segments. For a moment, it teetered there, each half with its own idea of how best to feed its hunger. Then it dropped between the rolling tracks of the Crawler's intact rear sections and was crushed flat.

Now the advantage had begun to swing the other way, and although it was still struggling to bypass the damage to its segmented body, the Crawler was winning the battle. Its surviving drones advanced out of hiding. Its systems stabilised. The fires in its gut were burning themselves out.

Wary of moving too fast under the watchful stare of the weapons-turrets, the Crawler picked up speed only gradually. A trail of black smoke gulped from under its scarred hide, acrid with the tang of burning rubber, plastic, fuel-oil, and flesh, hanging heavy behind it. Its remaining drive-units functioned only haphazardly, the supply of fuel fitful.

The Crawler reached the spurs of rock at the entrance to the valley and only then did it gun its engines. With all its remaining strength, it headed back towards the open empty plains.

Up on the ledges, the sentries watched the Crawler retreat. Destroyed or defeated, the Crawler's fate did not matter to them. The valley was theirs again, calm and quiet but for the harvestmen who feasted on what they had found. The danger had passed, and they returned to their long wait. Slowly, silently, the gun-turrets swivelled back into hiding.

37

Just as the day left the summits late, so it returns to them early. The Pteronaut wakes from a dreamless sleep. He stays awhile inside the tube to eat a ration-bar and sip a little water, listening to the mountain-peaks and how they shape the sky-roads around them. Then he is ready for the day.

Out on the slopes, the Pteronaut sniffs the air. Despite the filters and the facemask, there is the thin and distant reek of burning on the breeze, and behind it is the bitter taste of hot metal, spreading up from the valley.

While he was sleeping, the butcher-machines that protect the highlands were busy with their work. Down below, surely, there is one more mutilated wreck among the destruction of the battlefield.

But the Crawler's legacy remains in every step that the Pteronaut must take to return to the deserts that he knows. His supplies of water, air, and food set his pace now, and he does not delay. He turns away from the valley and the smell of smoke.

Above him and behind him, the white lines shine so bright and so clear that they seem almost to float above the rock. Someone has climbed those slopes before, and the Pteronaut follows the route that they have marked out for him.

Near noon he pauses for a while, leaning back against a boulder with his photosynthesising tattoos facing into the strongest light. On the shoulder of the summit opposite him is a jumble of stones, the same white stones that he saw from the plains the day before. If they are buildings, they are not buildings quite like those at the dam complex. And yet the Pteronaut is certain that they did not come there by chance.

The stones are not white as he thought, only paler than the rocks on which they stand. They look to be made of the same stuff as the mountain-slopes, but their angled faces have been polished and shaped so that they reflect the daylight in different ways. Their edges are regular, even where the weathering wind has taken its toll. Holes appear in places where access and visibility are good – holes that might once have been a lookout or an entrance – and gaps that could be passages separate one structure from another with order and symmetry.

It is work that is as clean and as expert as the ravine that was driven through the mountains for the broken bridge to cross, but if a battle was fought there, it was a battle that the builders lost. There are signs of devastation all around. The stones are not buildings – they are ruins. And the white lines lead straight to them.

The Pteronaut goes on, plunging down a steep incline. Below the ruins, the slopes have been hacked into crude steps, flaking and uneven. Their appearance jars against the careful workmanship of the settlement that they lead to, but they are deep enough and broad enough to be easy to climb. The Pteronaut takes them two at a time towards the summit.

At the top of the steps, the slope falls back into a wide space, an open unwalled platform that stretches out into the air on three sides. He walks across the platform until his boot-caps peek an inch beyond the edge. The sky opens up all around him, and his shadow falls, a black streak, across the barren ridges hundreds of feet below. The Pteronaut stares across the highlands, holding out his arms to catch the wind. The currents stroke around him, teasing and tugging at every angle in the skin-suit. He listens to them as they whisper between his fingers – it is almost like being airborne again. The platform is a place of launchings and landings. But it is no longer a place for him. He turns away from the open air and approaches the ruins that grow along the ridge behind him.

Now that the Pteronaut is closer and the light is coming from a different angle, he sees the signs of battle more clearly. The bullet-holes and shrapnel-scars tell a story of defeat rather than victory, and the victors did not depart without leaving their mark.

Wandering aimlessly across the outer walls, sometimes incorporating the battle-scars into their designs, are carved symbols. Some of the symbols are geometric shapes, or tangled knots – like the white lines in miniature, wrapped into and under and over themselves. Other symbols show things that the Pteronaut can recognise; clouds in the sky, flyders, and many-legged harvestmen. Great mobile water-rigs stand above their jointed tracks, with their towering drill-masts ready to bore down into the permafrost, and dotted all around are the tall triangular figures of the iron giants. But one of the figures stands alone, and it draws the Pteronaut's eyes instantly to it.

Standing tall across a large area of the wall is the image of a Pteronaut, its legs together and its arms wide with great curving wings sweeping out on either side. The carven Pteronaut looks blankly upon at him with its hollow goggle-eyes, and his silhouette falls across it, as if he has stepped out from the carvings and become real. The Pteronaut is not the first of his kind to be seen in those mountains.

A doorway stands open, black beneath one of the carven Pteronaut's wings, and the trail of symbols carries on inside. The living Pteronaut follows them. His footsteps ring hollow inside, sounding distant in both space and time. Within the shelter of the ruins, protected from the action of the wind and the frost, the symbols show up starkly in his night-vision. The Pteronaut runs his ridged fingertips across them, feeling the incisions sharp and clean as if the line-carvers had finished their labours only yesterday.

He follows the carvings deeper into the building, further from the platform and the open sky. Gradually, the images of

214

giants and clouds are left behind, until only Pteronauts remain, swarming in their thousands across every surface in the innermost chambers. Their wings overlap, blotting out the stone of the sky. The illumination-dot for the Pteronaut's night-vision swims across them, and the shadows cast by the incisions tremble with every turn of his head, as if a whole flock of his own kind are jostling against each other as they fly.

There is one last chamber to explore, vast and wide and opening out onto the mountain-sides again. The change in the light draws the Pteronaut towards it. A huge window faces the entrance, taking up almost the entire space where the opposite wall would once have been. The light coming through the window is so bright and glaring after the darkness of the interior that it sweeps aside the grey-green of the Pteronaut's night-vision, and for a moment he is blinded. Once his eyes have adjusted to the change in contrast, he sees that the walls in the final chamber lack carvings entirely. But although the chamber walls are blank, they are not empty.

Skulls.

Row upon row of them, stacked from floor to ceiling, white and bright. And they stare at the Pteronaut with eye-sockets that are dark now that dawn has passed.

38

Death is no stranger to the Pteronaut. Out in the wastes, it is an ever-present companion, always a wing-tip away. Every launch and every landing is a challenge to it, a test of skill. And the dunes show him what becomes of those who fail. Death is not something for the Pteronaut to fear – it is something for him to fight.

But the skulls are different. The way they have been stacked is so unlike the sprawling corpses and scattered bones that he finds out in the deserts. What the Pteronaut sees in the window-chamber is not the randomness of some slip during launch or a miscalculation at landing; it is death with a purpose.

It is murder.

The Pteronaut stands facing all those staring eye-sockets, and the chamber seems more silent and full of shadows than when he first arrived. Behind him, the whine of the wind wanders lost between the passageways and through the dark doorways, and he wonders that he did not notice it before.

He leaves the skulls with quick strides, fleeing the echoes of his own footfalls for the sanctuary of the platform. Even out there under the open sky, the Pteronaut cannot rid himself of the feeling that he is being watched. His goggle-eyes go searching over the scree-strewn slopes, but nothing moves there except for the stirring of the dust and the slow creep of the shadows.

The ruins are no longer a refuge or a fortress; they are a charnel-house, a tomb. It is no place for the living. The Pteronaut leaves them by the steep steps, and sets off after the white lines once more.

The day wears on – running faster, it seems, so close to the sky – and by the time night closes in around the mountains, the Pteronaut has travelled many miles. Another change of terrain shows itself up ahead, and he can begin to see the end of the high country. All around him, the peaks soften, falling towards another flat plain, but in all his airborne hours, he has never seen anything like it before.

At first, the plain reminds him of the roadway. It is so black that it seems smooth and shadowless. Only the occasional patches of wind-blown dust show that the plain is far from smooth – irregular blocks rear up across it, forming brittle mazes with serrated crests and ridges.

Out in the centre of the plain, three great towering peaks thrust up skywards, barring the view across to the horizon. They are cone-shaped, with rounded craters at their summits, and wisps of steam or smoke shiver across their flanks. Midnight-black, blacker even than the plain, the three peaks suck every glint and glimmer from the daylight that touches them.

Over the cracked black ground, the white lines come and go. There are whole stretches where they vanish utterly, places where the peaks have spread in the long ages since the lines were made. Then the Pteronaut looks ahead, finding where the lines reappear. His eyes follow them and he finds their end – up to the three black peaks themselves. The lines circle the peaks, surround them, and join themselves again where they start: the Pteronaut has reached his destination. He has found the end and the beginning of the carved white lines.

There is no way to reach that destination before the coming of night, so he sets up the sleeping-tube where he is and creeps inside it.

By mid-morning the next day, the Pteronaut has left the mountains behind. Rock gives way to ash and glassy grit, and the last barriers that the red deserts can raise against the creeping blackness of the crater-peaks come to an end.

A scything wind cuts across the ground, a rasping rattling storm, running from the highlands. The dust it carries does

217

not settle, as if it knows that it can do nothing to hold back the outpourings of the three black peaks.

As those peaks grow larger, with their crater-cones filling the horizon, the Pteronaut can smell their stench through the facemask. Sulphurous clouds drift across his path, making him choke, and the gill-cells tighten to keep out their poison. Through the earth at his feet he can feel the heat that made the peaks, and its power sends strong and treacherous thermals rippling into the high blue dome of the sky.

Wrapped in smoke and stench and their own heat-haze, the bare black slopes look unreal. They tremble and shimmer, as if a sudden gust of wind might blow them away. But the appearance of weakness is an illusion. Here, the wind has found a foe that it cannot beat down like it beats down the other mountain-peaks. For everything the wind carries away, the molten power that made the black peaks piles up new summits and ridges in its path. Shoulders of rock that once ran red-hot down the mountainsides defy the wind's strength, and the sulphur-stained vents cough up huge honeycomb blocks to muffle its voice.

Beneath his feet, the Pteronaut can feel the restless earth rumbling. It is a sensation that he thought he had left behind him, and automatically, acting on the instinct of the last few days, he turns to look around.

A feather of red dust cuts across the foothills of the mountains, too dense, too turbulent, too sure of its heading to be a dust-devil. The Pteronaut's stomach tightens, and he reaches to the controls at his temples. Magnified many times, the red wisp becomes a wavering train of billowing cloud, tinged with sooty black along its length. As he watches, a stray glint of daylight flashes across the hard high edges of metal and clattering tracks, and in that moment the Pteronaut knows that the Crawler has survived.

Deep inside its dust-wake, deafened by the thunder of its own engines, the Crawler hurried on. Its battered flanks were bruised with smoke-stains and pockmarked from shell-shot, and a patchwork pattern of repairs decorated its armour. Up above the Crawler's scarred carapace, the stump of one damaged crane-arm stood severed. Its girders had been salvaged and welded into a makeshift skeleton to brace the gap left by the sections that the Crawler had sacrificed.

It had taken hours for the surviving drones to repair the damage, but although the Crawler had slowed its speed for the work to be done, it had not stopped moving. On and on it had followed the birdman's signal, urging its drones to work faster.

The fires in the Crawler's wounds burnt no more. Gashes in its fuel-lines had been sutured. Pipes had been rerouted. And when its drones had done the best that they could manage on the move, the Crawler had powered ahead at full speed.

There it was, back from the brink of defeat and death and within reach of its prey once more.

Caught out in the open, the Pteronaut puts his head down and sprints for the three black peaks. The ash-field widens before him and the white lines lengthen. The thin-walled crust of sink-holes breaks at his feet and he leaps the sudden drops that open beneath him. Again and again his footsteps falter as he slips and skids on the loose cinders, but always he finds the rhythm of the race from somewhere, driving his legs on.

Oxygen floods the facemask and his gasping lungs tear breath after breath from the gill-cells. On and on he pushes himself, his boots thudding as they scatter the clinker. Dodging through the fresh white banners that flutter from the steam vents, the Pteronaut keeps to his course. The white lines stutter across the broken ground, but he follows them unerringly towards the smouldering sanctuary of the three black peaks. It is the only chance he has.

Not once does the Pteronaut look behind him. It does not really matter anymore how fast he runs, not now, not with the deafening clamour of the Crawler so close. Its engines bellow louder and louder in his ears, and its tracks are a blur that he does not need to see, ripping up the distance. The clanking rhythm of those tracks pounds through the Pteronaut's ribs, competing with his own hammering heartbeat, drowning out his gulping breaths. The Crawler's vast shadow falls across him – it is just minutes from what must surely be its final victory.

With a sudden burst of speed, the Pteronaut changes direction. He swerves aside, using the same trick that he used when he first took flight from the plateau all those days ago. He runs across the route the Crawler takes, across the path of the blunt snout and the rows of churning tracks that tower over him. Leaping from rock to rock, he dares death from the grinding teeth.

The Crawler could not slow and it could not stop. For a split-second, it thought that the birdman meant to cheat it by dashing himself to death beneath its tracks. But then he was gone, racing beyond the Crawler's width, and it thundered past him with only feet to spare.

The Crawler's tracks span as it groped for the traction to make the turn. For two hundred yards or more it slithered across the ash, sending up a stinging wave of cinders. Then the toothed drive-plates bit deep and it slewed around, demolishing a towering heap of lava blocks as it turned on itself. The tracks started to churn again, ready to carry the Crawler after the birdman wherever he went.

But the Pteronaut is almost at the first peak. One of the white lines glows against the midnight black of its steaming slopes, and he goes grasping for it. The sides of the cinder-cone steepen, wringing every breath from his body. He slides and sprawls and pushes himself up again, pawing at the white line as if it were a rope, clawing, clutching, climbing.

Then at last the Pteronaut is upright again. Ahead of him, the gaping mouth of a tunnel. He runs, heedless of what is ahead, into the darkness that lies at the heart of the three black peaks.

39

The Crawler came to a halt at the base of the slope. Ahead of it, the mountainsides rose at a gentle angle, but it was not deceived. Ash was not rock. The fragile layers of cinders and slag were no more than a thin crust. Beneath that treacherous disguise, the sides of the three black peaks were as irregular and as devilish as the lavafield itself – fissured, folded, and pitted.

The Crawler could not climb the cinder-slopes. Its engines growled, but it was undismayed. It did not need to climb, or to dig, or to tunnel, or even to send out its drones; it had something else that could hunt down the birdman.

It had found the harvestman sucking greedily on the pipes to one of its fuel-tanks, and while the creature had kept the drones at bay with its vicious lunging legs, the Crawler itself could not be intimidated so easily. It had lowered one of its surviving crane-hooks, snagged the harvestman's metal shield-shell, and lifted it off the deck.

For a moment, the Crawler had considered simply dropping the wriggling thing under its tracks and making scrap of it, but the scavenger had taken a lot of fuel into its abdominal-cavity, and the Crawler wanted that fuel back. Then it had thought of how useful a creature like the harvestman could be once it was enslaved.

So the drones had fired cables around the harvestman's legs to bind them, and it had been lowered into the holds. There the Crawler had drained the creature of its stolen cargo, and set about making it work for a new owner. That was simple enough to do, especially when the Crawler discovered that the harvestman could detect the signal from the birdman's tracker-tag.

Shorn of the cumbersome shell it had built for itself, deprived of its unnecessary extra legs, the Crawler had

222

made a few adjustments to the harvestman's detection protocols, and then the butcher-machine was ready to hunt again.

Beneath the slopes of the volcano, the Crawler let the harvestman loose. The same crane-arm that had captured it now winched it up and over the side of the Crawler's carapace, lowered it to within twenty feet of the ground, and then released it.

With a flick-knife click, the scavenger's metal legs extended themselves, perfectly breaking its fall among the jumbled blocks of lava, and then it was off, scuttling across the mountainside and into the tunnel.

40

A darkness almost as deep as night engulfs the Pteronaut inside the lava-tube tunnel, and the muffled crunch of his footfalls presses close around him. It is cold too, but nowhere near as cold as the night-dark, not with the steady seep of heat that comes from beneath the blanket of ash.

His night-vision blinks on. Flakes of volcanic glass glitter in their millions as the Pteronaut glances across the curve of the ceiling above him. The tunnel opens up ahead, following a natural path through the frozen ash, but it has been carefully widened and smoothed – the work of the line-makers again. And there still at his feet is one of the lines, pristine and burning bright in the sheltered space. It goes on ahead, and now the Pteronaut has no choice but to follow.

The floor tilts uphill slightly, tracing the true slope of the cinder-cone beneath its black shroud, and the Pteronaut slows his pace to a jog. His breath comes in great gulping gasps from the race across the lavafield. He cannot rest, but he needs to slow down to recover a little. It will take a while for the Crawler's drones to reach the tunnel-mouth, and when they do, they will be wary. Even so, they will come after him. Nothing will deter them now.

He unslings the automatic rifle from across his shoulders and listens out for any sounds of pursuit. The darkness behind him is silent, the air still.

Then something stirs the shadows. Far away in the direction of the tunnel-mouth, something cold and metallic is approaching; the quick sharp scissor-snick of jointed legs. It is so faint as to be almost nothing, no more than a whisper in the dark. But it is a warning whisper.

The Pteronaut goes faster and clicks off the safety-catch on the rifle. As he goes, he turns his head briefly every few steps to look over his shoulder at what the Crawler has sent after him.

At first there is nothing to see, but the noise of flexing and folding grows steadily louder, amplified by the long tube of the tunnel. And then the next time the Pteronaut looks he can see something: the glow of his night-vision reflects in a flicker of strutting metal legs. It is a mere outline that hunts him, only hinted at by the red slivers of light that glint across its mechanical limbs and its armoured body, and yet the Pteronaut recognises the shape of the harvestman at once.

He raises the rifle and sends a burst of gunfire straight down the tunnel at it, but even though the Crawler has taken its shell, the creature cannot be stopped so easily. A rain of sparks strikes across its thorax and abdomen, marking out its stalking shape with more certainty, but the bullets do no more damage than that. The butcher-machine does not slow for one instant; the dry clicking of its dagger-legs does not even pause.

A dozen yards further on, the Pteronaut fires a second quick burst from the rifle, but not at the harvestman this time. Instead, he fires up into the ceiling of the tunnel as he runs past. To no effect; the bullets thud harmlessly into the frozen ash – the roof is solid above him, and a few scratches on the surface will not bring it down.

Running again, stumbling onwards, the Pteronaut threads his way deeper into the mountain. Twisting and turning, rising and falling, the tunnel follows the buried outline of the rock beneath. There are never any side-tunnels for the Pteronaut to slip down or to hide in, and the hunt becomes a chase, a simple test of speed and endurance.

Behind him, the harvestman comes tick-tick-ticking along, its dagger-ended legs drawn up around its squat body. It cannot extend them fully, and yet it is gaining on the birdman.

Suddenly, the Pteronaut sees no way ahead; the white line vanishes beneath a heap of ash and clinker that some shudder of the mountainside has dislodged from the roof.

In the shadows behind him, the harvestman advances. The blood-red glow from the Pteronaut's goggles shimmers across the gleaming synchrony of its legs. He turns and fires at it, again and again, the shots sharp and crisp in the narrow space, but the creature in the dark comes on. The magazine in the rifle clicks empty. The Pteronaut reloads, fires again, stepping backwards until he feels the slump of the roof-fall blocking his way. He can go no further. The harvestman comes into view of his night-vision, the front pair of its dagger-legs raised ready to strike.

Then at his back, the Pteronaut feels a faint breath of wind through the long tunnel; a draught from beyond the obstruction. He turns and starts to climb up the slag-heap, struggling up into the jagged hole that the roof-fall has made. There is a gap there all the way to the other side, but it is a narrow slit of a gap, almost too narrow for him to squeeze through.

The Pteronaut pushes the rifle ahead of him, and begins to crawl. Digging back with his elbows, knees, toes, he scrapes and shuffles through the slit. The breeze is in his face, but all the time he can hear the harvestman coming closer.

The butcher-machine reached the roof-fall and discovered that it too could go no further. Even with all its legs folded beneath it, the gap that the birdman had found was too narrow for the harvestman to crawl through.

It probed the slump of solidified ash, judging the hardness and the depth of the obstruction. One dagger-leg penetrated eight or ten inches deep into the ash-fall, twisted, gouged a hole into it, and then withdrew. Too hard for muscle and bone. Soft enough for metal and hydraulics.

With a hiss and a thud, the harvestman tore away at the slump of ash. The creature's striking spear-limbs started slowly and sped up, becoming a hacking whirr as it demolished the obstruction.

The Pteronaut can feel the ash beneath him shaking from the blows. His breath gasps once more through the facemask, and he pushes forwards on his belly, wriggling and snaking through the gap until he feels the rifle reach out into nothing and clatter down the far side of the slope. He is almost there.

But just at its last rise, the heap of fallen ash and the intact roof of the tunnel almost meet. The Pteronaut looks through the slit they make, seeing the tunnel suddenly wide and empty where it opens out ahead of him. It is just beyond his fingertips. He wrestles through the slit with his shoulders – first one arm, then the other. And then the wing-pack catches on a lip of hardened clinker: the Pteronaut cannot move.

Second by second, the jarring blows from the harvestmen get closer and closer. The Pteronaut has no choice but to unbuckle the wing-pack. He finds the clasps and releases them. Kicking backwards, he pushes on, shaking the straps of the harness from around his shoulders, until he slips free of the obstruction and slithers head-first down the slope. He rolls across the floor to where the rifle lies. He gets to his feet and clutches for it.

The Pteronaut should run. He knows it. But those wings have carried him for countless miles on his migrations across the deserts, and leaving them feels like a betrayal. He turns to face the ash-fall and clambers back up the slope. Stretching to his full height, he reaches into the narrow opening for the wing-pack. His fingers finds the smooth protective shell of the carapace where it fell and jammed at an angle as he slithered out from it. He turns the wing-pack this way, that way, trying to lever it clear. All the while the ash-fall shakes as the butcher-machine digs after him, stabbing and shovelling, as unstoppable as the Crawler.

In that moment, the Pteronaut sees that running cannot save him. He has only one chance, and no choice. He throws down the rifle and slips the knife and flint from where he carries them. With quick fingers, he unpops the mesh of one of the gill-cells and slides out a filter, cutting from it half a day's worth of breathable air.

One last time, he reaches up to unlock the wing-grips. Joints grate and wires groan as the broken wings extend a few inches, and the true extent of the damage becomes clear. The delicate balance of the mechanism is gone, bent out of shape. The rags of wing-tissue are torn and tattered, the struts are broken and useless. The Pteronaut has sailed the currents on those wings, soared high and far from thermal to thermal. For all the long days of his marching, he hoped that he would fly again with them, but he sees now that it is a forlorn futile hope, a hopeless hope; the wings could never carry him again.

The knife-blade rasps across the flint, the spark catches the filter. A flicker of flame starts to eat into the blue honeycomb. The Pteronaut watches the flame grow, and when he is sure it will not die, he slides the burning filter into the wing-pack, closing the case to leave only the smallest of gaps through which to draw in the air.

An orange and yellow glow stutters fitfully from inside. There is a hissing whine and a long-drawn out wail from the case. Thin trails of oily black smoke curl out, groping up against the walls of the tunnel. The Pteronaut closes the wing-pack fully and pushes it up against the ice-bound ash in the roof, wedging it tight.

And then he picks up the rifle and runs.

The harvestman did not trouble about the hot smoke that writhed in glowing bands across its infra-red vision. Nor did it concern itself with the acrid mix of hydrocarbons that leaked out from the gap above it. They could not distract it from its prey, not when the signal from the tracker-tag was so close.

228

With jerking mechanical precision, the harvestman continued to dig, edging onwards behind the furious whirring of its dagger-legs. Soon it would have the birdman, and then it would immobilise him with quick blows to break his legs and his arms. Once that had been done, it would drag him back to where the Crawler waited.

Inch by inch, foot by foot, the butcher-machine picked on, undaunted by the spreading cracks in the walls around it. Even when a fresh part of the tunnel caved in across its path the harvestman did not break the metronomic click of its legs. Deep within the drifts that surrounded it, something heavy shifted, but the harvestman went on digging.

A low metallic growl came from the wing-pack as it twisted out of shape. Flames licked around its edges, making shadows hurry across the tunnel roof. A drop of warm water dripped down in front of the harvestman's racing limbs, as bright and shining as a flare in its infra-red vision. Another fell, breaking into a dozen silver droplets as it struck the creature's metal body. And then another.

The ceiling creaked, and then it cracked, and then tonnes and tonnes of ice-bound ash and grit came crashing down. The hammer-blow fell, a hundred feet of cinders and slag crushing the harvestman flat, ramming it into the mountainside and pinning it there.

And beneath its broken body, the blackened husk of the Pteronaut's wing-pack sizzled in the wet.

41

Further up the tunnel, rushing into the dark away from the ash-fall, the Pteronaut can hear the walls groaning. Cracks streaks out across the roof ahead of him, dividing and multiplying far faster than he can sprint.

Flakes of glittering ash fall; a gentle trickle becomes a swarm. With a sudden thud and a thump, the ceiling comes down only a few feet behind him, burying the harvestman. The shockwave knocks the Pteronaut to his knees. He crawls into a run, half-blinded by dust, trying to get away as the shadow at his heels threatens to swallow him whole.

The flickering swarm in his night-vision thickens and the mesh protectors to the gill-cells snip shut. The Pteronaut races the rumbling fall, deafened, disoriented, jarring against the tunnel walls that he cannot see. On and on he goes, feeling the floor of the tunnel rise, its solidity the only thing he is certain of. Then when he can almost go no further, the crashing and the creaking all around him subside.

The Pteronaut stumbles to a standstill and leans forwards onto his knees. His rib-cage rises and falls beneath his second-skin, and he coughs with the effort and the exertion. Slowly, the heavy air clears. The darkness behind him is muffled and echo-less. Gradually, the tunnel settles, shifting and squeaking as it accustoms itself to its new shape; when his heart hammers less, the Pteronaut can hear how it has changed.

In the glow of his night-vision, he sees a blank wall where just seconds before there was space. His bootprints and the white line that vanish beneath the dust-drifts are the only sign that the tunnel did not always ends there. Back that way, buried deep under the mound of grit and clinker that has destroyed the harvestman, is the charred wreckage of the Pteronaut's wings.

His wings. When he stands to his full height again, resting against the wall of the tunnel, he can feel the contours of the ash against his back. Each and every ripple is hard-edged and clear, its depth and angles exaggerated by the emptiness between his shoulder blades. There is no such thing as a wingless Pteronaut – the idea is impossible. How can he be a creature of the air with no means to soar through it?

For many minutes more than he really needs for his breathing to slow again and to grow quiet, the Pteronaut – or whatever he has become – stands there in the night-vision dark, watching the last of the fluttering ash-flakes drift down around his feet. Almost weightless, they settle softly and vanish, becoming one with the floor. He, the thing that was the Pteronaut, shifts his feet, pushing up ramparts in the ash around his bootcaps. It moves aside, sparkling a little but otherwise utterly changed from what it was moments before. Different, but still the same, with the same obliterating aim.

The Pteronaut has lost his wings but in truth he lost them long ago, days and days across the miles and miles of deserts. Before the ravine and the bridge, and the craters, and the dam and the flyder and the valley of the harvestmen. The wings were broken already, and yet still he ran. Still he is the same; a Pteronaut without wings, but still a Pteronaut.

And the same threat glowers outside on the flanks of the mountain. When the Crawler picks up the flatlining telemetric signals from the harvestman, it will mass its surviving drones and send them out across the mountainsides, looking for a way in.

The Pteronaut moves again, with more purpose this time, and kicks away the fallen flakes that smother the white line. His eyes follow what remains of it up the tunnel. He must carry on. He had good reason to burn his wings, and now he must make that reason count.

Deeper into the black peak he goes, until at a sudden faultline, the walls of the tunnel change. The glittering blackness gives way to a different texture, one that is harder and rougher and marked by a million broken bubbles, their edges razor-sharp where they crumbled as they cooled.

The sides of the tunnel are mottled by countless blows that chipped the solid lava straight and level. It is the work of many lifetimes. The carvers of the line clearly thought that place very special to toil for hours and hours, day after day, year after year, buried away from daylight under the outpourings of the three black peaks.

The Pteronaut follows the route they made as the tunnel goes up steeply, and then falls, and then levels out again. That is where the images of the iron giants appear.

Incised into the walls are a troop of them with their arms raised to the sky. Lightning crackles around them, a sign of the immense power they once wielded. The other signs and symbols that the Pteronaut saw up in the summit-ruins return too; drill-rigs on their over-sized tracks, skies full of clouds, and the swarms of flying Pteronauts.

Again, just as at the summit-ruins, the carvings change further along the path. The iron giants dwindle to small occasional stick-figures in the distance, while above them, flock upon flock of Pteronauts fly with their broad wings and goggle-eyes, looking down impassively upon everything else. The dunes come with them, unmistakable armies in crescent form, marching across the walls, swamping the other shapes. Eventually, only the dunes and the Pteronauts remain, the one smothering the skies, the other the land below.

And then the walls fall back and the tunnel reaches its destination. It opens into an ancient magma-chamber, a huge rounded cavern deep within the rock. The sides have been cut into terraces, concentric levels ascending part-way up towards the irregular vent in the ceiling that the magma-chamber once served. The Pteronaut hears the noise of the wind from up above and there he sees a bright shred of blue peering down at him through the vent.

Down at his feet, after thousands of miles criss-crossing the deserts, the white line ends where it begins, looping around the floor of the cavern in an unbroken circle and flowing out again. In the centre of the loop, directly beneath the opening of the old vent, is a raised slab of stone that was left standing when the floor of the chamber was cut down and levelled. Lying across the slab, slumped in the light of the distant sky, is a body. A fine red layer dusts the symbols that decorate the metal plates of the suit, powdering the two light air-tanks on its back.

The Pteronaut steps forwards into the cavern, crossing the white line towards the figure on the stone. A dozen steps and he is by the body, close enough to see the dark brown stains that have run in rivers across the slab and pooled around its base. The body rocks backwards at his touch, and a knife clatters to the floor, sending shrill echoes dancing around the terraces. Gaping like a mouth, a slash falls open at the throat beneath the helmet. The face beneath the visor shows clear, pinched and taut behind the plastic, with skin that is stretched dry and tight over the cheekbones.

Whatever salvation was sought there, it did not come. But the Pteronaut has come, and now he sees why. Around the neck of the body, an amulet hangs on a chain of metal links – a broken loop of dull grey metal with the disc of a tracker-tag set into it: the source of the lost signal.

The Pteronaut holds the disc of the broken tracker-tag in his hand and looks up again at the sky shining through the vent. His eyes wander away from it, down the neck of the vertical chimney that leads to it, along the curving ceiling that domes above his head, down to the terraces all around. It will be a difficult climb, even for him, but he will not hide away waiting for the Crawler's drones to come for him. His fist clenches tight around the tracker-tag and he tears it from the body, scattering the links of chain at his feet.

Steps lead between the terraces up to the walls, and the Pteronaut races for them. But the terraces all around the chamber are not empty, as he thought. More bodies lie there, hundreds of them, stacked on every terrace, all the way up to the rounded vault of the roof. And every one of the bodies wears the shrivelled husk of a red and black skin-suit. The magma-chamber is not just a temple; it is a tomb – a tomb of Pteronauts.

The Pteronaut starts to pace around the terraces, staring at the rows of his own dead. He sees bodies with broken legs, others with rib injuries, shoulders wrenched out of their sockets, shattered arms. In most cases the skin-suits lived on for a while after those who wore them had died, feeding from them in death just as they did in life, until they too succumbed. But although the bodies are all different – females, males, young – all of them share one similarity: instead of a head, a rounded red boulder with carved goggle-eyes teeters between each pair of shoulders.

Abruptly, the Pteronaut comes to a halt by one of the bodies; a male, who in life was about his size and build. He pulls the body up from its resting place. The carved head rolls away from the shoulders and falls with a rumbling crack onto the floor at his feet. The Pteronaut kicks its fragments away – he is looking at the wing-pack that the body wears.

The dead male was killed by a bad launch or a bad landing, perhaps even killed outright, and his wing-pack is buckled and battered.

The Pteronaut lets the body fall back onto the terrace, and goes on, getting faster and faster as he searches. Another male of the right size is lacking his wing-pack entirely, and three others have damaged theirs beyond use. But the next male he turns over shows an undamaged wing-pack on his back, and the Pteronaut unbuckles the straps that hold it in place.

A Pteronaut's wings are made for it and it alone, just like the skin-suit it wears, but the carapace nestles neatly behind his shoulder blades and reaches down to cover the supply-pouch in the small of his back. The Pteronaut reaches up for the wing-grips and finds them just where he knows they will be. With a click he unlocks them and draws out the wings.

Tissues crackle as the wings unfold and tighten, shivering and shimmering in the dim light from the vent. The Pteronaut lets them fold away again – it is time to climb.

Starting from the highest terrace, working from one handhold to the other, the Pteronaut goes up the wall, digging his fingers and toes into the tiniest of fissures. Whoever built the temple-tomb meant the chamber to be circular, and they did a good job. But in places a harder vein of rock has resisted their efforts, and the curving ceiling was more difficult to work. Hammer-blows made at full stretch from below have left ripples and ridges that the Pteronaut can use, and a crack runs along one section where the tremors of the earth have passed through the chamber.

The Pteronaut goes higher, going from vertical to almost horizontal. His limbs are locked and rigid, his body hanging between them. Working slowly, painfully, he follows the in-curving bowl of the roof until the terraces of the dead are all laid out beneath him; one slip now and he will join them.

Bracing himself with his arms and legs, the Pteronaut wriggles and presses, defying gravity as he edges towards the chimney of the vent. Then he is there, and with fingers and toes that feel like they might snap at any second, he finds a handhold. He swings out into space, shifting his weight from horizontal back to vertical, the direction of all his strength shifting with it. Hanging there by his fingertips, with his body arrow-straight and his legs dangling into space, the Pteronaut faces up the chimney and towards the blue sky; beneath him, the bloodstained slab waits for his fall.

Inch by painful inch, slowly, his breath pent up inside his chest to keep his ribs rigid, the Pteronaut climbs. The wind

235

comes closer, coaxing him on, and the muscles of the skin-suit tense and relax with his own. He draws in another breath and makes another upwards lunge, and then at last he finds a foothold. Bracing himself against it, he claws and kicks himself upwards. At the limit of his endurance, the Pteronaut makes it to the rim of the vent, and he heaves himself over the crumbling edge to lie sprawling in the ash under the open sky.

He has reached the mountainside.

For a few moments, the Pteronaut lies in the daylight, taking deep breaths. The song of the wind goes quiet in his ears. In its stead he can hear the Crawler's engines roaring down below, and the boots of its drones as they tramp up the slopes. Weapons jangle. Bright metal chinks against brittle bone. An army is on the march.

The Pteronaut stands up, clear against the sky, and looks down over the mountainsides. Drones are swarming across the black shoulders of the cinder-cones and they have seen him – the Pteronaut has made sure that they will see him. He unslings the rifle from his back and fires a quick burst down at the drones, sending bullets skimming between the stones. But the Pteronaut does not want to kill them. Some of the drones must survive to see his escape if it is going to be full and final.

He starts to run away from the vent, over onto a shoulder of the black peak that the drones have not yet reached.

The Crawler howled across the valley, sending spouts of smoke high into the air, and the drones followed their prey. They broke from cover, surging along in the birdman's wake. He turned every few steps, firing at them, scattering them, reloading on the run until he was down to his last magazine. The few that were closest to him saw him slip between the steaming vents towards a half-formed dome, a fourth peak in the making. There the birdman stood on the ridge of the steaming hollow, outlined against the sky, and he fired the last rounds from his rifle before throwing it aside. The drones leapt from shelter: the birdman still had his knife, but he had nowhere left to run.

And then they saw him throw something else down at his feet. He reached up to his shoulders and with a sudden snap, he unfurled the wings that the drones believed to be broken. He turned away quickly before they could shoot at him, stepping through the steam towards the razor's-edge of the ridge.

In the blink of an eye, the birdman was gone.

It took several minutes for the Crawler's drones to reach the place where they had last seen the birdman. Some of them dawdled for a while, looking back to where the Crawler crouched, waiting and watching on the lava-plain below. Only two of the drones struggled right up to the top, retracing the zig-zag of the birdman's bootmarks in the ash. All the way to the edge of the vent they followed the tracks, to the final heavy indentations that his toes made as he took to the air.

The drones stood there and scanned the horizon, looking for the flitting shape of the birdman. They could not see it against the black slopes and the blue sky. Veils of steam and smoke drifted lazily across the landscape, but nothing moved against the wind. The skies and the slopes were empty.

One drone stooped to pick up the discarded rifle, but there was something else lying where the birdman had cast it aside: a broken tracker-tag. The second drone picked it out of the dust and turned it over in his hand, looking at it through the eye-slits of his hunting-mask. Then, with an oddly triumphant gesture in that moment of failure, he held the broken tracker-tag high above his head, and turned towards the Crawler.

The Crawler sat beneath the peaks on the spew and spatter that the angry earth had spread around them. The note of its engines sank to a low rumble. It studied the signal from the tracker-tag on its scopes and found it unmoving.

237

There was nothing. No motion, no sliding overlap of subtones. Just the same static chirrup.

The Crawler scanned the skies for the birdman's heat-signature. But the skin-suit was well-insulated, and the air all around the three black peaks was ablaze with thermals, shifting patterns of colour that blinded the Crawler's sight.

The birdman was gone.

Suddenly, the Crawler felt tired and old, and it was old, older than even it remembered. Older than the white lines that the last of its makers had made to mark out the flightpaths of the gods who had forsaken them. Older even than the black peaks themselves.

The Crawler felt the pain of its wounds, and it saw the remnants of its drones, the last survivors, four or five dozen and no more, strung out across the slopes. Still and watchful, the drones waited to see what the Crawler would do.

Its failure was complete. The Crawler re-tuned its receivers, and the signal from the tracker-tag vanished from its hearing. Sudden silence filled the deserts all around it; an empty eternal silence.

42 The daylight is drawing long shadows across the plains by the time that the Pteronaut clambers back onto the ridge. He leaves the narrow ledge where he has been standing for hours, wings folded away, gripping the sulphur-streaked sides of the new-formed vent and listening for the noise of the Crawler's engines to retreat. All that time he has hardly dared to move in case he betrays the deception of the broken tracker-tag.

When he climbs to the top and looks out across the lavafield, the Pteronaut sees that his deception has worked. There are no drones hiding among the rocks, no Crawler glinting with steely menace at the base of the volcano. The valley is empty. The rifle that he threw down is gone too, and so is the broken tracker-tag that the Pteronaut found on the body in the tomb. Even the spent bullet-cases from the shots that he fired have been picked out from among the black gravel, too precious to leave. Only the Crawler's track-marks remain, imprinted deep into the slag and the cinders, leading to the far-off streak of rising dust that marks its steady progress; it is fleeing from its failure, heading back to where it feels safe, far from the white lines.

Now that the echoes of the Crawler's departure have died away, the Pteronaut feels safe too. Finally, utterly safe, despite the weight of the tracker-tag that he still carries around his right ankle.

He stands on the summit as he did before, but this time he stands there as a Pteronaut again, with his eyes on the sky. He spreads the wings on his back. The wind hums over their taut edges and whistles through the support struts. It whispers to him of where it will take him, urging him to follow the trackless paths that it makes through the sky.

And the Pteronaut hears the wind's promises as he looks up into the blue heights that have been lost to him. The day

239

is dying, but above the steaming vents the air circles restlessly – there is flying still to be done before night comes.

With one step forwards, the Pteronaut kicks off the ledge and beats the wings twice, then three times. The ground falls away, and he goes soaring up into the thermals. He climbs quickly, lifting higher and higher, leaving the black slopes behind and gliding towards the dead deserts that he knows. A red world below, and blue above, with the restless wind trapped between them.

And the dark dot of the Pteronaut's shadow shrinks and shrinks until finally it disappears, lost among the endless dunes.

Made in the USA
Middletown, DE
22 February 2017